SIZZLE

A Novel

JULIE GARWOOD

BALLANTINE BOOKS • NEW YORK

2011 Ballantine Books Mass Market Edition

Copyright © 2009 by Julie Garwood

Published in the United States by Ballantine Books, an imprint of The Random House Publishing Group, a division of Random House, Inc., New York.

BALLANTINE and colophon are registered trademarks of Random House, Inc.

Originally published in hardcover in the United States by Ballantine Books, an imprint of The Random House Publishing Group, a division of Random House, Inc., in 2009.

ISBN 978-0-345-50078-6

Cover design: Christopher Sergio
Cover photograph: Jupiterimages/Getty Images

Printed in the United States of America

www.ballantinebooks.com

9 8 7 6 5 4 3 2 1

In memory of
Thomas Edward Murphy III

Our Tommy

One of the brightest lights in my life
"Giddyup"

ONE

THEY CALLED HIM A HERO FOR DOING HIS JOB. And if that weren't bad enough, damn if they weren't making him talk about it.

Special Agent Samuel Wellington Kincaid received a standing ovation when he finished his lecture. He gave a quick nod then tried to leave the podium and the auditorium, but he was pulled back by another FBI agent who insisted that, as soon as the cheering and clapping stopped, Sam answer questions.

Knowing he should cooperate, he nodded again and waited for the audience of cadets and future FBI agents to quiet down. Like most people, Sam hated giving speeches, especially those concerning his work in intelligence, but this was a training seminar and a goodwill mission, and he had been ordered by his superiors to talk about his role in the dramatic capture of the notorious Edward Chester, a radical white supremacist and one of the most elusive criminals in many years.

Despite his reluctance, Sam had been scheduled to conduct five of these seminars around the country. He'd already completed the first in D.C., and this one in Chicago was the second. Next week he would fly to Seattle for the third and then on to Los Angeles. His final stop would be at the naval base in San Diego where he would address Navy SEAL trainees. Inwardly, he groaned at the thought of three more appearances in front of inquisitive audiences who wanted only to hear sensational details of the capture.

This particular audience, however, also wanted to hear how Sam, while helping out on another case, saved the life of Alec Buchanan, a local Chicago FBI agent. The incident had happened six weeks ago, and since then, a few stories had been circulating. Agent Buchanan had been on medical leave, so they weren't able to get any facts from him. Before Sam was introduced to the crowd, he had been warned about their curiosity and the questions he might face. Was it true Agent Kincaid had gone into a blazing house to get Buchanan? How many gunmen were in the house when he'd broken in? Had he carried Buchanan out seconds before the house exploded?

What happened was a matter of public record. Sam still didn't want to go into it, but now that he stood at the podium, he was trapped by a group who wanted all the gory details.

Yet the first question Sam was asked had nothing to do with the Chester case or Alec Buchanan. It was the same one that was asked almost every time Sam was introduced. "Agent Kincaid, I couldn't help but notice your accent. Is it . . . Scottish?" a female cadet asked.

"Yes it is." Sam was accustomed to people's curiosity about his background, and so his answer was polite but brief.

"How is that possible?"

He smiled. "I'm from Scotland, and that's probably why I have a bit of an accent."

The cadet blushed. Not wanting to embarrass her, Sam continued, "What you really want to know is how someone from Scotland could become an FBI agent, right?"

"Yes, sir."

"I have dual citizenship," he explained. "I was born in the United States, but I was raised in the Highlands of Scotland. I did my undergraduate work at Princeton, my postgraduate work at Oxford, then moved to D.C. to get my law degree. I started with the FBI just after I passed the bar."

Sam evaded disclosing anything more about his personal life by calling on another eager cadet whose hand was raised, and for the next twenty minutes he was bombarded with questions.

Toward the end of Sam's lecture, Agent Alec Buchanan and his FBI partner, Jack MacAlister, slipped into the room and took seats near the rear door. Alec, still recovering from the wound to his back, shifted forward to find a comfortable position. Neither federal agent had seen Sam for a few weeks, but during the time they had spent with him in D.C., he'd become a good friend.

Jack leaned toward Alec to whisper. "He really hates doing this, doesn't he?"

Alec grinned. "Yeah, he does."

"We ought to mess with him a little bit."

"What have you got in mind?"

"I could raise my hand and ask him a couple of questions about his sex life."

Alec laughed. A woman in front of him turned around to glare but changed her mind when she saw him. Instead, she smiled.

Jack lowered his voice again. "How long is Sam going to be in Chicago? I forgot to ask when I picked him up at the airport."

"Two nights. He's staying with Regan and me, but I had to promise him that my wife wouldn't cry all over him again."

Giving an understanding nod, Jack said, "She's a crier all right."

"I believe your fiancée shed a few tears at the hospital."

"True," he admitted. "Will Sam join our poker game tomorrow night?"

"That's the plan."

"Can he play?"

"I sure hope not."

"Man, listen to that brogue. He's really miserable up there. Should we save him?"

Alec took a second to watch Sam, who was turning from one questioner to another, and replied, "Nah."

The two agents thoroughly enjoyed watching Sam squirm in the limelight. Although he looked composed, it was apparent he was nervous because his Scottish brogue got thicker with each sentence he uttered. Alec also noticed that, during his lecture, Sam never used the word "I" when describing his accomplishments. He was humble, self-effacing, and impressive. As Alec had discovered firsthand, Sam was also as hard as steel and as unfeeling as a machine when it was necessary.

Sam was a skilled agent, proficient in gathering intelligence and carrying out missions, but his real expertise was in languages. Truth be told, the only languages he couldn't translate were those he hadn't been exposed to. As he had explained to the cadet who was curious about his accent, most of his childhood was spent in Scotland. What he had not mentioned was the fact that, as the son of career diplomats, he had either lived in or traveled to almost every country of the world. Languages came to him easily.

It was this linguistic proficiency that had saved Alec Buchanan's life.

The Chicago office had sent Alec and Jack to D.C. to follow a lead on a suspected arms dealer. A low-level informant was ready to give them the names of men who, for a price, could help them. While Jack headed off to get background information on a couple of people, Alec planned to make contact with the informant to gain his trust. There was no guarantee that anything would come from the meeting, but the D.C. office insisted on sending along audio equipment to record the conversation anyway. And even though the informant spoke some English, they thought it would be prudent to have a translator on hand.

What was supposed to be a quick meet-and-greet turned into a nightmare.

Sam Kincaid happened to be in the D.C. headquarters at the time finishing a case report. He was reading the last page on the computer screen when the director called him into his office. He asked Sam for a favor. An agent from Chicago was in town to question a possible informant, the director explained, and the translator, who was sitting in a van a block away from the house where they were meeting, was having difficulty.

The director handed Sam a file and said, "This has all the information on the case thus far, along with photos of those involved."

Sam quickly looked it over and handed the file back.

"The safe house is real close," the director told him. "Shouldn't take long. It might even be over before you get there."

Fifteen minutes later Sam was sitting in the van with the driver, Agent Tom Murphy, and the translator, who introduced himself as Evan Bradshaw. Sam took one look at the perplexed young man at the console and summed up the situation immediately: rookie. Evan handed Sam his earphones and moved aside to give him his chair. "They've been talking for about an hour."

Sam slipped the earphones on and listened for a minute, then turned around to find Evan sliding the van door open to leave.

"Hey . . ." Sam called.

"Yes?"

"They're speaking English," he pointed out, trying not to sound exasperated.

"I know, I know," he answered. "But every now and then the guy says a sentence or two in a dialect I've never heard. I can't make heads or tails of it."

He got out of the van and, before he pulled the door closed, said, "I think Agent Buchanan ought to pull the plug on this one. I hope you can understand what the man's saying. Good luck."

Only Murphy and Sam remained. For several minutes Sam listened to the conversation, which continued in English. Suddenly he heard two men burst into the house and begin barking orders in another language. Sam understood every word, but he only needed to translate one sentence to know that they were planning to kill the informant and Alec, then blow up the house. The charges had already been set.

"There's a bomb in the house. Call it in and stay in the van," Sam shouted as he ripped the van door open. He hit the ground running, pulling his Glock from its holster. He leapt over a fence and raced across the yard. At the sound of a gunshot, he increased his stride and, using his forearm to protect his eyes, crashed through a bay window.

He landed on his feet and took in the scene all at once. The informant, blood oozing from a bullet wound to the head, lay crumpled on the floor. Agent Buchanan was slumped in a chair, his white shirt covered in blood. A gunman running toward the front door whirled around in surprise when Sam crashed through the window. Another gunman stood behind Buchanan's chair. He raised his gun to the back of Alec Buchanan's head and shouted, "If you—"

Those were his last words. Sam fired his gun. His bullet struck the man between the eyes. Sam spun to his left and fired several times in the vicinity of the second gunman, forcing him to dive for cover. In a rage, the man rolled, then sprang to his feet. Sam shot him as he was bringing his weapon up.

Not wasting a second, Sam rushed to the unconscious Alec Buchanan, lifted him over his shoulder, and carried him out of the house. He managed to get him across the street and behind a huge oak tree when the house exploded. The force was so great the trunk of the tree shook. Fiery debris rained down on them.

Seconds later, the van screeched to a halt in front of them, and Murphy leapt out to help get Alec inside. While Sam applied pressure to Alec's wound to stem the flow of blood, Murphy threw the van in gear and sped away from the fire, stopping at the end of the street to summon an ambulance.

Sirens screamed in the night, and within minutes two paramedics were transferring Alec into the ambulance. He had been stabbed in the back, just above the right kidney. They worked quickly to stabilize him. Sam rode with them to the hospital, and though it was only a couple of miles away, it seemed to take forever to get there.

"How's he doing?" Sam asked once they were well on their way.

"He's stable," the female paramedic said, "but he's lost a lot of blood." She looked over at Sam and added, "It looks like you're wearing most of it."

Sam sat back. The adrenaline was still racing through his veins, and it was difficult for him to sit still. He could feel the sticky wetness of the blood on his shirt.

The other paramedic was adjusting Alec's IV when he noticed blood dripping from Sam's arm. He reached out and pushed the sleeve up to expose shards of glass embedded in Sam's skin.

"You've got to get that cleaned out and stitched."

Unconcerned, Sam tugged the sleeve down. He saw the lights and the emergency entrance sign and felt immediate relief.

As Alec was being rolled into surgery minutes later, Sam called his superior, Special Agent in Charge Coleman, and told him what had happened. Coleman had already heard some of the details from Agent Murphy and had called the Chicago FBI to notify Alec's boss, Special Agent Margaret Pittman. She would make the dreaded calls to Alec's wife and family.

"I should be at the hospital soon," Coleman said. "Buchanan's partner, Agent MacAlister, has already been located, and he's on his way there, too."

Sam disconnected the call, then went into the emergency room. It was a surprisingly slow night in the D.C. trauma center. He had to wait only an hour for one of the physicians on duty to take a look at his arm. After he'd been sewn back together and the injury was wrapped, he headed up to the surgical waiting room.

Sam had never met Alec Buchanan before tonight, but he wasn't going to leave the hospital until he knew the agent was going to make it.

When Sam stepped off the elevator on the surgical

floor, Coleman was standing in front of him. He recognized several agents in the waiting room. Coleman motioned him toward the end of the long hallway to talk in private, and Sam explained everything that had happened from the moment he had entered the van.

The surgeon nearly ran into them as he rounded the corner on his way to the waiting room. He raised both eyebrows when he saw Sam's blood-soaked shirt. "You were with Agent Buchanan?"

"Yes," Sam answered.

He nodded. "Thought as much. Agent Buchanan came through the surgery just fine, and I expect him to make a full recovery." After a few words on what Alec could expect in the upcoming weeks, the surgeon shook their hands and left them.

The adrenaline long gone, Sam was suddenly exhausted. Thinking he wasn't needed at the hospital any longer, he headed downstairs. Agent Murphy met him at the emergency room entrance. He reached up and patted Sam on the shoulder. "Good job, sir," he said and then offered to drive him home.

The second his apartment door closed behind him, Sam stripped out of his clothes and headed to his shower. Following the doctor's orders to keep his bandage dry, he held his arm outside the shower curtain while he washed away the blood and grime of his day. Minutes later he was sprawled on his sofa sound asleep with the BBC blaring on the television.

He didn't wake until seven the following morning. His first order of business was to call the hospital to get a report on Alec. He knew that complications after surgery were routine, and he wanted to make certain Alec was still alive. When he was told the patient's condition was good, he breathed a sigh of relief.

Sam didn't know anything about Alec Buchanan, but he felt a professional bond with the fellow agent and a sense of responsibility to check on his progress. He planned to stop by the hospital that afternoon just to look in on him to make sure he was out of danger.

He certainly didn't plan to stay.

Agent Jack MacAlister had other ideas.

Sam had just gotten dressed in a pair of old jeans and a navy blue T-shirt when he heard someone pounding on his door. His gun was clipped to his waist, and he flipped the snap holding the gun in the holster in case the man telling him to open the damn door was a nutcase.

The visitor turned out to be Buchanan's partner, Agent MacAlister, and Sam's first impression was that he *was* a nutcase.

As soon as Sam opened the door, MacAlister shoved a Starbucks coffee and a pineapple Danish at him.

"Come on, let's go."

The two men were the same height and stood eye to eye. Sam backed up so MacAlister could come inside. From the FBI-issue gun he was wearing, Sam knew he was an agent.

"Okay. Who are you, and where are we going?"

"I'm Jack MacAlister."

"Buchanan's partner."

"That's right. You can call me Jack, and we're going to the hospital. Alec wants to see you."

"He's talking already?"

Jack nodded. "He's not only talking, he's complaining—a sure sign he's on the mend. We better hurry. Alec's wife, Regan, flew in last night, but the rest of the family are going to get to the hospital anytime now, and if you don't get in and out before they all arrive, you won't get out of there for a week."

Sam smiled.

"I'm not joking," Jack said. "Alec's got a lot of family, and most of them are on their way here. Are you going to eat that Danish?"

Sam handed the pastry back to him then grabbed his sunglasses and keys and followed him out the door.

ALEC WAS IN A private room and, fortunately, alone. He was sitting up in bed with the television remote in his hand. He looked bad, like vampires had feasted on him, but his eyes were alert.

"You want some company?" Jack asked as he walked in. He tried to shove Sam in front of him, but Sam didn't budge. He did give Jack an incredulous look, though.

Jack leaned against the window ledge and folded his arms across his chest. He nodded to the IV. "You getting your breakfast?"

Sam approached the side of the bed. "How're you feeling?"

"Like I got stabbed in the back. You're Sam Kincaid, aren't you?"

"Yes."

"Thanks for getting me out of that house."

"No problem."

Alec asked if Sam would mind answering a couple of questions about what everyone was now calling "the event." It was Jack, however, who asked the most questions. After a half hour or so, Sam could see that Alec was fading.

"You need to get some sleep. I'll see you around," Sam said.

He and Jack walked down the hall together. "It's good to know he's going to be okay," Sam said. "From what I've heard the other agents say, he's a good one."

"The best," Jack answered, "but don't let him know I said so. There'd be no living with him."

Three men who resembled Alec Buchanan were headed toward them. All, Sam noticed, wore guns. A distinguished older man followed them. He had his arm around the shoulder of a pretty young woman.

Jack chuckled. "You're about to meet some Buchanans. They have a way of making you feel like family. And I should warn you . . . once you're in, there's no getting out."

He wasn't exaggerating.

Over the next couple of weeks, Sam got to know the family very well, and Alec and Jack did become Sam's good friends. And friends were supposed to help each other out when needed, right? Like today.

Sam, still standing at the podium, spied the two agents sitting in the back row of the auditorium.

He gave Alec and Jack the "get me out of here" look. They didn't respond. Either they were oblivious to his distress, or they were so thoroughly enjoying his misery, they were pretending not to notice. He opted for the second choice and decided to get even.

"I see Alec Buchanan is with us," he announced to the crowd. "Perhaps we could get him up here to say a few words."

With that, the whole room erupted in wild applause and turned to face Alec.

Alec looked shell-shocked, and Sam responded to his startled expression with a quick nod and a satisfied smile. Slipping his hands into his pockets, he whistled a cheerful tune as he left the podium and strolled out of the auditorium.

TWO

GRANDMOTHER WAS STEALING HOLY WATER
again.

Lyra Prescott didn't have to guess why Father
Henry was calling. As soon as she saw the caller
ID, she knew it was about her beloved grandmother, the eccentric woman who had practically
raised Lyra.

Her cell phone sat in her hand. She had switched
the ringer off, but when she looked down, she saw
his name and number. Even if she wanted to talk
to the priest—which she didn't—she couldn't answer the phone right now. She was in the back of
a classroom trying to pay attention while Professor Mahler assigned subjects for the documentary
films his students were about to do. He was also
sharing his cynical opinions about the people of
Los Angeles.

Mahler, a handsome man in his forties, was a
noted professor who had published several books
about documentary filmmaking, and who had
won an award for his exposé of a notorious crime
family—a fact he liked to mention in almost every

lecture he gave. He was also a left-wing activist who tended to go overboard with his projects and opinions. He had the reputation of being arrogant and difficult, and rumor had it that his wife had walked out on him.

Lyra would have felt sorry for him if he weren't so egotistical. She couldn't agree with a word he was saying. The professor invariably made sweeping statements. "No one in this community takes care of what he has. When people get bored with something, they throw it away. Have you seen pictures of the landfills out here? Disgusting," he muttered. "I hope one of you will choose that topic for your documentary."

A hand shot up. "I'll take it."

Mahler nodded, poured water from his disposable plastic bottle—which Lyra thought was hypocritical—and took a drink before continuing his rant. "Instead of fixing a bicycle or a car, they buy a new one. And it's not just possessions," he added, wagging his finger at them. "They destroy homes and then abandon them."

"How often do you want us to check in with you while we're working on our documentaries?" a student asked.

"Not this time," he answered. "There will be no coddling from me."

Several members of the class looked at one another. Some seemed ready to laugh. When had Mahler ever coddled them?

"I don't want to see what you have when you're halfway done, and I don't want to hear about any problems. I want to watch the films when they're finished, and I want to be surprised, pleased, and—dare I imagine?—dazzled. Yes, you heard me. Dazzled. Now who wants to take on the corrupt mortgage industry?" he asked.

Another hand shot up.

"All right, Peter," Mahler said. "Put the topic and your name on the sign-up sheet on my desk. You too, Phillip," he said to the student who wanted landfills.

The professor gestured behind him toward his office. It was connected to the classroom by a door he kept wide open whenever he was teaching.

Without breaking his stride, he continued. "And the malls. Don't get me started on those structures. They keep building more and more of them, letting the old ones sit empty until someone comes along and tears them down or burns them."

"I'll take the malls," another student called out.

The professor nodded and gave suggestions on how to go about the project.

Lyra wasn't paying attention to his instructions. She was staring through the open door at a colorful poster hanging on the wall behind the professor's desk in his office. The words on the poster said, "Paraiso Park. First Annual Festival." It showed a lovely place that was clean and beautifully landscaped. Next to that poster was another one, a grim, black-and-white photo of industrial smokestacks. There were no words on this poster, and she couldn't tell where the photo had been taken. What a contradiction in subjects, she thought. She much preferred to look at the bold colors of Paraiso Park.

She raised her hand.

"Yes, Lyra?" Professor Mahler said.

"What about neighborhood parks? I'd like to take that subject."

"Excellent," he replied. "Do you know that most parks have a ten-year lifespan?"

She thought his remark ludicrous but didn't want to antagonize him, so she didn't argue. Everyone in his class had learned early in the semester never to disagree. Several students tried to dispute his comments in the beginning, and every time they explained their positions, the professor would rub his chin, pretend to be listening, and say, "Uh hum, uh hum," and then declare that the students were completely wrong. He never forgot who had argued with him and usually repaid those students with horrid assignments. Lyra was too close to the finish line to get on his bad side.

"No, Professor, I didn't know that." *Because it isn't true,* she thought.

"The equipment is broken by then. Even the chains holding the swings are gone or rusted out, and picnic tables are destroyed. Vandals and gangs move in and take over."

Lyra was determined to prove him wrong. She chose to do her documentary on beautiful Paraiso Park.

Two weeks later she deeply regretted her choice.

IT WAS AN UNUSUALLY hot and humid afternoon in Los Angeles, and Lyra was knee-deep in garbage that reeked to high heaven. She had just covered her nose and mouth with a scarf when her phone rang. She took one look at the display screen, saw

Father Henry's name, and let the call go to voice mail. Now wasn't a good time to have yet another lengthy visit with the priest. It had been two weeks since their last conversation, and she had assumed the problem with her grandmother had been solved. If that were the case, however, why would he be calling now? She knew she'd have to talk to him eventually, but Father Henry's complaints would have to wait. Once Lyra was back inside her air-conditioned apartment and had showered and changed into clean clothes, she would be in better shape to take on the priest.

Lyra's documentary project wasn't turning out to be what she had expected. Her initial plan had been to do a film about a happy place, a place where families gathered for carefree afternoons. It had been inspired by the poster in Professor Mahler's office.

In her preliminary research, she ran across a photo of a killer slide that had been built into an extremely steep hill in the middle of a neighborhood park. The photo showed children lined up to climb the steps to the top. They looked so eager and happy, one could almost hear their laughter. The photo had been taken just six years ago.

At first, Lyra didn't have a firm idea on what the theme of her documentary was going to be, but she thought that, if she walked around the area, she would come up with some sort of angle. A community coming together maybe? Or perhaps the joy in simple things? She did know she wanted the piece to be uplifting. Yes, light and uplifting. Maybe with a touch of humor.

Even with her GPS, she had difficulty finding the right place. The park was more than an hour away from her apartment, and when she finally pulled onto a gravel road, she thought she'd taken a wrong turn. Then she spotted what was left of the slide and was heartsick. Weeds obscured most of it, but what she could see was rusty and broken. Trash was everywhere . . . piles of it. She saw as many used needles as old newspapers and disposable diapers. The park was so contaminated with filth, climbing the hill now would be hazardous. The transformation from beautiful to beastly in such a short time was devastating.

What had happened here? Was Professor Mahler right? Were people destructive by nature? Lyra still refused to accept her professor's negative philosophy. She had driven through many neighborhoods with pristine parks and public areas that were meticulously kept, so she knew they existed. This one was different. What had destroyed this park in only a few years? She was determined to get answers.

She began with city officials. One city councilman she asked told her that gangs had moved into the neighborhood, and the park had become their battleground. It was a war over turf, he explained, and families had moved away. Another politician told her that a new highway cut through two neighborhoods, and families moved out, which was why the park was abandoned. Both politicians stopped talking to her when she asked if they knew the park was now a toxic wasteland. Apparently that wasn't their problem.

Lyra went to public records and newspaper archives to research the park further. She found photos of happy families strolling along a flower-bordered path with their picnic baskets. Children playing tag on the side of a hill. If she didn't know better, she would have thought these pictures were of an entirely different place.

She decided that her documentary would not only show the ravaged park, but it would also expose the people whose disregard had caused such devastation. She would intersperse these old photos with new ones of the men and women who frequented the wasteland now to dump their trash and, in some instances, their toxic waste.

Because these polluting people were breaking the law, she felt no compunction to shield their faces. Lyra's SUV had been a deterrent to anyone throwing trash on the site, so she decided to take secret photos of the perpetrators. A digital time-lapse camera with an intervalometer would give her continuous shots. She set it to take a picture every five seconds and connected a backup battery to ensure she'd get up to twenty-four hours of images. She hid the camera in a weatherproof box and anchored it down with rocks. Placed high up on the hill and surrounded by so much disgusting garbage, she knew no one would find it.

Every afternoon after class she drove back to the dump site, checked the memory card, and reprogrammed the camera to begin taking pictures for another day. She wished there was a way for the public to see what the litterers were doing, the young man dressed in a crisp blue shirt and striped tie and a sparkling white lab coat dumping plastic containers filled with used hypodermic needles that he removed from the trunk of his Saab, or the teenagers in tattered jeans and dirty T-shirts throwing old car batteries from the back of their pickup truck, but the reality was that no one but her professor and a few of the students in her film class would see her documentary.

After two weeks, she had enough images. She drove to the dumpsite with the intention of getting her camera and never ever going back. She looked forward to a full twenty-four hours of not inhaling the god-awful stench of rotting fruit.

But plans have a way of changing. She had just dismantled the camera and put it inside its case to take home when she spotted a dark sedan speeding down the narrow road that wound around the hill and through the park. Whoever was driving the car was in a hurry. Gravel dust sprayed up behind it as it took a sharp curve.

The car disappeared from view at the bottom of the hill. Lyra looked back in the direction the car had come from, and her curiosity was piqued. The road narrowed to little more than an overgrown path and disappeared as it wound upward. Thinking there had been little to see, she'd never really explored the other side of the hill. She decided to hike the rest of the way up now to take a look.

Good thing she wore her boots. The climb was difficult. It was made even more miserable by the heat and the stench wafting up from the dump sites. Finally, at the high point, she tramped through some dead shrubs and maneuvered around an uprooted tree to get a clear view. What she saw stunned her.

Down below lay a flat area about the size of a baseball diamond. It, too, had been the victim of vandals. Trash was scattered everywhere. But something even stranger captured Lyra's attention. It was so out of place. In the middle of all the rubble and litter was a beautiful little garden. A tiny patch of grass, looking like it had been freshly cut, was lush and green and edged with thriving flower beds. None of the trash touched the grass, as though it knew that doing so would defile this exquisite and most unexpected beauty.

Lyra stared at the amazing sight. How did this happen? Such a lovely spot in the middle of this cesspool.

Someone was obviously caring for the garden and cutting the grass, and she wanted to know why. She hiked back down the hill to her car to fetch her camera. A half hour later she found a suitable spot well-hidden by the dead shrubs and anchored the camera in the weatherproof box. She made sure the eye of the camera was focused on the road and the garden beyond to capture images of anyone coming or going. After inserting a new memory card, she set the timer.

This meant a couple more weeks of hiking back and forth. It probably wouldn't amount to anything, but then again maybe it would. She imagined all sorts of possibilities. Maybe an elderly gentleman had planted the flowers in memory of his dead wife. Perhaps this was the spot where he'd met her, or perhaps this was where he had taken her on their first date. Her mind then turned to a darker scenario. Maybe this was the spot where he'd killed his wife and buried her. Wracked with guilt, he had planted the flowers. The possibilities were endless.

Walking back to her car with the sun beating down, her face as sweaty and wet as the back of her neck and her soaked blouse sticking to her, she found herself smiling in spite of her discomfort. What would her parents think if they could see their daughter now, wearing old jeans and heavy hiking boots to protect her feet from used needles on the ground? They would be properly appalled, Lyra knew. Then again her mother and father were properly appalled at just about everything she did.

She finally reached her SUV, started the engine, quickly turned on the air conditioner, then pulled her boots off and slipped on flip-flops.

Once she had cooled down, she decided to call Father Henry. Better to get it over with than have it hanging over her, she thought.

She was given a reprieve. The priest wasn't home. The secretary informed her that Father wouldn't be back until the following evening. Lyra tried not to sound jubilant when she left a message on his voice mail, telling him that she was so sorry she had missed his call and that she very much looked forward to talking to him at his convenience.

Lying to a priest might well get her some extra time in purgatory. She couldn't worry about it now, though. She had a lot of work to get done before tomorrow, and she was anxious to get started on the latest batch of pictures.

Traffic was heavy, and it took her an excruciating hour and forty-five minutes to get back home. She pulled up to the gate of her apartment parking lot, and once she punched in the code, the wrought-iron gates swung open, and she drove through to her assigned parking space. Grabbing her back-pack from the seat next to her, she got out of the car and locked it. She climbed the stairs to her apartment and fumbled through her bag, looking for her key. Not finding it, she pushed the buzzer at her door.

A woman's voice immediately came through the door. "Yes?"

"It's me, Sidney," Lyra said. "My key's some-where in my bag and I'm too tired to look for it. Could you let me in?"

The lock on the door clicked.

Lyra's roommate, Sidney Buchanan, swung the door wide. Wearing faded gray sweatpants rolled at the waist, a white tank top, and fuzzy pink slip-pers, Sidney had one pencil between her lips and another one sticking out of the haphazard bun on the top of her head.

She reached out to relieve Lyra of her backpack before taking the pencil out of her mouth to talk. "You look like you've just been through a car wash without a car," she said sympathetically.

Lyra slumped into their only easy chair and ex-haled loudly. "I've had an exhausting day. How about you?"

"Oh, the usual," Sidney chirped. "I had brunch with Leonardo DiCaprio. He tried to talk me into flying to Cabo with him this afternoon, but I had already set up a meeting with Spielberg and Lucas. They're just relentless about the movie they want me to direct, but I said I needed more time to think about it. Then I had drinks with Robert Pattinson and dinner with Chace Crawford. Oh, and Zac Efron has been calling nonstop. I'm telling you, if they don't stop fighting over me, I'm just not going to see any of them ever again."

As Lyra was laughing, Sidney sat down on the floor inside a semicircle of scattered film reels and a stack of papers. "Actually," she said, "I haven't left the apartment all day. In fact, I don't think I've left it all week." She glanced up at the window. "Is it night already?" she groaned. "If I don't have this project ready to hand in tomorrow, I'm in deep trouble." She picked up a couple of loose pages and stacked them on the pile. Taking a deep breath, she said, "I can do this. I can do this."

Lyra lifted her tired body out of the chair. "I'll take a shower, and then if you need my help, I'm yours."

Sidney gave her an appreciative smile. "Thanks, but I think I've got it under control. It's just going to take time."

Lyra and Sidney were more like sisters than roommates. They met the summer before their second year at the university at a film festival where they had both volunteered to act as assistants to the presenters. Lyra's roommate had just graduated and moved back to Fargo, and Sidney's lease was up. Her apartment was three times the size of Lyra's, but it was an hour away and didn't have security. She asked Lyra if she could move in with her. The apartment was tiny, but both of them could walk to class if they wanted to.

It was an easy adjustment because they were so much alike. The same age, they both came from large close families who at times could be over-protective. They both loved classic rock and dark chocolate. Their ambitions were slightly different, though. Sidney wanted to someday create movies that would set the cinematic world on fire. Lyra wanted to write and produce documentaries.

After her four years at the university, Lyra had graduated with honors. When the opportunity came for her and Sidney to study at a prestigious California film school, they both jumped at it.

As Lyra was reaching the end of her studies, she was thinking about what she was going to do when she was finished. Jobs were being offered, but they were all wrong for her, and a little bit of panic was creeping in. All of that would have to be put aside today, though. She had more immediate concerns to deal with.

She had just stepped out of the shower when she heard the phone ring.

"Want me to get that?" Sidney called out.

"No, I'll get it," Lyra answered. Wrapped in a towel with her hair dripping water down her back she hurried to get the call, sighing when she saw who it was. "Hello, Father Henry. How nice to hear from you." That lie could cost her another month in purgatory. "How have you been?"

The priest didn't waste any time on chitchat. "Lyra, she's at it again."

There was no question as to who "she" was: Lyra's grandmother, or Gigi, as Lyra had called her since childhood. Lyra frowned. "Was it the holy water from the back of the church?"

Of course it was the holy water from the back of the church. That was the only holy water her grandmother was interested in.

The funny thing was, as much as she dreaded talking to him, Lyra really liked the priest. He was a kind man, usually very laidback, with a great sense of humor. He was quite good-looking, too, though noticing that a priest was handsome was probably frowned upon by the church.

"Now, Lyra, you know it's always the water from the font."

She walked into her ridiculously small bedroom and tripped over a shoe box. Hopping on one foot, she made it to the bed and dropped down.

"Father, I'm so sorry for the inconvenience," she said as she rubbed her foot. "You know she is . . ." Her voice trailed off. How did one accurately describe her grandmother?

"Stubborn," he suggested.

"Yes, but she's a dear, sweet woman, and her heart is—"

Ignoring her praise, he continued, "Outrageously superstitious?"

"Yes, but—"

"You need to have another talk with her."

"Yes, all right."

"When?"

"Soon."

"How soon?"

He wasn't going to let her wiggle out of it. "This weekend. I'll leave after my last class on Friday," she promised. "Is there a way you could stop by while I'm there? Perhaps between the two of us we could talk some sense into her." Fat chance, she thought, but didn't dare say.

Father Henry was appeased . . . for the moment anyway.

Lyra tried to put the worry about Gigi aside for now and concentrate on the work she needed to get done before she went to bed. This weekend she would surely come up with a solution that would appease both her grandmother and the priest. Until then, she was determined not to think about it.

She put on a pair of old-fashioned pajamas, then went back into the bathroom to smooth on moisturizer. Her face was sunburned. She blamed it on her afternoon climbing the hill. She also blamed it on Dr. Keaton, the professor of her afternoon class. He had insisted on lecturing outside by the commons where there wasn't a single shade tree. The professor lounged under a huge black umbrella while his students baked in the sun. To be touched by nature, he'd said. The only thing that had touched Lyra was the sun. She'd used sunscreen, of course, but she had started splashing water from her water bottle on her face into the second hour of his lecture and had apparently wiped off the protection.

Sidney smiled when she saw what Lyra was wearing. "New pj's?" she asked.

Lyra nodded. She went to the kitchen and returned with a bottle of water.

Sidney tilted her head and studied her friend for several seconds.

Lyra noticed. "What?"

"How come, even with a sunburn and dressed in 1950s pajamas, you still look stunning?"

"Okay, what do you want to borrow?"

"Nothing."

"Then why the compliments?"

"I just think it's disgusting," she explained with a grin. "I always feel like the homely stepchild when we go out together."

Lyra wasn't buying it. "Oh, please. I'm ordinary. You're the one with the strawberry blond hair and gorgeous eyes."

"I'm the girl next door. You're the sexy one. I make men smile. You make them pant."

Lyra laughed. "You're crazy. Men adore you."

Sidney shrugged. "Some do," she said. "I suppose it's because I know how to flirt."

"Yes, you do. You've turned it into an art form."

"I *am* good at it," she admitted. She pulled out her T-shirt and said, "I'm thinking about implants."

Lyra had just taken a drink and nearly choked on the water. "You're what?"

"Implants," she repeated with a straight face. "If I get them, I'm going for gigantic, like Professor Pierson. Perky Pierson."

"Those aren't real?"

"They're up around her neck," Sidney said. "There's no way they can be real."

"You aren't really thinking about getting implants, are you?"

"Of course not. You're so easy to rattle." Swiftly changing the subject, she asked, "Did your grandmother send you those pajamas?"

"Yes, she did," Lyra replied as she sat down across from her friend and picked up a laptop.

"What was the occasion?"

"Early birthday gift."

"She doesn't ever get you anything else, does she?"

"Not for a long, long time."

"What about your brothers? Does she get them pajamas, too?" she asked, smiling as she tried to picture Lyra's brothers wearing them.

"Watches," she replied. "Watches or alarm clocks every holiday."

"I think your grandmother is a genius. Think about it. She's eliminated the agony of trying to figure out what everyone wants, and she never has to fight the crowds or worry about costs. Christmas shopping must be a breeze."

"You're right, it is," Lyra agreed. "You really should meet her. She's the only member of my dysfunctional family you haven't met, and I know you'll like her. Why don't you drive down to San Diego with me this weekend? I promised Father Henry I'd have another talk with her. I'm planning to leave after class Friday afternoon. Please come. It'll be a nice getaway for you."

"I wish I could, but I can't. I've got two projects due the end of next week and both of them need a little more work. I'm going to be in the film lab all weekend."

"Is there anything I can do to help?"

"You've got your own project to finish. How's it going, by the way?"

"Almost done," she said. "I want to add a few more photos of the oh-so-lovely men and women dumping their trash, but I've got all the pictures I need."

"That's great. You've got to be happy you don't have to spend hours every day driving back and forth to the dump in all that traffic."

"No, I'm still doing that."

"You just said you weren't taking any more photos . . ."

"I've got another project going now. It's not really a project, I guess. I'm just curious."

She told Sidney about the patch of grass and flowers she'd found on the other side of the hill. "It was so . . . surprising, and I admit, I'm fascinated."

"So you set your camera to take pictures of what? The grass growing?"

"No, I want to find out who's cutting the grass and tending the flowers. More important, I'm curious as to why. I've got all sorts of theories, but my favorite is a lost love. Maybe that little patch of grass is where they liked to picnic or—"

"You're a hopeless romantic, Lyra. You're going to keep driving back and forth just to satisfy your curiosity."

"It's not as crazy as it sounds," she protested. "And I'm only going to keep the camera there for a week at the most . . . okay, maybe two weeks at the most. Is there any of that chocolate left?" she asked.

The swift change in topic didn't bother Sidney,

as she often did the very same thing. Since they'd been friends and roommates for a long while now, each understood how the other's mind worked.

"No, you ate the last of it last night, and yes, it is, too, crazy. Driving back and forth in Los Angeles for your documentary was necessary, but continuing to battle the traffic for hours on end for no apparent reason . . . that's absolutely crazy."

"Maybe it is, but I'm going to keep on doing it. Wait just a minute, I didn't eat any chocolate last night."

Sidney grinned. "Okay, I ate the last of it."

She got up and went into the kitchen and came back a minute later with a box of Cocoa Puffs cereal and a bottle of flavored water. When she sat down, she took a fistful of cereal and handed the box to Lyra.

"You didn't see it, Sidney," she said as she scooped out some cereal.

"See what?" she asked, reaching for the box.

"This little oasis the size of our parking space with lush green grass and pretty flowers around the border. It's almost a perfect square," she added. "And in the most bizarre place, surrounded by horrible, smelly trash. You really should come with me and see it."

Sidney surprised her by agreeing. "You're right. I should. Maybe then I'll be as intrigued as you are. I'll ride with you one afternoon next week. You know what I'm thinking? That grass could be covering a grave."

"I considered that possibility."

"Wouldn't that be something? A wife killed her

husband, or a husband killed his wife, then dug a hole and buried her."

"And he then planted flowers and cuts the grass out of guilt?"

Sidney laughed. "I guess a murderous husband wouldn't bother cutting the grass." She then suggested several other theories, all involving murder and mayhem. After suggesting one rather gruesome possibility, she was ready to buy a shovel and start digging to find out if there really was a body.

"Why is it you can only come up with brutal crimes?" Lyra asked.

Sidney shrugged. "Probably because so many of my brothers are in law enforcement. I've heard a lot of stories around the dining room table, and I guess it's made me cynical."

Lyra disagreed. She didn't think Sidney was cynical; she just had an overactive imagination, which was why she was going to be great in the field she had chosen.

"We should get to work," Lyra suggested. "Or neither of us will get any sleep tonight."

Sidney agreed, and for the next several hours both of them worked in silence. Lyra finished around midnight and headed to her bedroom.

"What time will you leave for your grandmother's?"

"Around three. I want to beat some of the going-home-from-work traffic if possible. Why?"

"Could you take those reels back for me? They have to be checked in by five on Friday, and I'll be across campus all day. It'll be a big help . . ."

"I'll take them. It's on my way."

Tuesday, after class, Lyra went into Dr. Mahler's office to discuss her extra-credit project. She told him about the garden she'd found at the back of the dump site and explained how she wanted to do a very short film about it.

"Have you finished your documentary about . . . what was it you chose?"

"Parks," she answered. "I decided to do my film on Paraiso Park, and that's where I found the pretty little garden."

He looked astounded. He braced his arms on his desktop. "Whatever possessed you to do Paraiso Park? That's over an hour away. How did you even know about it?"

She tilted her head toward the poster on the wall. "I got the idea from you, Professor. You and your poster."

He leaned back in his swivel chair to look over his shoulder at the wall. "I've had that hanging there for so long I forget about it. I grew up right next to the park," he explained. "I got that poster at the first annual festival. Moved the following year." He looked at Lyra. "Has it deteriorated? It has, hasn't it?"

"Yes, it has."

She told him how she had been filming cars and trucks dumping their trash.

"And now you want to start filming the garden on the other side of the hill?"

"I already have started filming. I switch the memory card every day. I haven't had time to look at any of it yet. I thought I'd get your approval for the extra credit—"

"Uh hum, uh hum . . ."

Uh oh, he was rubbing his chin. He was going to squelch the project.

"It's intriguing," he admitted. "I'll tell you what. Your grade is dependent on your documentary. Once you've handed it in, then maybe you can tackle the garden film. I'm concerned that it's too much like your documentary. It's the same notion, the same setting . . . but it's up to you. Just finish one before you start on another."

Lyra thought about Mahler's advice as she left his office. He was right. She needed to finish the important project first, but in the meantime, she'd let the camera at the park keep taking pictures.

Friday afternoon, Lyra thought she could beat the L.A. traffic, at least until she got to the Interstate, but there was a four-car pileup and that meant she had to take a detour. She had driven the route before, cutting through the most beautiful neighborhoods. The speed limit was much slower, but Lyra didn't mind. It was a lovely day, and she enjoyed looking at the manicured lawns and gardens.

She was driving down Walnut when she saw the sign. "Yard Sale."

THREE

MILO SMITH WAS AN IDIOT. HE WAS ALSO A fraud and a braggart.

And he didn't have a clue. Not only did he think he was brilliant, but he actually believed that everyone else in the collection agency he worked for thought so, too. His employer, Mr. Merriam, rarely gave compliments to any of his seventy-plus employees, but just last month Milo overheard him remark to an associate that Milo had proven himself invaluable time and time again. Milo interpreted the comment to mean that Mr. Merriam would lean on him more for his "specialized" overtime work.

Like the other employees, Milo wanted to climb up the company ladder. He openly talked about that goal, yet he never discussed his number one secret goal because he knew none of them would understand. They might even laugh at him.

Milo wanted to be James Bond. Oh, he wasn't crazy. He knew James Bond was just a character in the movies. Milo had grown up watching 007 and had seen every Bond movie so many times he'd lost count. He could repeat word for word all of the lines Bond said. Milo's miserable childhood had disappeared as soon as one of the movies started, and for a couple of hours he wasn't the scrawny kid who got smacked around by his old man. No, Milo was James Bond.

As an adult, Milo had gotten into the habit of praising himself. Was it any wonder he had accomplished so much at such an early age? He was exact; he followed directions—no matter how complicated or convoluted—and like all professionals, he never missed a deadline. Best of all, he kept his emotions out of the job.

He couldn't say the same for his ego.

Milo was a hit man. Sort of. To date he had never actually killed anyone, but that was yet another fact he discreetly kept to himself.

Luck got him into the profession, being in the right place at the right time. Kind of like those pretty movie stars who got discovered while they were sipping Cokes at the drugstore fountain. Yeah, just like that.

Milo got discovered by Mr. Merriam, who happened to be walking by when Milo was beating the crap out of one of his neighbors. Mr. Merriam plucked him right out of that alley and hired him on the spot. Milo was given a tiny cubicle with a phone and a list of people to harass and threaten if they didn't pay their debt. The collection agency was legit. A couple of credit card companies used them, and Mr. Merriam made a healthy income.

But the boss had a couple of side businesses, too. Milo didn't know what they were, but there were times when the boss's "clients" disappointed him, and action needed to be taken.

Milo had been working at the agency for about eight months when the boss called him into his office. Most of the other employees had gone home, and the second shift was just starting. Mr. Merriam came right out and asked Milo if he had ever killed anyone.

Feeling clever and important, Milo didn't quite answer the question. Instead, he told the boss that he had never had any problem taking a life. He guessed he was just a natural. If he hadn't gone to work for the collection agency, he said, killing for hire might have become his chosen profession. He was that good, he boasted.

Mr. Merriam was convinced of Milo's sincerity and loyalty. He gave Milo his first killing assignment that night. Because he was pleased with that outcome, more jobs came in the months that followed.

Milo's ego swelled to an even greater dimension because of the confidence Mr. Merriam was showing in him. He decided his experience and know-how should be shared with others, and so, after completing several assignments, he began to compile a list of the lessons he had learned, thinking that, when he was old and ready to retire, he could pass these lessons down to another hit man just starting out.

First lesson: wear disposable clothes.

Case in point: Marshall Delmar Jr., Milo's first assignment.

Delmar was an investment counselor who had

convinced Mr. Merriam to put money into a company that went belly-up. Mr. Merriam would have taken the loss in stride if he hadn't found out that the slimy Delmar had sold all his shares and made a handsome profit right before the company crashed. Mr. Merriam was certain that Delmar had known the stock was going to plunge, and because he committed the sin of not sharing that information with Mr. Merriam, Delmar needed to die with all possible haste. Mr. Merriam gave Milo no other instructions than to make the death look like an accident.

Once the hit was carried out, Milo returned to Mr. Merriam and proudly stated that the police report would say that Delmar's death was the result of a fall, that he had stumbled and hit his head on the sharp edge of his desk.

Mr. Merriam was impressed with the report, and frankly, so was Milo. How Delmar had *actually* met his demise was vastly different from the version Milo had concocted and then decided to believe.

Marshall Delmar lived in an overstuffed, Spanish-style house in the pretentious neighborhood known as Vista Del Pacifico. If one stood on the tiled roof of the two-story house and squinted into the sun, one might get a glimpse of the ocean on a cloudless day, which was why the home was considered ocean view and, therefore, cost millions of dollars.

Getting inside the house turned out to be surprisingly easy. Delmar was hosting a large dinner party that evening, and servants were coming and going through the kitchen entrance assisting the caterers with their trays and glassware.

Milo had done his preliminary surveillance. He knew all about the party and which catering company Delmar had hired. The staff were required to wear black pants, long-sleeved black shirts buttoned to the neck, and black shoes. Milo dressed accordingly and was able to walk in unnoticed carrying a silver tray he had lifted from the back of the caterer's van. It was a hot summer night and no one was wearing a wrap or a coat, so he hid in the coat closet just off the foyer and patiently waited until the house had quieted down, and Delmar, a confirmed bachelor, was alone.

It was after one o'clock in the morning when Delmar turned the lights off, locked the front door, and crossed the foyer to his library.

Milo continued to wait, his hope that Delmar would retreat to his bedroom and go to sleep. Milo would use a pillow to suffocate him, and if Delmar didn't struggle, he was certain he could make it look like the man died in his sleep.

But Delmar was screwing up the plan. He didn't appear to be going to bed anytime soon. Milo couldn't wait any longer. Perhaps Delmar had fallen asleep at his desk. Milo silently opened the closet door and crept across the foyer to look. Slipping on a black mask he'd stolen off a Zorro mannequin at a costume shop, he peeked inside and saw Delmar sitting at his desk, pen in hand, flipping through what appeared to be legal documents.

The library was in shadows. The lamp on the

desk cast only a narrow light over the papers. The air-conditioning was running full blast, making the room frigid, but Delmar, Milo noticed, was sweating profusely. He panted as though he'd just run a couple of miles, which was kind of funny since Delmar was a good hundred and fifty, maybe two hundred, pounds overweight. Milo didn't have any trouble sneaking inside without being noticed. He pressed against the wall hidden in darkness. Standing motionless for several seconds, he took shallow breaths as he thought about his contingency plan.

Then he remembered he didn't have a contingency plan. Stupid, stupid, he berated himself. Now what was he going to do? He didn't have a gun with him because he was supposed to make the murder look like an accident, and a bullet hole would be a dead giveaway.

He chewed on his lower lip while he tried to think of a clever way to do the man in. Suddenly Delmar dropped his pen and began to rub his left arm. He groaned loudly.

Hit him. That's it. That's what Milo could do. He would hit him in the head and make it look like he killed himself falling into the stone fireplace.

Feeling much more in control now that he had formulated a plan of action, Milo stepped forward, but then he realized he didn't have anything to whack the man with. He should have thought of that, he chided himself as he frantically looked around for a weapon to use. He backed up slowly and once again pressed against the wall out of Delmar's line of vision.

No heavy candlestick or bookend . . . nothing. There wasn't even a poker from the fireplace he could use.

In a panic now, he edged his way back to the foyer. Maybe he could fetch a heavy utensil from the kitchen. In his haste to retreat, he tripped over his own feet and fell sideways to the floor. Unfortunately, he made a little noise. He quickly scrambled to his feet and whirled around to see if Delmar was going to scream or, worse, come after him with a gun.

He peeked into the library and couldn't believe his good luck. Delmar didn't seem to hear or notice him. Delmar's behavior was odd, though. His right hand had gone to his chest, and he slumped toward the light. His complexion was rapidly turning the color of a day-old corpse as he struggled for breath.

Suddenly Delmar lurched up from his chair, staggered backward, then turned in a feeble attempt to reach for the phone. He never made it. He fell hard and struck his head on the corner of the desk, then crashed to the floor and lay there in a heap, blood shooting from his skull.

Was he dead? Milo rushed forward to check for a pulse. Tripping on the edge of the rug, he lost his balance and landed with a thud on top of Delmar. When Milo regained his feet, his shirt and pants were covered in Delmar's blood. He stared down at the lifeless face until he was absolutely certain the man was dead. It wasn't until he thought he heard someone coming that he finally moved. Maybe it was just the sound of his heartbeat roaring in his ears, but he wasn't taking any chances. He skidded across the hardwood floor, ran out the back door, and kept on running the three long blocks to his car. He was halfway home before he realized he was still wearing his mask, an error he didn't mention when he was writing about his lessons learned. After all, legends didn't make mistakes, did they?

Lesson two: bring food for the dogs.

Case in point: Jimmy Barrows.

Barrows was a meaner than usual loan shark who was squeezing Mr. Merriam's nephew for payment. Milo had been instructed to kill Barrows with one shot between the eyes. Mr. Merriam wanted to send a message that no one messed with his family.

After this job was completed, Milo reported to Mr. Merriam that he'd had a little trouble with a couple of Barrows's pesky, yapping dogs. Still, he swore, he had made the kill with little fuss at all.

Well, not quite. The real story was much more painful and embarrassing than Milo would admit.

Mr. Merriam had given him a photo of the loan shark, and one look at the man convinced Milo that killing him was going to be a walk in the park. Barrows wasn't big, maybe five-two or five-three, and he couldn't have weighed more than a hundred ten pounds with clothes on, but Milo knew he had to be cautious. Size didn't matter if Barrows happened to be holding a gun in his hand. Milo doubted he was carrying, though. Rumor had it that Barrows was a prissy man who didn't like to do anything he considered unpleasant. His clothing and his manners were as meticulous as his

well-manicured hands. He left the unpleasant-
ness to the people who worked for him, but Milo
planned to make sure none of them were around
when he walked in pretending to be in need of
money.

The loan shark business was an odd profession
for someone as cultured as Barrows. He was the
complete opposite of what Milo thought a loan
shark should be, a thug.

Barrows worked out of a converted storefront
on Second and Cypress Lane. It was in a bad-ass
part of town where anyone who stood on the corner more than fifteen minutes was bound to get
stabbed.

Milo had no intention of lingering. He spotted
Barrows through the glass window sitting on a
sofa across from his desk, sorting through bank
receipts. He was dressed in a black suit with a red-
and-white-striped tie, and draped on the other
end of the sofa was a brown fur coat. Must belong to his wife, Milo thought, and he wondered
what he could get if he tried to fence it.

"Are you Barrows?" Milo asked as he approached.

"*Mr.* Barrows," the loan shark corrected in a
peevish tone of voice.

"I need a loan," Milo said. "I've got some papers
here you could look at and maybe keep as collat-
eral." He reached into his raincoat, pulled out his
.38 and pointed it at the loan shark.

Barrows froze when he saw the gun. Almost
instantly he recovered and relaxed against the
cushions. "Are you here to rob me?" he asked

calmly. "If so, you're going to be disappointed. I don't keep any money here."

"I'm not here to rob you. The man I work for wants to send a message."

"Oh? And who do you work for?"

"Never you mind."

It seemed odd to Milo that having a gun pointed at his head didn't seem to faze Barrows.

"All right then," Barrows responded. "What message does this mysterious man want to send?"

"He wants you and everyone else to know that you don't mess with his family."

"Then you simply must tell me who he is." He sounded amused as he added, "What family can't I mess with?" Barrows's right hand was slowly edging down between the cushions.

"Keep your hands where I can see them," Milo ordered.

He steadied his aim and pulled the trigger. Nothing happened. In his haste, he had forgotten to flip the safety off. He was about to correct his mistake when, out of the corner of his eye, he saw the fur coat moving. Spooked, he took a hasty step back and lowered his gun just a little. The heads of two dogs, Shelties, emerged from under the fur showing their razor-sharp teeth and growling.

"Show some love," Barrows ordered.

Confused, Milo jerked back. "What?"

The animals understood the command and came flying at him. Milo half turned toward them and got off one shot quite by accident. The bullet went wide and struck the wall.

The sound scared the dogs, and both of them

looked at their owner, who very calmly repeated the command. "Show some love."

The demon dogs came at Milo again. In a panic, he turned his back on the animals, thinking to get the hell out of there, but was stopped in his tracks by his own piercing scream. One of the dogs had clamped down on his backside, digging his teeth in. Milo whirled in a circle thinking to fling the animal off him, but try as he might, he couldn't shake the cur loose.

The other dog sprang at Milo's throat. He tried to knock him away with his gun, but the dog was quick and took a bite out of his hand. Milo barely noticed. The pain the ass dog was causing was so excruciating he couldn't stop yelping.

The second dog let go of Milo's hand long enough to drop to the floor, bounce back up like a damn tennis ball, and go for Milo's throat again.

Barrows had pulled his gun from between the cushions but didn't fire. He assumed the threat was over. Vastly entertained, he watched his dogs in action.

Milo did the unthinkable. He dropped his weapon. The bouncing dog caught it in its teeth before it hit the ground, and boom . . . a bullet discharged hitting Barrows in the chest. For a split second Milo froze. The damn dog was a better shot than he was.

The noise freaked the dogs again. They let go and ran back to the sofa to wait for the next kill order from their boss.

Barrows was dead. The crimson color from his tie seemed to be oozing down his impeccably laundered white shirt. The bullet must have gone through his heart, killing him instantly. He died with the amused expression still on his face.

Thankfully, Milo had the presence of mind to snatch his gun and shove it back into his pocket before he ran out the door. He couldn't stop crying. People gave him strange looks as he limped the several blocks to his car, but he didn't care. Let them stare. His ass was on fire and he could feel the blood from the wound dripping down the back of his leg. Lucky for him, no one in that particular neighborhood talked to the police.

Damn dogs. Should have killed them, too.

He reached his car, got inside, and howled when he sat down. He gripped the steering wheel with both hands and continued crying all the way to the hospital.

Needless to say, he didn't mention these details as he talked to Mr. Merriam about his experience. He didn't want to tarnish his image. Mr. Merriam only cared about results.

The third lesson he had learned was still so raw he couldn't put any kind of spin on it yet, couldn't even think about it without shuddering.

Lesson three: learn to swim before you try to kill someone beside a swimming pool.

Case in point: George Villard.

Milo still had nightmares about that one. Villard, the man he'd been ordered to kill, was a bodybuilder. He was also a notorious drunk and womanizer. Mr. Merriam hadn't given Milo any background information on this assignment. His only orders were to get rid of Villard, and do it immediately.

Milo didn't have time to research or plan. He made sure there were bullets in his gun and headed out. By the time he found the house in the maze of twists and turns up in the hills, it was after midnight. Villard was in his backyard next to his kidney-shaped pool. Milo hid in the shrubs observing his target, who was teetering on his feet. It was only a matter of minutes before the hulk passed out.

As drunk as Villard was, Milo figured he wouldn't put up much of a fight, but he was wrong about that. Milo burst through the bushes and was fumbling to get his gun out of his raincoat pocket when Villard spotted him and his weapon and attacked, getting in one solid punch before tossing Milo into the pool.

Milo tried to dog paddle to the side and climb out, but his clothes and his panic worked against him. He was going under for the third time when, with one hand, Villard hauled him out and began screaming questions at him.

"Who sent you? Was it Jo Ann's husband or Crystal's? Tell me," he yelled. His head rolled to the side and his eyes drooped as he slurred the words of his demand. Suddenly jerking his head up, he kicked Milo in the stomach. "Answer me, damn it!"

Milo couldn't speak. Flopping around on the concrete like a dying carp, he was fully occupied with choking on all the water he'd taken in.

Impatient to get answers, Villard kicked him again. "Was it Lenny? It was, wasn't it? That no-good bastard." He gave him another vicious kick in his side and snarled, "You're going to tell me who sent you, and then I'm going to throw you back in the pool and watch you drown."

The threat wasn't much of an incentive to cooperate, Milo thought, though he doubted Villard, in his drunken stupor, realized it. As inebriated as he was, the bodybuilder could still do some damage. Milo wanted to run away, but he was afraid to even move, afraid to reach for his gun—which he wasn't sure would work since it, too, was probably waterlogged—afraid to provoke the drooling muscleman in any way.

While Milo desperately tried to think of a plan to save himself, Villard began blinking furiously and squinting down at him, obviously trying to concentrate. He must have remembered what he was doing because he suddenly nodded and smiled, then swung his foot back to kick Milo again, but the vast amount of alcohol he had consumed interfered with his balance. His body swayed; his eyes closed, and still grasping his glass in his hand, he plunged headfirst into the pool. He was too drunk to know he was drowning.

The death was ruled accidental.

It was another near disaster for Milo, yes, but as he did with the other hits, he took credit, and in Mr. Merriam's eyes, he had a perfect record. Three for three. Merriam was so impressed, he gave Milo a bonus for a job well done.

Two weeks later on a Thursday afternoon Milo

was called into Mr. Merriam's office for a new assignment.

His boss usually wasn't one for idle chitchat, but today he wanted to talk.

"You may have noticed how distracted I've been this past couple of weeks."

Milo hadn't noticed, but he thought maybe he should have, and so he nodded. "Yes, sir, I have," he lied.

"I've got a situation, and you're the man for the job. This one is going to be tricky and will require a little more guile. You understand?"

"Yes, sure," he lied again. Guile? He'd never heard the word before. He wasn't about to admit it, though, for showing his ignorance might diminish his standing with Mr. Merriam, and he couldn't have that. Just as soon as he left the office, he would find out what guile was and where he could get some.

"A business associate I once considered a friend screwed me. Screwed me good. Bill Rooney is his name," he added with a sneer. "I took that weasel to dinner more than once, sat down across from him and broke bread with him, and what does he do in return? He stabs me in the back, that's what. He's got something I want."

Milo didn't know if he should say something sympathetic or not, so he stayed silent and waited.

"Just goes to show, you can't mix business with pleasure. I learned my lesson, and Rooney's about to learn his. I've got the edge here because Rooney doesn't know I found out."

He pulled the chair out from behind the desk

and sat down. "I discovered quite by accident where he's hiding it. I knew he had a safe in his office. Everyone knows. It's the first thing you see when you walk in the door. It's big and must be a hundred years old."

He opened a carved wooden box on his desk and reached inside for a cigar. He stuck the stogie between his lips and continued talking as he struck a match and sucked the flame into the tobacco. "He doesn't have to worry someone's gonna pick it up, and run out the door with it. It would take a crane to lift it."

He motioned for Milo to take a seat before continuing. "Rooney wants everyone to see the safe. Naturally, they'd think that's where he keeps his valuables. Right? The shmuck. It's all a sham. Turns out he's got another safe in his office. It's built into the floor under the desk. I got the combination. Let me tell you, that took some doing."

"Do you want me to break into his office—"

"No, no, I've got Charlie on that. I want you to take care of Rooney and his wife."

Though Milo knew Merriam's office was soundproof and was checked for bugs at least once a day, he skittishly glanced around the room. "You want his wife dead, too?"

"That's right. Rooney might have told her what he did. Keep her alive, and she could go to the feds. Too risky. So here's how I want it to go down. Rooney always leaves his office at four o'clock on the dot, and it takes him an hour to get home. He never goes out on Friday night. Never," he stressed. "He's predictable and that's going to work for us.

He takes his loudmouth wife out every Saturday night, and Sunday he rests up for his mistress. He sees her every Monday and Wednesday.

"I want this to look like a murder-suicide. Wife kills husband, then kills herself. The police will investigate, of course, and they'll find out about the mistress. They'll assume the wife found out, too, and that's why she killed him. Everyone knows she's got a hell of a temper."

"When do you want this done?"

"Tomorrow night at five o'clock. Charlie's going into Rooney's office then, and he'll be in and out of there in no time. If there's a problem, he'll let me know, and I'll call you. Take this cell phone," he ordered, tossing it to Milo. "It can't be traced. Don't kill anyone until you hear from me. Got that?"

Once again, Milo was being rushed. He didn't have time to do much surveillance, but he vowed there weren't going to be any glitches this time. He drove through Rooney's neighborhood the next morning to familiarize himself with the layout and to see if there were any nosy neighbors. Once he'd checked out all the entrances into Rooney's house, he drove to a grocery store about a mile away. Milo purchased a couple of pounds of hamburger meat he planned to stuff in his pockets just in case there was a dog lurking inside the house.

He still had a lot of time on his hands, so he strolled back to his car, pulled out one of the girly magazines he kept under the seat for those times when he needed a little pick-me-up, and flipped through it to pass the time.

At 3:30 he put the magazine away and headed over to Rooney's. His house sat in the middle of a long, gently-sloping hill, and Milo's plan was to park at the top where he would have a clear view of the driveway. As soon as Mr. Merriam called, Milo would sneak into the house and take care of business. While he waited, he would put the cell phone to his ear and pretend he'd pulled over to talk. Nothing suspicious about that.

The plan was flawless.

FOUR

MILO SLAMMED ON THE BRAKES AND STARED
in astonishment at the mob gathered on the
lawn in front of Rooney's house.

They were everywhere, hordes of men and
women—no, no, mostly women—all carrying
away as much as they could hold in their arms. A
couple of them, Milo noticed, had that same
glazed look of unadulterated joy he sometimes
saw on the faces of the men who frequented strip
clubs with him.

The Rooneys were having a yard sale.

"Now what am I supposed to do?" he muttered. The question was followed by a stream of
curses. He couldn't call his boss because that was
against the rules, so he guessed he would just have
to wait until Mr. Merriam called him.

A yard sale. He cursed again. In such an exclusive neighborhood, this kind of middle-class activity seemed out of place. Rich people threw stuff
away. They didn't sell it.

A couple of women, red-faced and screaming,
were fighting a tug of war over a leather chair.

Look at them, Milo thought with disgust. Someone else's junk had become their treasure. Slap down a dime or a dollar, and a piece of crap was all theirs. *He* would never touch anyone else's used stuff. He had more class than that.

The front doors of the house were wide open, and a steady stream of shoppers came and went. One carried a pretty lamp, the cord dragging behind her. Another had what looked like a fancy humidor. He noticed she had a bottle tucked under her arm. Then he saw another woman carrying out two bottles of wine. More followed. Were the Rooneys emptying their bar or maybe their wine cellar? Why would they do that? Were they moving or something?

Milo checked the time. Rooney should be pulling into his driveway any minute now, unless he didn't work at the office today. That was a possibility. Maybe he was at home helping. Mr. Merriam had given Milo a photo of the couple, but so far he hadn't spotted either husband or wife. Bill and Barbara. Cute the way their names went together, he thought. They sure weren't cute in the photo, though. Bill looked like he was wearing a shag rug on his big head, and Barbara—or "loudmouth Babs" as Mr. Merriam called her—had had one too many face-lifts. Her lips ended where her ears began.

Yard sale. Mr. Merriam wasn't going to believe this. Surely he wouldn't want Milo to continue with the job. There were close to forty people in the yard alone, and God only knew how many more were inside the house.

A woman dressed in a pale gray maid's uniform came out of the house with a stack of books and CDs. She ran down the steps, dropping a couple of the CDs, but she didn't stop to pick them up. Pushing another woman aside, she raced across the lawn. Her expression was frantic. She slowed down long enough to dump all the books and CDs in a pile, then furtively glanced over her shoulder at the front door and ran like hell down the street.

What was that all about? Milo watched her disappear around the corner before he turned back to the crowd. He shook his head at the frenzy of bargain hunters darting from one pile to another, snatching up their booty as though it would disappear if they didn't have their hands on it. His gaze stopped at one woman who didn't seem caught up in the chaos. She knelt on the grass beside the pyramid of books gently picking them up and examining them one at a time. He couldn't see much of her. Her long dark hair hid her face, and frenzied people pouring in and out of the house kept blocking his view.

Finally the dark-haired woman stood and he got a better look. He whistled. A real knockout, this one. *Real* nice body. He tried to picture her without clothes, which was a pleasant little fantasy, until he realized he was beginning to react physically. Now wasn't the time. He tried to look away but couldn't. Dressed in jeans and a pink T-shirt, she definitely wasn't trying to sell her attributes. Yet on her, the clothes looked sexy. She was even sexier than the Bond girls. She was tall and slender, not skinny like those stick runway

models, more like the athletic type with curves in all
the right places. Bet she's a dancer, Milo thought.

She turned her head as she reached for another
book, and Milo caught a glimpse of her face. Beautiful. He couldn't remember the faces of the Bond
girls. He'd never really bothered to look at their
faces, and yet he couldn't take his eyes off of hers.

With all the good stuff, why was she wasting her
time on that junk? Must be the brainy type, he
concluded.

He continued to stare as she carried a stack of
books to the street. She was taking such care with
them, cradling them as though they were important.

She drove a Ford SUV maybe five or six years
old. The back was open, and he could see that it
was already crammed full of books and what
looked like a box of DVDs and CDs. A beauty
like her should be driving a brand-new car every
year.

"Throw out the junk books, lady," he said, exasperated. "Go for the good stuff. If you don't want
any of it, you can sell it on eBay and get yourself a
new car."

A parking spot opened directly across the street
from her car. Milo threw his into gear and nearly
sideswiped an Acura as he pulled into the space.

If he could only get a photo of her, he wouldn't
need a girly magazine to take the pressure off.
She'd do the trick all right. Yeah, he definitely
needed a picture. He didn't have a camera with
him, but his cell phone had one, and it would have

to do. He pulled it out of his pocket and held it up, then waited for her to turn around so he could get a clear shot. Just as he pressed, she moved, so he took several more.

None of them were probably any good. He deleted them and gave up. He guessed he would have to memorize her face and body for his evening entertainment.

Now what was she doing? She'd closed the back door but kept glancing at the yard. She went around to the backseat, opened the door, and crossed the yard again, making one last trip for books.

Milo was so busy watching the knockout he didn't notice Babs Rooney approaching until she stopped the beautiful woman and added more books to her pile. Babs said something to the book lover, then handed her an expensive-looking camera. He couldn't tell if it was a video camera or one of those fancy new digitals, but it looked brand new and was probably worth a lot of money. The woman wouldn't take it, but Babs insisted and put the camera on top of the books. He looked at the SUV again and noticed the university sticker in the window. A student then. No wonder she liked books.

He couldn't believe what he did next. He got out of his car to get closer to her, forgetting in his haste that he had placed the cell phone Mr. Merriam had given him in his lap. It clattered to the street and bounced under the car. He had to get down on his stomach to reach far enough under the car to get it. Cursing profusely, he tossed the phone onto the front seat and started out again. It took balls, but he was going to talk to her, maybe even flirt. Who knows? She might like the macho type. If she were to blow him off or laugh at him, no big deal, none of his friends would ever find out.

Opportunity struck. She dropped one of the books. Milo raced to pick it up.

"I got it. I got it," he shouted, sounding ridiculously excited.

He put the book on top of her stack. "Here you are, Miss . . ."

The camera slipped but Milo grabbed it and tucked it into the crook of her arm. He couldn't remember if he said anything else after that or not. Gorgeous green eyes. He'd never seen that exact color before.

"You could be in movies," he blurted. "Are you?"

She shook her head.

He swallowed. "You go to school around here?"

"Yes, I do," she answered, smiling.

Nice voice. Southern tinge to it. She was walking away. "Wait," he called, running after her. "I want to help you carry those books."

"No, thank you. I've got it."

He froze in his tracks and frantically tried to think of something else to say to keep her there.

Too late. She was leaving. His mind was still blank. He hadn't even said thank you. Yeah, thank you. He could say that, but why would he be thanking her? No, that wouldn't work. He had to come up with something else.

And she was gone. He wanted to scream, but he had to think fast. Her car was pulling away. As he watched it disappear down the street, he zeroed in on her license plate and quickly memorized the number. He fumbled in his pockets and found a pen. Grabbing a stray book lying at his feet, he ripped out a page and quickly wrote down the number. A gratified smile spread across his face. He was pretty smart after all. Now all he had to do was use her license number to get her name and address, and then he could pretend to run into her again.

"If I were still married, I'd buy my husband those new Callaway clubs," a woman behind him said and drew his attention.

Hey, wait a minute. Maybe it wasn't all junk. "Did you say new?" he asked her.

"Yes."

"How much?"

She looked confused. "It's free." Sweeping her arm toward the lawn, she said, "Everything's free. Didn't you read the sign?" She looked toward the corner of the yard by the driveway. "Oh, I see. It fell over. Maybe I ought to take those clubs . . . my nephew—"

"Where are they?" he interrupted.

"In those bushes over there. I think the owner's wife threw them there."

Milo didn't give the woman time to get them. He dove into the shrubbery and retrieved the golf clubs. They were brand new, and he was careful with them when he put them in the trunk of his car. New clubs would get him more money on eBay than scratched ones. He noticed an older man carrying a small flat-screen television out the door. "I gotta get in on that," he whispered.

Time got away from him as he searched for more stuff. Yes, it was secondhand stuff, but what he took wasn't junk, and best of all, he didn't pay a cent for it. He was going to make a fortune on eBay. Milo was suddenly feeling superior again. He wasn't at all like those other yard-sale freaks.

He was squeezing behind the wheel, trying not to knock over the food processor that hadn't even been taken out of its box, when Merriam's cell phone rang. It took five rings before Milo could get to it under the silverware.

"Yes?"

"Where have you been?" The fury in Mr. Merriam's voice came across loud and clear. "I've called four times."

"I've been sitting here waiting for your call. I swear this is the first time the phone rang. The signal's weak . . . maybe that's why . . ."

Milo felt like such a fool. How could he have forgotten why he was at the Rooneys?

"Cheap, throwaway phones," Mr. Merriam railed. "Listen to me. I'm calling it off."

"You don't want me to—"

"That's right, I don't. Someone lied to me, convinced me something I wanted was in Rooney's office safe, but it wasn't there."

Milo was watching the street and saw Rooney's car turning the corner. "He's coming this way now."

"Excellent. I've got Charlie Brody and Lou Stack headed over there. You stay where you are. They might need your help getting Rooney to talk."

"I don't think that's gonna work, sir. See . . . uh . . . there's this situation here."

"What?"

"There's this situation," he repeated. "Rooney's wife is having a yard sale."

"A what?"

"A yard sale, and there's like a hundred people here," he exaggerated. "They're going in and out of the house, too. The wife is getting rid of everything."

"You sit there and wait," Merriam ordered. "I need to talk to Charlie and Stack, then I'll get back to you."

Milo decided he'd better not put the phone down, fearing he'd lose it again, so he put it on the dashboard and sat back to wait.

Rooney's BMW screeched to a stop in the driveway. He hadn't even gotten out of the car before he started screaming.

"Put that down. What are you doing?" he roared. "Put that back. You there . . . get away from that." He ripped a stack of clothes out of a woman's arms and shoved her. "You get out of here, right this minute."

Milo felt as though he was watching a slapstick movie. Rooney's behavior was hilarious. His face was bloodred, and he hurled through the crowd knocking people aside as he bellowed for his wife.

"Here we go," Milo whispered. He spotted Babs coming around the side of the house, a complacent smile on her face. She was apparently used to her husband's rants and raves.

"What have you done?" Rooney shouted. He tripped over a stack of books. "Oh my God. You didn't touch anything in my study, did you? You did, you did. Do you realize what you've done? Is everything gone? Everything in there gone?"

Babs's expression didn't waver. "Every article from your precious library is out here . . . what's left of it."

He shook his head in disbelief and ran inside. Babs stayed in the yard. Continuing to smile, she turned to the crowd warily watching her and called out, "Everything's still free. Go ahead and take whatever you want, but you'd better hurry. My husband has a foul temper, and it's going to get ugly."

She seemed utterly unfazed by the possibility.

Milo watched from his car and decided that, despite her creepy face-lifts and inflated lips, Babs was fairly classy. Classy dresser anyway. She had on a knockout, rhinestone-embellished, lime green velour jogging suit with matching high heels. He could see her red-painted toes peeking through the openings.

Milo wasn't sure how long he should wait. Mr. Merriam had told him not to do anything until he heard from him, but people were heading to their cars now. Once they were gone, one or both of the Rooneys would surely notice he was still there.

The Rooneys made the decision for him. Milo got so caught up in their argument, he couldn't leave.

Babs shoved her hands in the pockets of her jacket and appeared to be bracing herself for the confrontation when her husband flew out the front door, shrieking like a wounded hyena.

"You stupid bitch. What were you thinking? Don't you know what you've done? You've thrown away a gold mine. A gold mine worth millions of dollars."

His gaze darted around the yard. He locked in on a pile of miscellaneous items and raced across the yard. "Maybe it's still here . . . maybe it's not too late." He dropped to the ground and began to search frantically. "Maybe it's buried on the bottom." Throwing notebooks and ashtrays and picture frames in the air, he pleaded, "Please, please, God, don't let it be gone. Don't let it be gone."

"That's rich. You praying to God. You hypocrite," Babs said scornfully.

Ignoring his wife, he continued the search until he was convinced what he was looking for wasn't to be found. Still on his knees, he turned to her. "Why? Why did you do this to me? He's going to come after me. He won't just kill me. He'll go after you, too. That's right. He can't take the chance I didn't tell you about it. Why?" he repeated on a sob. "Why did you—"

"You wouldn't take me to New York."

His mouth dropped open. "New York?" he shouted. "You did all this because I wouldn't take you to New York?"

Babs held up her left hand, looked at the diamond wedding ring, sighed loudly, then took the ring off and threw it at her husband. It landed in the grass next to him.

"What are you . . . are you nuts?" he gasped as he pawed the grass searching for it.

She shoved her hands back in her pockets and glared at him. "You knew how much I wanted to see the shows on Broadway. You told me you couldn't spare the time, remember? I begged and begged you. It didn't matter, though. Yet you did find the time to take another woman to New York. How many shows did you see with *her*?"

As though the wind had just been knocked out of him, Rooney slumped back on his haunches. "This is all because—"

"How could you think I wouldn't find out? You cheated on me, but unlike you, I have loyal friends. Susan saw you on the plane. She told me the woman you were with was hanging all over you."

He stumbled getting to his feet. "I'm going to kill you," he growled through clenched teeth.

Babs pulled a gun from her pocket. "No, you're not. I'm going to kill you."

Milo was mesmerized by what he was witnessing and was afraid to blink for fear he'd miss something. Would she really do it? What kind of a gun was it? Looked like a .38 or a .45. Wish he could get closer to see. Maybe even steal it. He could always use another piece.

And that ring. He had to get it before anyone else did. His gaze bounced back and forth between the ring in the grass and the gun. Should he try to stop the crazy woman? Mr. Merriam needed to find out where Rooney had hidden whatever it was he'd taken. Was it the same thing that Rooney was desperate to find now? Milo's boss should have told him what the mystery item was so he could look for it in all the junk in the yard.

Milo glanced back at Babs when she began to laugh. It was a weird sound, somewhere between a snort and a cough. She held her smile as she took aim and fired. She hit Rooney in the chest, took a couple of steps forward, and fired again.

Milo heard a woman scream, looked in his rearview mirror, and saw a couple standing in front of their car. The man held a phone up snapping a picture of the scene. Milo ducked down to be out of camera range. When he dared to raise his head to peek over the dashboard, Babs was standing over her husband, staring down at him, probably making sure he was dead. She must have been convinced because she lowered the gun and calmly walked into her house. Milo had hoped that she would drop the gun so he could snatch it, but she held on to it. He craned his neck to watch her close the door. A second later he heard another gunshot. It came from inside the house. Had she just killed herself, or was she shooting holes in another one of his treasures?

Men and women were cautiously making their way toward the body on the grass. Milo immediately jumped to the conclusion that they were all thinking about stealing the ring.

"Oh no you don't," he muttered as he jumped out of the car and sprinted over to Rooney's side. He knew exactly where the ring had landed and knelt down next to it. With his right hand he pretended to check for a pulse while he lifted the ring with his left hand and tucked it into his pocket.

"Is he dead?" a woman called out.

Milo nodded. He didn't look at the woman because he didn't want anyone to get a good look at him.

"I called nine-one-one," another shouted.

As the curious moved forward, Milo hurried back to his car. He kept his head down as he started the motor. He would wait until he could leave without being noticed, and since he didn't want anyone recording his license plate, he would have to back up and turn around at the top of the hill. If he backed into the first drive, the trees would block the view.

Though he was dying to take the ring out of his pocket and look it over, he didn't dare. Someone might walk by and notice what he was doing. He nearly jumped out of his skin when his cell phone rang.

"Yes?"

"You can go on home. Charlie Brody and Lou Stack will take care of the Rooneys."

"There's a new situation here . . ."

"Yeah, yeah, I know, the yard sale. Charlie and Stack will take them somewhere quiet. They're experts. They'll get Rooney to talk."

"Sir, it's going to take more than an expert. I'm looking at Rooney right now, and I'm telling you, he ain't gonna be talking to anybody."

FIVE

SOMETIMES THE WORRY ABOUT HER GRAND-
mother would become so intense, Lyra would
get sick to her stomach and couldn't eat. During
the Dr. Timothy Freeman debacle, she'd lost seven
pounds, but once the noted psychiatrist gave the
court his findings regarding Gigi's mental health,
Lyra had quickly regained the weight.

Her grandmother's son, Christopher Prescott,
Jr., and his wife, Judith—who also happened to be
Lyra's parents, though she was loathe to admit
it—initiated the shenanigans when one night at
dinner Gigi announced that she was going to
make an appointment with her attorney to tweak
some of the conditions of her trust. Since Gigi was
spending time with a widowed gentleman she
spoke fondly of, her son, with his wife's guidance,
jumped to the conclusion that Gigi was going to
include said gentleman in her will. God forbid,
she might even decide to leave everything to him.
The possibility that they could be bilked out of
her fortune gave Lyra's parents chills. They had
become quite accustomed to the lifestyle her

money provided, and they wanted nothing to change.

Christopher cunningly waited until Lyra's two brothers, Owen and Cooper, were out of the country on business before taking action. Using Gigi's advanced age as a matter of concern, he and his attorney filed papers requesting guardianship. The petition cited mental incapacity and asked the court to give Christopher power of attorney over all financial and medical decisions.

Dr. Freeman was called in to evaluate her grandmother. An efficient, no-nonsense physician, the doctor was also a kind man, and Gigi liked him. He administered a multitude of tests to determine her mental state, spending several two-hour sessions with her discussing everything from Christopher Columbus to the space shuttle. With her full cooperation, he admitted her to a nearby hospital for a complete physical examination including a CT scan.

The results of the tests were just as Lyra had expected and prayed for. Aside from some arthritis in her grandmother's knees and hands, she was in excellent health, and mentally she was sharp as a tack. She wasn't suffering from Alzheimer's disease or any other form of dementia, and contrary to strong suggestions made by her daughter-in-law, Gigi wasn't exhibiting any signs of senility.

The truly surprising moment came at the end of the hearing. The judge had been given a copy of Gigi's trust, and just before he rendered his verdict, he asked Christopher Prescott if he had taken the time to read it.

"No, Your Honor, I haven't," Christopher admitted. "But my mother had my full approval when she made changes to her trust three or four years ago."

The judge nodded. "And at that time, did you believe your mother was of sound mind?"

"Absolutely," he answered. "It's only lately that she has exhibited signs of . . . confusion."

The judge held up the trust papers. "I see that you were given two hundred thousand at the time she had the trust rewritten."

"Yes, I was given that amount, but I assure you, I wouldn't have accepted it if I had thought she was unable to make sound judgments."

"For the record, Mr. Prescott, the conditions of the trust state that if your mother should become incapacitated, her granddaughter, Lyra Decoursey Prescott, would become her guardian. She would have power of attorney over her medical and financial decisions."

"But I am executor of the estate when my mother dies," Christopher said.

The judge shook his head. "No, you are not."

Christopher's mouth dropped open. His expression was almost as comical as his wife's. Judith looked as though she'd just stepped off a Tilt-a-Whirl.

The judge promptly dismissed the case, ruling that Gigi was quite able to handle her own finances.

Throughout the tiresome ordeal, Gigi remained unruffled. After the hearing, she'd patted her son's arm, kissed her daughter-in-law on the cheek, then hooked her arm through Lyra's and suggested she take all of them out to dinner at her favorite restaurant.

At an early age, Lyra had recognized what an amazing woman her grandmother was, but after the hearing she realized all over again she was a force to be reckoned with. What was the expression? Oh, yes, crazy like a fox. That was her Gigi, all right. She had so charmed the psychiatrist and the judge that, when the results of the tests came in, they seemed just as pleased as Lyra. Gigi always knew exactly what she was doing . . . and why.

Despite the victory in court, Lyra was sure that her despicable father wasn't going to stop trying to get control of his mother's money, which meant that he wouldn't give up on his shameful attempts to prove her incompetent. Her grandmother had managed to win this round, but Lyra worried that next time might prove more difficult.

Gigi was certainly not helping her cause. Now and then she did things that might be construed as downright bizarre.

In the past nine months, she had remodeled her downstairs bathroom three times. Lyra's stomach started hurting after the second complete remodel. First, Gigi had the bath expanded, eliminating a storage closet for space. A few weeks later, she wanted it changed again, so she had a shower and a new pedestal sink installed, new floor, too. Once that was finished, she decided she wanted to go modern. She had the fixtures, the shower, and the sink ripped out and donated to Habitat for Humanity. The contractor, a sweet, patient man named Harlan Fishwater, didn't complain. He put in a travertine marble floor, a rich wood cabinet with a granite countertop, and a water bowl that sat on top. He also replaced the wallpaper for the third time.

Harlan was going to start building shelves in the attic next while Gigi talked to an architect about remodeling her brand-new kitchen. That was when Lyra started losing weight again, concerned that Christopher and Judith would find another excuse to pounce. Despite Gigi's assurances that everything was just fine, Lyra couldn't understand her behavior—that is, until she found out quite by chance that Harlan was struggling to support his five children and a wife who had been laid off from her job. Harlan did fine work, but with the downturn in the economy, there weren't many people interested in remodeling their homes. Gigi's generous response had been to keep him busy.

But this was hardly the only time Gigi's actions might be considered peculiar. The weekend that she took off without telling anyone came to mind. By the time she returned home, Lyra was frantic, and her grandmother—though sorry she'd caused any worry—absolutely refused to say where she'd gone.

Disappearing for days on end . . . that's what Lyra's father would say as he once again built his case.

And then there was the holy water. What in heaven's name was that all about?

Lyra was thankful the traffic on the I-5 was light as she headed south. A stress-free drive would give her some much-needed time to figure out what to do before Father Henry visited.

She sped up to merge into another lane. A car cut her off and she swerved sharply. Books and DVDs flew everywhere, reminding her that she needed to do something about them. She shook her head as she recalled her experience that afternoon.

The yard sale had grabbed her attention when she was taking a shortcut through the posh neighborhood. Ever since she was a child, Lyra had been fascinated by these rituals, where people displayed their personal belongings to the world in hopes of bringing in a little cash.

While other people saw the sales as occasions to pick up cheap items, Lyra saw them as stories. As she would browse among the articles the owners had chosen to discard, she would create a narrative about the people and their lives. It was a strange thing to do, but as long as no one else knew about it, she didn't care. Lyra used the stories she made up as creative exercises.

She usually didn't look at clothing, but in one sale she saw a beautiful white wedding dress, vintage 1970, the tags still on. Obviously no one had worn it. In a box filled with pieces of jewelry, Lyra found a bracelet inscribed "Love you forever, John." Lyra's imagination took over, and she envisioned a young couple madly in love and on their way to the altar. Had the woman changed her mind or had he? One dramatic story emerged and then another, all triggered by that little price tag and an inscription.

The sale that caught her attention today was

particularly odd. Lyra couldn't quite make out the story behind this one yet. The frantic woman throwing all of her treasures out had a noticeably strange look in her eyes. She seemed desperate to be rid of everything, shouting to people to just take whatever they wanted.

Lyra's downfall was books. She couldn't walk by one without looking at it, so naturally she had been drawn to the pile in the center of the yard. When she knelt and picked up a couple, she was amazed at what she found. Some of them were quite old. She opened a worn copy of *The Grapes of Wrath* and looked at the title page. Clearly inscribed on it was John Steinbeck's signature. She carefully turned the page and looked at the copyright, realizing it had to be a first edition. Gently laying the book down, she reached for another, *The Lord of the Rings*. Inside was Tolkien's signature. She went through a dozen other classic books and found four more signed copies. She couldn't believe what she was seeing. In this pile, haphazardly strewn across the grass, there had to be a fortune in first edition and inscribed volumes. Surely the hysterical woman rushing around the lawn had no idea what she was giving away.

Lyra tried to explain to the woman that the books were worth a great deal of money, but she didn't seem to care. In fact, she screamed at Lyra that, if the books weren't taken, she would build a bonfire and throw them all in. Appalled, Lyra sifted through the stacks and took as many as she could to her car.

On the drive to her grandmother's, Lyra struggled

to decide what to do with them. Until she could come up with an answer, she would have to store them in a safe place. These were valuable editions, and she couldn't risk anything happening to them. Gigi's house was small, and Lyra felt it would be an imposition to ask her to keep them there. The apartment she shared with Sidney was also out of the question: it was already packed to the rafters with books and clothes. There simply wasn't room for more. That left the family ranch in Texas. Lyra and her two brothers had inherited the fifteen-thousand-acre spread from their grandfather.

She pulled off at an exit and called the house-keeper to tell him that she was shipping a few boxes of books. They should arrive within the next week, and would he please put them in her bedroom.

Lyra finished the call, then turned into a McDonald's parking lot and used her GPS to find the nearest pack-and-mail store. As she was unloading the books, she saw the box of DVDs and CDs. She'd forgotten she'd picked them up as well. Not wanting to take the time to sort through them all now, she decided to ship them to the ranch, too. Forty-five minutes later, she was back on the highway and the books, CDs, and DVDs were on their way to Texas. One problem solved. Now on to another.

Gigi lived in a quiet community north of San Diego. Her neighborhood, a row of eleven houses painted in bright pastel colors, had been lovingly preserved from another era and had escaped the ravages of progress. The homes, lined up on the east side of the street, had unobstructed views of the ocean. The pier was less than a mile away, and so were the shops. A coffee shop, a grocery market, and a flower and fruit stand were all within walking distance.

Gigi's garage sat behind her house, and the only way to get to it was from the side street. Lyra pulled in, parked the car, and walked between the houses to get to the gate of the picket fence surrounding her grandmother's tiny front yard.

Lyra had a key, but decided to knock. Her grandmother opened the door seconds later.

"Lyra Decoursey Prescott, what on earth are you doing on my porch?"

Trying not to smile, Gigi was obviously pleased that Lyra was home, though she wasn't ready to admit it just yet. She stepped back so her granddaughter could get past her and asked, "Did the phone company go bust? Is that why you couldn't call ahead and tell me you were coming?"

Lyra kissed her grandmother on the cheek. "I know, I should have called."

"Then why didn't you? If I had known you were coming, I would have made your favorite seafood chowder."

"Any chance you still could?"

Before Gigi could answer, Lyra carried her bag and laptop upstairs to her bedroom. When she came back down, her grandmother was in the kitchen rummaging through her pots and pans.

"Aren't you happy to see me?" Lyra asked.

"Of course I am," she grumbled. "We'll have to go to the market first thing in the morning. I'll need fresh fish for my chowder. I'd better make a list, or I'm sure to forget something. There's iced tea in the refrigerator."

"Sweet tea or regular?"

"Regular."

Lyra poured herself a glass and sat down at the table. "This is good," she said.

Her grandmother found the big pot she was looking for and put it on the stove. "I always add a hint of lemon to my tea. Why are you here, Lyra? You haven't gone through your trust fund so soon, have you? No, of course you haven't. Your grandfather would roll over in his grave if he thought you were frittering that money away."

Lyra laughed. "I haven't touched my trust fund," she said. "And I don't need any money."

Gigi nervously wiped her hands on a towel. "Then it's your school, isn't it? What's happened? You were doing so well . . ."

"I'm not having any problems with my classes," she assured her. "I'm doing fine."

"How many more weeks do you have? Three? Four?" her grandmother asked as she opened a drawer, took out a pink notepad and pencil, and sat down across from Lyra. "I'm out of potatoes, and if I don't write it down now, I'll forget. I know why you're here. It's your father, isn't it?"

"You mean your son."

"And your mother," she continued as though Lyra hadn't interrupted her. "They've upset you again, have they?"

"No, *they* haven't upset me," she answered. "I haven't spoken to those people in quite a while, and I don't intend to anytime soon."

Gigi smiled. "Dear, you really should stop calling them 'those people.'"

I was being kind, Lyra thought. She could come up with a lot worse to call her ungrateful, pretentious, greedy parents.

"Father Henry called me."

Gigi put her pencil down and let out a sigh. "He's a bit of a tattletale, isn't he? Don't get me wrong. He's a nice man," she hastened to add, "but he gets so worked up over every little thing. He's going to end up with heart problems if he doesn't learn to relax. Stress can kill," she added with a nod.

"Grandmother, *you're* the one who's causing him stress! Father Henry is very unhappy with you."

Gigi scoffed at the notion. "Taking a little water isn't hurting anyone. And I always replace it. I don't leave the tub empty."

"It's not a tub, it's a font," she corrected. "And what do you mean, you replace it?"

"I take a couple of big bottles of Perrier with me, and after I've helped myself to what I need, I pour in the Perrier."

"You pour sparkling water—"

"That's right, dear."

The priest wasn't going to like hearing that one bit. "When you talk to Father Henry, it might be a good idea not to mention the sparkling water."

"When I talk to him?"

"I've invited him over to the house tomorrow. Perhaps he could join us for dinner."

"I like to be sociable, and this is your home, but I would like to know why you invited him."

"Gigi, you know very well why." Threading her fingers through her hair in frustration, she said, "I'm hoping he can talk some sense into you. He's warned you before about stealing holy water. Why do you keep doing it?"

"*Stealing* is such an ugly word. I'm *taking* the holy water. *Taking*," she emphasized. "The answer to your question is outside. Stand on the porch and look over at Mrs. Castman's yard. Pay particular attention to her flower beds and her planters. Compare her yard to mine."

"But Gigi . . ."

Waving her hand, she said, "Go on now."

Arguing was pointless. Lyra went out on the porch, checked both minuscule yards, then walked back into the kitchen.

"And what did you observe?" her grandmother asked.

"Mrs. Castman's flowers are blooming, and yours aren't."

"Hers are thriving, Lyra, and mine are withering away," she corrected. "Same thing happened last year and the year before. This spring I decided I would buy exactly what she did and water just as often. And look at the results. My yard gets as much sun as hers," she added. "Then I saw her coming out of church one Sunday with a big plastic jug of water. I knew where she got it. I followed her home, and lo and behold, she sprinkled the holy water all over her planters and her flowers. And that, young lady, is why I'm taking holy water."

How did one argue with such logic?

Lyra was not looking forward to the priest's visit tomorrow. If Father Henry stayed for dinner, would he make it to dessert without storming out in frustration?

SIX

FATHER HENRY HAD A LOVELY EVENING. HE'D called ahead to tell Lyra that he'd arrive at the house after saying five o'clock mass. His intention was to have a stern conversation with Gigi Prescott and be back at the rectory by six-thirty to eat cold leftovers, but the spicy aromas wafting from Gigi's kitchen made his stomach grumble, and it took very little coaxing to get him to stay for dinner.

The meal Lyra's grandmother prepared was fit for a king. It was all part of her master plan to disarm the priest. With Lyra's help she served spinach salad, prime rib with Yorkshire pudding, her special eight-thousand-calorie potatoes, and fresh asparagus. For dessert, she offered homemade apple pie with cinnamon ice cream.

Father was tall and slender, yet this evening he ate enough for three lumberjacks. Lyra couldn't figure out where he was putting it all. Gigi had decided against making her chowder in favor of red meat, arguing that all men liked beef, or at least most did. The priest was obviously a fan. He had two extra helpings.

Gigi served Father Henry coffee in the living room, then suggested they go out on the porch and sit in the wicker rockers while they discussed the holy water "situation."

Lyra stayed inside. She didn't want her grandmother to feel that she and the priest were ganging up on her. Because of their soft voices and the rising wind, Lyra couldn't hear any of the conversation, but she did hear Father laugh, and thought that must be a good sign. When Father Henry called out to Lyra to say good-bye, she decided to walk with him to his car. She wanted to find out how the "situation" was resolved.

"Your grandmother has given me her word she'll leave the holy water alone. I suggested alternatives . . . several, as a matter of fact," the priest said.

"And?"

He shook his head. "She explained it wouldn't be the same."

"But she did promise not to take any more holy water from the font?"

"That's right."

"Okay, but if anything else involving my grandmother should occur, will you call me, and only me? I don't think it's necessary to involve any other family members."

"She gave me her word," he reminded her.

Yeah, right, Lyra thought. "And I'm certain she has the best intentions," she said.

He was catching on. "I'll call you."

"Thank you." Relieved, she smiled.

He opened the car door, paused, then said, "If

she should slip up again and take a little more holy water, ask her not to replace it with sparkling water. It was still fizzing when Bill Bradshaw, one of our parishoners, happened by. He thought it was a miracle. If the pastor had seen that, he would not have been amused."

Lyra didn't start laughing until Father Henry's car had turned the corner. As she was walking up the porch steps, her eye caught a slight movement of Mrs. Castman's curtains. Lyra smiled to herself. The neighbor's curiosity must be killing her. Lyra went into the house and carried the dishes from the dining room to the kitchen. While she was loading the dishwasher, she heard laughter coming from the living room. She peeked in to find Gigi entertaining a couple from down the street. By the time Lyra finished cleaning up, Gigi's company had increased to six. Earlier Lyra had wondered why her grandmother had made two pies. Now she understood. Friends and neighbors often dropped in to visit, and Gigi always fed them. She was a wonderful hostess. When Lyra was a little girl, she would sit on the stairs, out of sight, and listen to her grandmother tell the most wonderful stories. From an early age, Lyra wanted to be just like her. And no wonder. To Lyra, Grandmother Prescott was the epitome of the genteel southern lady.

Born Lyra Colette Decoursey in Alexandria, South Carolina, a charming little town an hour from Charleston, Gigi was raised as the privileged child of Beauregard Decoursey, owner of Alexandria's single industry, the Decoursey Textile Mill.

She attended the finest boarding schools in Europe, and one month after her return home at eighteen, she met Tobias Christopher Prescott, a man her father called an upstart oil baron from the uncivilized state of Texas.

A year later, she married Tobias in the most lavish affair Alexandria had ever seen. Gigi told her namesake years later how she promised to love and honor her husband on that day, but she deliberately left out the word "obey" from her vows. Obeying a husband was just plain nonsense. Her grandmother was stubborn even back then, but Grandfather Tobias must not have minded his wife's attitude, for their marriage was strong and happy and lasted forty-two years.

Lyra knew she would never find a man like Grandfather Tobias. He was bigger than life. She doubted there were even any men like him around these days. The men she dated were self-centered, money-loving, sex-addicted chauvinists who expected to hook up with a woman two hours after meeting her. Needless to say, they were disappointed and a little shocked when Lyra said no and went home alone.

Love wasn't for her, she supposed. She was so tired of dating jerks, it just wasn't worth it. She was happy being single. Why change what worked?

It was after eleven when Lyra went downstairs to make sure the doors were locked and to say good night to her grandmother. Gigi's bedroom was tucked in the back of the house on the main floor. Her door was open, and she was tying the belt of her robe.

She saw Lyra in the doorway and said, "It was a nice day, wasn't it?"

"It was." Lyra came into the room and sat on the side of Gigi's bed. "Do you get that much company every night?"

"No, of course not, though the Parkers—they're the couple who live two doors down in the pink bungalow—like to check on me."

"I'm glad they do." Lyra's eyes settled on the framed photo on the dresser: her grandparents arm in arm standing in front of two horses.

"Do you ever miss the ranch?"

"Oh, yes, of course I do. It was my home for most of my life."

"I sometimes think you left there to get away from my parents."

Gigi looked sheepish, and deftly dodged the issue. "I love California. The move has been good for me."

Lyra smiled. "Do you miss Grandpa Tobias?"

"Yes, I do. I liked being married," she said.

"Ever think about getting married again? Grandpa Tobias would want you to be happy."

"No, no, I could never marry again. I believe you only get one, Lyra, and Tobias was my one."

"One what?"

"One true love. Now go to bed."

"I didn't realize you were such a romantic," Lyra said as she kissed her grandmother good night.

Once she was settled in bed, Lyra thought about all that her grandparents had accomplished. They had turned their small Texas ranch into an empire of fifteen thousand acres that produced oil and cattle and thoroughbred horses. It was a wonderful place to raise a family, and the couple had hoped for a house full of children, but they were able to have only one. They showered their son, Christopher, with love and attention and expected that he would take over the ranch one day. He grew up with every advantage, but showed little interest in the family business. After college he married Dallas socialite Judith Thorndyke and moved back to the ranch and, regardless of his parents' efforts, managed to shirk any of the responsibility that came with living there. Lyra's parents' lives were filled with exotic trips and social obligations, interrupted briefly by three pregnancies. Lyra's two brothers, Owen and Cooper, were born a year apart. Lyra came along five years later.

Despite the fact that her parents were seldom around, Lyra's childhood on the ranch was idyllic, thanks to Gigi and Grandpa Tobias. While Christopher and Judith were jet-setting around the world, Owen, Cooper, and Lyra grew up under the loving and watchful eyes of their grandparents. They were encouraged to explore and to pursue their passions. For Owen and Cooper, that was the ranch. Lyra's interests took a more artistic path: she fell in love with filmmaking.

Lyra's parents were deeply disappointed by their daughter's peculiar interests. They had hoped she would take her place in society by marrying into a wealthy and prominent family. Gigi, however, encouraged Lyra to pursue her dream. After Lyra finished college, her grandmother turned the ranch over to Owen and Cooper and moved to California.

Lyra had decided to stay there in order to study at one of the country's best film schools, and Gigi wanted to be nearby. For that and so much else in her life, Lyra was eternally grateful to Gigi. And she was also very protective of her.

Although her grandmother was a wonderful woman, she wasn't perfect by any means. She held grudges. She only discussed politics with Democrats because, in her outrageously biased opinion, they were intelligent and sensible, and Republicans weren't. She was stubborn and she was superstitious. And if one considered stealing holy water a crime, then Gigi was also a thief.

After mass on Sunday morning, Lyra went with Gigi to the market. They strolled among the vendors and bought oranges and grapes and bunches of bright-colored daisies, then they stopped for lunch at a cafe overlooking the beach before walking home. Lyra loved these quiet times they shared, but she knew she had to get back to Los Angeles, so by mid-afternoon, she had hugged her grandmother good-bye and was back on the freeway heading north.

As she turned the corner onto her street, her phone rang. She pulled over, put the car in park, and answered. Cooper was on the line.

"How's Gigi?" her brother asked.

"She's great."

"Still ornery?"

"Oh, yes."

"Then she's doing okay. I still think she should come back to the ranch where Owen and I can keep an eye on her."

"She doesn't want to come back, and she doesn't need a babysitter. She's perfectly capable of taking care of herself."

"Hey, I'm just as protective of her as you are. Listen, the reason I called . . . You're not going to like this . . ."

"Tell me, Cooper. Just tell me," she repeated impatiently.

"Mom and Dad just bought a house in La Jolla, not far from Gigi."

"What?" Lyra nearly dropped the phone. "Why'd they do that?"

"Dad said they want to be nearby should Gigi need them in her final years."

"Oh, right," she scoffed. "They're treating her as though she's ancient. She's in her seventies, and in this day and age that isn't old. Besides, she's in perfect health—"

Cooper interrupted her tirade. "I'm just telling you what they said."

"I'm not buying it, and neither should you. Their only real motivation is Gigi's money. They want to be near *it* far more than they do *her*. I swear I can't understand why Gigi puts up with such blatant greed."

"It could be because he's her son," Cooper said.

Ignoring that truth, Lyra said, "Every time those people do something horrible and I suggest she never speak to them again, she always says the same thing, 'Don't let it worry you,' and that's the end of the discussion."

"Like I said, he's her son."

"I know," she said.

"I've got to go. You doing okay?"

"I'm fine," she sighed.

"Stay in touch." And with that, he was gone.

Lyra took a deep breath. She was determined not to let Cooper's news upset her. She had a busy week ahead, but it would be an easy one if she stayed focused and calm. She wasn't about to let this or anything else rile her.

She could hear her grandmother's words echoing in her head: "Don't let it worry you. Don't let it worry you."

SEVEN

LYRA DIDN'T HEED THE WARNING SIGNS.
  She had punched in the code to open the parking lot's electronic gate, and as soon as she had pulled through and the gate had closed behind her, she was home.

A big luxury sedan was parked in Mrs. Eckhard's assigned spot next to Lyra's. It sat on the line separating one space from another, and she could barely get her door open. Mrs. Eckhard's Prius was at the airport for another week while she was in Hawaii. Lyra was collecting her mail for her. So who was using the space and being so careless about the way he parked?

She grabbed her purse and her keys in one hand and her overnight bag in the other. As she struggled to squeeze past the ridiculously big car, she noticed a triangular rental car sticker in the corner of the back window, and when she turned to cross the lot, she saw the trunk lid was slightly open.

One of the apartments on the second level had the television blaring. It wasn't until she climbed the outside stairs and moved down the external corridor to her apartment that she realized the noise was coming from her own living room. It sounded as though cartoons were playing. That didn't make any sense. Sidney's car was in her assigned parking spot, so presumably she was home, but she'd be the last person Lyra would expect to be watching cartoons. Yet Lyra clearly heard "Yabba dabba do" coming through the door. She slowed her pace as she approached, perplexed at the sight of scratches on the new nickel-plated lock and a split in the wall at the doorjamb.

Finally, the warning bells went off. Was Sidney inside, and if so, who was with her? Lyra leaned closer to the door and nearly jumped out of her skin when she heard a man's voice.

"Turn that down," he shouted. "It's giving me a headache."

Seconds later, the television's volume was lowered. Then Lyra heard another man talking.

"Why do we have to wait until she wakes up to carry her down to the car and dump her in the trunk?"

"That's not why we're waiting. It's because it isn't dark yet. You want someone to see you?"

"No, but why don't we just tie her up here?"

"You left the rope and the duct tape in the car, that's why."

"So why was that my job? You could have carried it up. And what are we gonna do if she don't wake up? You hit her pretty hard."

"Hey, she was making too much of a racket. I had to hit her to shut her up. If we had found what we were looking for, we would have been out of here."

Lyra moved away from the door as quietly as possible and then ran around the walkway to the back of the building. Her heart racing, she called 911. Lyra told the operator what was happening, and though her voice was shaking, she tried to answer the questions as succinctly as possible. The operator dispatched the police to her address and instructed Lyra to stay on the line. Lyra couldn't do that. She kept the line open but put the phone on top of her overnight bag, then opened the side flap of her purse and found the small canister of pepper spray. She had no intention of going into the apartment unless she heard Sidney. She would wait for the police, but in case something did happen, she needed another weapon. She looked around her. What could she use?

Her car . . . She flew down the stairs and hit the remote on her keychain to pop open the trunk. She found the L-shaped lug wrench and raced back up to her apartment door to listen while she prayed for the sound of sirens. What was taking them so long!

Pepper spray in left hand poised to fire, a lug wrench in the other, Lyra was ready. Scared to death, but ready.

She leaned toward the door to listen for Sidney's voice. The television was still tuned to the cartoon channel. The men inside were silent. What were they doing? She held her breath while she waited.

When she thought she couldn't stand it another second, they resumed talking.

"Maybe I did hit her too hard. See if she's still breathing."

As if on cue, Sidney groaned loudly.

"She's breathing, all right. Seems to be coming around. Should I tape her mouth?"

"See if there's tape in the kitchen. Can't think where else it would be in this crackerbox apartment. And while you're in there, see if there's any beer."

"Okay. Okay. Maybe after I tape her, I'll take her into the bedroom. Have a little fun while we wait, you know?"

"She's got a fine bod, doesn't she? First, get the tape and my beer, then you can do what you want with her."

"Oh, no," Lyra whispered.

She heard sirens in the distance. Thank God.

Suddenly, Sidney screamed, and Lyra knew she couldn't wait any longer. Ringing the doorbell, she stepped to the side so she couldn't be seen through the peephole.

She heard a loud whisper from the other side of the door. "Keep your hand over her mouth."

A rustling sound and then nothing. Lyra held her breath waiting. An eternity seemed to pass, and nothing but silence came from inside her apartment. Then she heard faint whispering and a scuffle. She had to do something! Edging toward the door, she carefully inserted her key. With one motion, she unlocked the door and pushed it open as she jumped out of sight. Swinging the lug wrench back, she waited.

A man bolted out the door with a gun aimed to

fire. He was huge, wide in the chest and stomach. He wore a black ski mask, and all she could see of his face were his beady eyes. As soon as he turned in her direction, she sprayed. He screamed and grabbed at his eyes. Lyra swung the wrench with all her might at the hand holding the gun. The weapon discharged before it flew out of sight, the bullet grazing her leg.

Stumbling back into the apartment, the man shouted to his cohort. "Get her, get her. Don't let her grab my gun."

Right . . . the gun. Lyra spun around to look for it, but it must have fallen through the railing. The other man tossed Sidney aside as he reached into his own pocket for a gun. He started running toward the door and Lyra, but was stopped in his tracks when Sidney swung a table lamp full force into the side of his head. Howling, he tripped and went tumbling into the sofa.

Lyra rushed forward to pull Sidney outside. Her friend looked dazed and confused. In seconds, the two thugs would be coming out after them.

"We've got to get out of here," Lyra urgently whispered.

A shot rang out, hitting the doorjamb. They ran down the stairs and ducked beneath them. On the ground a few feet away, Lyra spotted ski mask's gun. She had it in her hand a second later.

"Stay behind the post," she told Sidney as she lifted the gun and took aim toward the stairs, waiting for the two men to emerge. When nothing happened, she took hold of Sidney's hand and led her into a hallway that connected the front of the building to the back. Standing against the wall in the shadows, they heard footsteps pounding down the apartment complex's front stairs. Lyra leaned forward just enough to see the two men jump into the rented sedan next to hers. They threw the car in reverse and tore out of the parking lot, slowing only to let the electronic gate open automatically. Their tires screeched as they careened out of the lot and disappeared down the street.

Lyra slumped back against the wall and finally took a breath. "Are you all right?" Lyra whispered.

"I think so. You?"

"Still scared."

"Me, too."

Seconds later, two police cars, lights flashing, slammed to a stop in front of their apartment building. Four policemen threw the doors open and got out with guns drawn.

Lyra stepped from the hallway, bent down and put the gun on the ground, and motioned for Sidney to come forward. Police surrounded them.

"She needs an ambulance," Lyra said. "I think she has a concussion."

"I'm all right," Sidney insisted.

"We got reports of gunshots. An ambulance is on its way," a policeman said. Noticing that Sidney was swaying on her feet, he led her to the steps to sit down while he took a look at her head.

Two paramedics arrived on the scene a minute later. One tended to Sidney, and the other examined Lyra's leg wound. While he was applying antiseptic and a tiny Band-aid to the minor cut, two police officers questioned her. She couldn't tell them how the men had gotten into the apartment or what they wanted.

"We don't have anything of value except our laptops," she told them. "I did hear one of them say they were going to take Sidney somewhere when it got dark."

"Then how did they get in?" one policeman asked.

Sidney heard the question and came to stand beside Lyra. "They were already in the living room when I came home, and they weren't interested in robbing us. They were waiting," she explained.

"Waiting?" Lyra asked. "Waiting for what?"

"You," Sidney answered. "Lyra, they were waiting for you."

EIGHT

SIDNEY KNEW THEY NEEDED HELP.
Even with a police car stationed outside the gate, she didn't feel safe.

Deciding whom to call was the problem. Of her six brothers, three were FBI agents and one was a federal attorney. Even her sister, Jordan, was married to an FBI agent. All of them would come if she needed them, which was a blessing, but it could also be a curse. Her brothers could be overly protective.

Siblings in large families usually found it impossible to keep secrets from one another, and the Buchanan brothers were no different when it came to their two sisters. If either Jordan or Sidney were in trouble, all the brothers rushed to get in the middle of it, and they couldn't understand why their sisters weren't grateful for their assistance. The lack of appreciation didn't stop them, though. Fortunately, not all of the brothers were available to interfere. The youngest, Zachary, was in the Air Force Academy and, therefore, out of the loop. He and Michael, a Navy SEAL, were usually the last to know what was going on.

Sidney was the quiet one in the family. She was an observer, not a participant, which was why she, like Lyra, was going to be so good in the field they had chosen. She was also independent and determined to live her life on her own terms. In general, she wanted her brothers to stay out of her business and let her make her own decisions—good or bad—but what happened this afternoon was different. Lyra needed their help. Sidney realized that her best friend was in serious danger. Hopefully, one of her brothers would figure out why.

Sidney decided to wait until they were done at the hospital before making the call. Lyra had followed the ambulance in her car so that Sidney would have a way home.

The physician on duty in the emergency room examined Sidney and then ordered an X-ray and a CT scan. "To be safe," he said. The results were good. Sidney had a mild concussion, but it wasn't necessary for her to stay overnight. On the drive back home, she nagged Lyra to stop at the store to get some desperately needed chocolate, and Lyra gave in.

"I called maintenance," Lyra said when they were back in traffic.

"What for?"

"The apartment door. Hank should be putting the frame back together now. If those men broke the lock, Hank will put a new one in. I chose this apartment because it was so close to campus but also because I thought it was safe. The electronic gate and the proximity to the police station . . . safety outweighed how tiny the apartment was. How did they get inside the main entrance?"

"They probably followed another tenant in. Getting into our apartment was easier. That front door is so old, one good kick and they're inside."

"They tried the lock first," Lyra said. "There were scratches all over it."

"I noticed that," Sidney admitted, "but I didn't notice the frame was messed up until I was walking inside." She shook her head. "I wasn't paying attention. I've gotten lazy."

"Me, too," Lyra said. "Tell me what happened next."

"One of them grabbed me. The other guy pulled out a photo, looked at it, and shook his head. He said, 'It's the other one.'"

"The other one?"

"You, Lyra."

Lyra slowed down when they reached their street. They could both see their apartment door. Hank wasn't working on it.

He must have already finished, Lyra thought. She pulled up to the gate and pushed the numbers. The parking lot gate slowly opened.

"Did you see the photo? Where did they get a picture of me?" she asked as she drove through.

"Someone's been watching you. The photo was of the two of us walking across the quad."

"This is so creepy," Lyra whispered. She pulled into her parking spot and turned off the motor.

"Yes, it is," Sidney agreed. "The one holding me loosened his grip, and I kicked him hard you know where. That got him mad and he punched me right under the chin. Knocked me out. I'm kind of surprised I didn't chip a tooth. I don't know how long I was out, but when I woke up, I stayed still and kept my eyes closed so I could listen to them talking. They were waiting for you to get home, and were planning to take you somewhere. I think they wanted you to give them something."

"What?"

"I have no idea. Neither of them said what they were after. That's all I got before you opened the door."

"Come on. Let's go upstairs. I want this day to end."

"I want chocolate," Sidney said as she followed Lyra, who had pepper spray and her keys in her hands and a box of chocolates tucked under her arm.

"I want a Taser," Lyra said. "And mace . . . lots of mace."

"Are either of those legal in California?"

Lyra shrugged.

Sidney followed her toward the apartment building.

"How's your poor little leg?" Sidney asked. "I can't believe you were shot and didn't say anything when the police got here."

Lyra laughed. "No big deal. The paramedic was so sweet. How's your head?"

"Throbbing."

Once up the stairs, they hesitantly approached their door. The same lock was there, scratches and all, but the frame was repaired.

"We should get a second deadbolt," Sidney suggested.

Lyra agreed. "Definitely."

"Wait until you see what they did to the bedrooms. They were definitely looking for something."

"Jewelry and money?"

"We don't have any jewelry or money."

"I'll go in first," Lyra said, holding up the pepper spray as she unlocked the door and pushed it open. Blessedly, the apartment was empty. And an awful mess. It would take a solid day to get everything straightened. Drawers had been pulled out, clothes ripped from their hangers, and mattresses overturned.

"I'm going to call my sister," Sidney said. "But I'll make my bed first because I'm going to be on the phone all night."

"I'll make your bed. You relax. Jordan's a talker, huh?"

"Not really. We'll probably only talk for ten minutes, but she'll tell her husband what happened, and he'll tell my brothers, and you can bet that soon enough all of them will be calling you and me."

"They don't need to talk to me. You can tell them what happened."

"Lyra, you're part of the family now. You've known Alec and Dylan and Nick and Theo and Jordan's hunky husband, Noah, for a long time. Not only are you my best friend," she added, "but you saved my life today. It's the one benefit of being related to so many men in law enforcement. Of course they're going to help you."

Lyra smiled. "Yes, you're right. They'll help figure this out." *Thank God,* she silently added.

"Are you going to call Gigi or your brothers?"

"Oh, no," she said. "Gigi would worry, and my brothers . . . you know how they are."

"They'll drag you back to the ranch and put armed guards around you."

"Exactly," she agreed. She headed to the bedrooms. "I'll make the beds while you call Jordan. Then I'm taking a hot shower and finishing my paper on Katherine Hepburn films. It's due tomorrow."

"Who's class?"

"Linden's. He's such a hardnose."

Lyra got busy while Sidney looked for her cell phone. She found it under a table, plugged it in to charge it, then used the apartment phone to call Jordan.

"Is it too late to call?" she asked when her sister answered.

"No, of course not," Jordan assured her.

"Is Noah home?"

"He's right here. You want to talk to him?"

"Yes, please."

"Are you all right?" Jordan asked, worry in her voice.

"I'm fine."

Jordan handed the phone over to her husband, telling him that Sidney wanted to talk to him.

"Hey, sugar, what's going on?"

"Listen . . . something happened today . . ."

NINE

SIDNEY WAS ON THE PHONE UNTIL AFTER MID-night. Just as she had predicted, she had to tell the entire story to Noah, then to Theo, Dylan, Nick, and Alec.

Alec was the last to get through to her. "Who have you been talking to?"

"Our brothers."

"You should have done a conference call. Would have saved you some time."

Why hadn't she thought of that?

"Yes, I should have. Or you could have—"

"I talked to Noah," he said. "He told me what happened. Do you have any idea what the men wanted?"

"All I know is that they were looking for Lyra. Detective O'Malley spent an hour with us at the hospital asking questions, but neither of us could come up with an explanation." Her voice shook. "Alec, they were really creepy. I've never been so terrified."

"Do you know how lucky you were?"

Of course she did. "Do you know how many

times I've been asked that? I have a concussion. That isn't lucky," she said just to be obstinate.

"It could have been much, much worse. Lyra used pepper spray, huh?"

"And a lug wrench."

"Going in . . . that took guts. Still, she should have waited for the police."

"She had called them, and she was waiting," Sidney explained. "But then Lyra heard the two guys getting even more violent, and she decided she couldn't wait any longer."

"You both could have been . . ." He didn't finish his thought.

"Lyra wants to get a Taser."

"A what?"

"A Taser," she answered. "I don't think she cares if it's legal here or not. Oh, and mace. She wants to get mace."

"Let me talk to her. Can you put her on the line?"

"She's asleep. Do you want me to wake her?"

"No, I'll talk to her tomorrow. I was going to ask if you two are nervous about sleeping there tonight, but Lyra obviously isn't. What about you?"

"There's a nice policeman outside, and he's going to be there the rest of the night. That's a real deterrent, right? Besides, I don't think they'd come back. You don't either, do you?" she asked worriedly.

"Probably not."

"And I'm exhausted. I'll sleep. What do you mean, probably not?"

"You'll be okay tonight. What's your schedule tomorrow?"

"Classes."

"Both of you?"

"Yes, but not the same classes. Why?"

"E-mail me Lyra's schedule, and yours, too."

"What are you going to do?"

"I'll talk to some people early in the morning, and I'm going to send some help. I wish I could come out there, but I can't. I promise I'll send someone almost as good."

"I see you're still arrogant," she said, smiling. "This someone will take good care of Lyra. You trust him, right?"

"Yes," he assured. "And just to be on the safe side, I'm gonna get someone to watch over you until we figure this out."

"Alec, you're being so sweet. I'm starting to understand why someone as beautiful as Regan married you."

He laughed. "She lowered her standards. Talk to you tomorrow."

Sidney hung up the phone, then went to the window to see if the police car was still there. It was parked under a streetlight, so anyone approaching the apartment would definitely see it. Sidney checked the door, put a kitchen chair in front of it, and looked out the window once again before finally getting ready for bed. She wished she had a baseball bat for protection, but she didn't, so she grabbed a kitchen broom. She might be able to do some damage with that.

She fell asleep gripping the broom handle.

*   *   *

"WHERE ARE YOU, SAM?"

"Seattle."

"You owe me a favor," Alec said.

"Saving your ass makes me owe you a favor?"

"That's how we do it in the United States."

"Listen, Buchanan, I'm kind of busy . . ."

"Ask her to get dressed. This is important."

"Hold on."

Alec was left waiting for two maybe three minutes, then Sam was back on the line.

"Okay, you've ruined my evening. What do you want?"

"When are you going to Los Angeles?"

"I leave tomorrow. Why?"

Alec told him about Sidney and her roommate, Lyra. "I can't get out there, and Lyra's in trouble. I thought maybe you could step in for me. You've got the time off—"

"Sure, I'll do it. What about your sister? Is she in danger?"

"I don't think so, but I'm not taking any chances. I'm gonna ask Max Stevens to watch out for her."

"How long do you think I'll be on this?"

"I honestly don't know. I'll talk to the detectives tomorrow, but I don't think they have anything."

"When do you need me there?"

"As soon as."

"Yeah, okay."

"And Sam?"

"What?"

"Thanks."

*　　*　　*

LYRA HAD COMPLETED HER paper and had fallen asleep on her laptop. Fortunately, the lid was closed so she didn't drool all over the keyboard. She slept hard and didn't really wake up until she showered the next morning. She dressed in jeans and a light blue T-shirt. Usually she wore flats, but today she decided to wear running shoes because they were more practical, and she could run like lightning if she needed to.

"Do you think we should move?" Lyra asked Sidney while they ate cereal.

"I don't know. If we asked the super to put in a new door, maybe we'd feel safe here again."

"I don't know about that."

"Alec called," Sidney said. She repeated what her brother had told her. "I gave him our schedules. Whoever he sends will have to find us."

"I'm kind of nervous," Lyra admitted.

"Me, too."

"Listen, don't go anywhere on campus alone."

"Good idea. You shouldn't be alone either."

"We've got to leave, or we'll be late."

Sidney moved the chair away from the door, unlocked it, and pulled it open. Then she yelped. A man was standing a foot away from her.

"Sorry," he said. "Did I scare you?"

"No," she lied. "Who are you?" She realized after she asked the question how rude she'd sounded.

"If you're Sidney, I'm your shadow. Alec sent me."

Tall, dark hair, lovely smile. She noticed it all in a

flash. He could pass for a hunky graduate student, she thought.

"Do you have a gun?" she asked.

"Sure do."

She smiled. "Let's go. Lyra, hurry up. I've got a class at ten, remember? And so do you."

Lyra walked around the corner looking at her iPhone. "Pierson canceled. I don't have to be there until eleven."

"We just promised not to go anywhere on campus alone."

"She won't be alone," Max said. "Agent Kincaid is five minutes away."

Lyra looked up from her phone and put her hand out to Sidney's protector. "I'm Lyra Prescott. And you are . . . ?"

He took her hand. "Max Stevens," he said. He turned to Sidney. "Shouldn't we get going?"

Sidney grabbed her bag and said, "Lead the way."

He started down the stairs. As Sidney followed him, she turned back to Lyra wide-eyed and mouthed the word "Wow."

Smiling at Sidney, Lyra shut the apartment door. The fact that Max carried a gun and could protect her friend was all that really mattered to her. When it came down to it, looks weren't important.

TEN

AGENT SAMUEL KINCAID WAS ONE GORGEOUS man.

Pepper spray in hand, Lyra opened the door, looked up into his eyes, and promptly forgot how to breathe.

She had never had such an oh-my-God reaction to any man before, and she had met plenty of pretty men since moving to Los Angeles. They were everywhere—in restaurants, theaters, gyms, universities, beaches, even churches. This man wouldn't be called pretty, actually. He was too rugged, too masculine, and very, very sexy. He was tall—she was considered above average in height and she barely reached his shoulders. He had sandy blond hair and piercing blue eyes. His facial bone structure was just about perfect—lovely straight nose, sexy mouth, chiseled chin.

Yes. Gorgeous, all right.

Enough, she told herself. So he was the sexiest man she had ever seen. Big deal.

"You gonna spray me with that?" he asked in a low voice with an intriguing accent.

"What? Oh, no, no." She lowered the pepper spray, thrust out her hand, and said, "Lyra. I'm Lyra . . ." Why couldn't she remember her name?

"Prescott?" he suggested.

How sweet. He was helping her out.

"Yes, Prescott," she agreed.

His eyes sparkled. Did he know how discombobulated she felt? Apparently so, since he had to tell her her own last name.

He shook her hand while introducing himself. "Agent Samuel Kincaid. You can call me Sam. You and I are going to be tight for a while."

"The accent . . . Scotland, right?"

"Yes."

"You saved Alec Buchanan's life."

He didn't comment but said, "You want to let me come inside?"

"Of course." She hastily got out of the way. As he passed her, he reached down and took the pepper spray out of her hand.

Sam was looking around the room, and she couldn't imagine what he must be thinking . . . probably that she and Sidney lived like pigs.

She hurriedly said, "The men who came here last night tore the place apart, and Sidney and I haven't had time to clean it up yet. I don't know if they found what they were looking for or not."

He turned to her. "From what Alec told me, *you* were what they were looking for."

"I know, but if they were waiting for me, why tear up the apartment? I think they were after something else."

"Could be," he said. "Tell you what, while you're

packing your things, you might do an inventory, see if anything is missing."

"While I'm packing?"

"Yes. We aren't going to be staying here."

"We?"

"Like I said, you and I are going to be real tight for a while."

"So you're my shadow?"

"That's right. Alec sent me your schedule. We should get going if you're going to make your ten o'clock class."

"My ten o'clock was canceled. My next one is at eleven."

"Good. That will give me time to check things out on campus. Don't forget, the guys who broke in last night are still out there."

A chill ran down her spine, and she nodded that she understood.

She went into her bedroom, looked in the mirror over her chest of drawers, and ran her fingers through her disheveled hair. Then she put on lip gloss, dabbed a little perfume behind her ears, and picked up her backpack. Slipping a strap over her shoulder, she walked back into the living room. "Okay, I'm ready."

He opened the door for her. She smiled and said, "I'm not so sure Professor Mahler will let you stay in the classroom. He doesn't like anything establishment . . . such as the FBI."

"Yeah? I'll bet he lets me stay. I can be a real charmer."

Ten minutes later, Sam walked close to her side as they headed across campus. She noticed his gaze taking it all in, watching the roofs, the people in the quad, the street. Impressive, she thought. A casual observer wouldn't notice what he was doing.

"Lyra? We need to establish some ground rules."

"Like what?"

"It's important that you do what I ask. I'm here to protect you, so if I tell you to drop or to run, do it immediately. No questions or arguments. I might have to use my gun, and I don't want you in the way."

He was scaring her. She nodded. "I understand."

"Good. Later, I'll want you to tell me exactly what happened last night."

"I thought you already knew."

"I do, but I want to hear it from you."

Two female students walked by, their eyes glued on Sam. Lyra certainly couldn't blame them. She heard one of them whisper that Sam had a gun.

"How am I going to explain your constant presence at my side?"

"Say whatever you want."

Except for the gun, he didn't look like an agent. He was wearing worn jeans with a Polo T-shirt. As they walked toward the classroom building and he was telling her how much he liked the campus, she was thinking how much she liked his sexy brogue. She hoped Professor Mahler didn't make a fuss or throw him out. She'd hate for Sam to have to stand in the hall for an hour.

"We're early," Lyra said as they approached the classroom. "You could probably talk to Dr. Mahler now in his office. I'll introduce you."

Lyra led the way through the classroom to Mahler's office as students filed in behind them. She knocked on the professor's door and said, "Dr. Mahler, it's Lyra Prescott. I have an FBI agent with me who—"

"FBI?" he roared. The door was flung open and within seconds his face was beet red.

"Told you he'd be difficult," she whispered.

Sam smiled. "I'll take it from here." With that, he walked past Mahler into his office and closed the door behind him.

Lyra wanted to press her ear to the door to hear what was being said, but she resisted the urge. She wouldn't have been surprised to hear the professor shouting, but neither he nor Sam had raised his voice. Dr. Mahler was probably in shock that an FBI agent was standing in his office. Sam represented everything that Mahler thought was wrong with this country. "Big Brother"—that's what he called law enforcement officers. Fortunately, with her academic work almost done, she wouldn't have to hear his bunk much longer.

The door opened and Sam emerged. Winking at Lyra and nodding to two gaping graduate students, he walked to the last row of chairs where Lyra had dropped her backpack. He took a seat and leaned back.

Lyra sat next to him and took out her laptop. "What did you say to him?" she asked.

"Not much."

Lyra was skeptical. Maybe Sam used brute force to get his way . . . or maybe he really was a charmer.

Dr. Mahler entered the classroom. His face was pale, and he glanced furtively at Sam.

Lyra leaned close to Sam and whispered. "Okay. What did *he* say?"

Sam grinned. "He's real happy I'm here."

ELEVEN

MAHLER'S CLASS LASTED TWENTY-FIVE MIN-utes instead of the usual fifty. Lyra was sure Sam was the reason. The FBI agent stood for every-thing Mahler despised, and the professor couldn't wait to get him out of his classroom. He obviously blamed Lyra, and he wasn't going to be forgiving or understanding. His hateful glances in her direc-tion told her as much.

There goes the grade, she thought with a sinking feeling.

She knew the professor wanted to blow up at her, but he couldn't with Sam in the room. He wouldn't forget, though. Lyra had witnessed his temper the first of April when another graduate student, Carl, dared to suggest that Big Brother wasn't watching anyone or invading anyone's privacy because Big Brother didn't exist. As soon as Mahler could catch his breath, he went ballistic. He called Carl a right-wing baboon and a puppet for the establishment. He was berating Carl's work and was threatening to throw him out of class when Carl jumped up and said, "April fools, Professor!"

Taken aback, Mahler blinked furiously and rubbed his chin. "April fools . . ." he repeated.

Carl stood there sweating bullets until a slow smile appeared on the professor's face. He pointed a finger at the student. "Good one, Carl. You really got me."

The professor laughed, and Carl's career in film was saved.

Lyra had dealt with difficult professors before, but none with an ego the size of Mahler's. She'd heard his wife had left him. She probably walked out on him because she made the mistake of having a different point of view, Lyra thought. She couldn't even imagine being married to such an obnoxious man.

Students were filing out of the classroom. Lyra slipped her laptop into her backpack and threw the strap over her shoulder to leave, but Sam put his hand on her arm to indicate that she should wait.

Carl and another grad student, Eli, filed past in the row ahead.

"It was nice knowing you, Lyra," Carl whispered.

"It's not that bad," she protested. "Mahler will get over it."

Carl shook his head. "Have you learned nothing from the April fools debacle?"

"I'm really going to miss you," Eli added, grinning, "when you get kicked out."

"Oh, stop it," she said, exasperated. "The professor isn't going to throw me out."

She knew they were having a fine time teasing her, but there was a kernel of truth in their jibes. Mahler would do something to get even . . . like ripping her documentary apart. If that happened, she'd go to war with him. She'd start with the head of the department, get someone else who knew what he was doing to look at her film . . . unless of course it really was awful and should be ripped apart.

Her mind was racing until she heard Eli say, "You're gonna have to sleep with him, I suppose. Then he'll get past it."

Lyra's mouth dropped open. "That's not funny. To think . . ." She shuddered. "It makes me sick to my stomach."

Carl looked at Sam. "Eli was kidding. Lyra doesn't sleep with anyone."

"I've got to get to the lab," Lyra quickly blurted to change the subject.

"You haven't introduced us," Carl said. He and Eli simultaneously turned their eyes toward the gun at Sam's side.

Lyra introduced Sam to her friends.

"You a cop?" Eli asked.

"FBI," Sam answered without further explanation.

"You're the real deal? You're not just acting like an FBI agent to give Mahler a nervous breakdown, are you?"

"No," Sam answered.

"So how come you're with Lyra?"

"He's a friend," she said, hoping to end the conversation. "Sam, we really need to get going."

Carl and Eli followed them outside the building and stopped on the steps watching as Lyra and Sam walked across the campus. When they turned to walk parallel to the street, Sam moved to block Lyra from the passing traffic.

"I didn't think they needed to know the real reason you're here," she explained, anticipating that he would ask that question.

Sam glanced over his shoulder at her friends. Carl and Eli hadn't moved. Both were looking wistfully at Lyra.

"Have you ever gone out with either one of those guys?" he asked.

"No."

"But they've asked, haven't they?"

She looked up at him. "Yes, they have. They're nice guys."

He surprised her by laughing. "What's so funny?" she asked.

"I doubt they'd appreciate being described as nice." He glanced at her with a mischievous glint in his eyes. "How do they know so much about your sleeping habits?"

Lyra could feel her face turning red. "They don't," she answered. "They just know I wouldn't sleep with *them*."

"You're picky, huh?"

"Very," she said emphatically, as she turned onto a sidewalk that led to a small windowless building. "Here we are. I'll be in the lab for a couple of hours finishing my editing. Then I'm officially done. You can drop me off and do whatever while I'm—" She stopped talking when he shook his head. "I just thought you might—"

"No." His voice was firm. "You need to start taking this seriously, Lyra."

She nodded. "I know."

He opened the door for her and followed her up the stairs. "What's your schedule tomorrow?"

"No classes."

"That's good. We can get away from here. If you're not following your normal routine, it will make it harder for them to find you."

"Meaning the men who broke into our apartment?"

"Yes."

"Where are we moving?"

"I don't know yet. Alec will tell us."

"Will Sidney be coming with us?"

"No."

He didn't elaborate, but she knew what his silence implied: that it would be too dangerous for Sidney to be around her.

For the next two hours Sam either sat beside her with his arm on the back of her chair or stood in front of the door watching her screen as she manipulated the images. The film was only twenty minutes long, but Lyra was being meticulous as she did her final edit. Once it was complete, she played it from start to finish.

Sam stood behind her to watch. The documentary was amazing, and so was she. Lyra narrated the film, and her voice was both sultry and sweet— a contradiction to the images he was seeing on the screen. She had managed to get nearly every license plate on the cars and trucks that drove into the park to dump their toxic waste. She got the people's faces on camera as well. Atta girl, he thought, smiling. If

the police got hold of her movie, arrests and con-
victions would be a slam dunk.

Lyra burned three extra disks before finally
standing and stretching her arms over her head.
"I'm completely done. All I have to do is hand it
in, and I'll do that next week."

"Why not today?"

"Are you kidding? I'll wait until the professor
gets over . . . you . . . as in FBI you."

"He would be that petty?"

"Probably not, but why take the chance? Are
you hungry? I'm starving."

She assembled her things, and Sam held the door
for her as she stepped outside. She had been sitting
in the dark for so long, the sun nearly blinded her.
Sam took his sunglasses from his pocket and offered them to her.

She shook her head appreciatively. "Thanks. I'm
fine."

A T.A. passed her. "Hey, Lyra, I heard what
happened last night. Glad you're okay."

Three more students commented on yesterday's
incident before she'd crossed the quad.

"News travels fast around here," she said as she
quickened her pace.

"Someone's waving to you," Sam told her a
minute later.

Oh, damn, she thought. Jean Lillard, Mahler's
personal assistant, was running toward them, her
long tie-dyed skirt flapping in the wind and her
Earth Mother shoes clomping on the concrete
sidewalk.

Trying to catch her breath, Jean panted, "The professor wants to see you right away . . . in his office."

"Now? Do you know what he wants?"

"I think he has another project for you. Don't frown, Lyra. It's all good."

All good? Nothing about Mahler was all good. Since Jean was obviously loyal to the man, Lyra kept her opinion to herself.

Ten minutes later she was knocking on the professor's door.

He looked up from a stack of papers. "Come in. Come in," he called out.

"You wanted to see me?" She approached his desk while Sam waited in the doorway.

"First of all, I want to apologize for my outburst. I simply overreacted," he explained, his gaze bouncing back and forth between Lyra and Sam. "I just heard what happened to you last night. Horrible, horrible crime these days. It's not safe anywhere. I certainly understand why you would call your friend for help," he added, pointing to Sam.

Before she could answer, he asked another question. "You and your roommate are all right, aren't you?"

"Yes, we're fine."

"Good. Now to the reason you're here. Carl mentioned in passing that you and he are both close to finishing your projects."

"Yes, Professor."

Lyra quickly assessed the situation. Mahler seemed to be in an uncharacteristically good mood. If she handed her project in now, she might benefit from it. She took one of the DVDs out of her bag and put it on the desk. "Here it is. All finished."

He beamed. "Excellent. You're the first to turn in your work. Are you pleased with it? Or do you feel you rushed it?"

"I don't think I rushed it. I'm proud of the work."

Mahler nodded. "Because you finished first, you get the opportunity to do a short subject. If I think it's good enough, it will be entered into the Dalton competition."

The Dalton was an award given for the best children's short film, fiction or nonfiction. Lyra didn't know the first thing about doing a children's film— didn't know much about children either—but how could she pass up the chance to be entered in a major competition?

"I know you're working on another project for extra credit . . . what did you call it . . . The Garden?" Mahler asked.

"Yes."

"I think it's a great idea, and you could do the two projects simultaneously, but they probably would be better if you concentrated on one at a time. Are you interested in doing the childen's short?"

"Oh, yes, I'd love to do it," she rushed out without further thought.

He handed her a folder. "There are the rules for the competition. You're allowed to do fiction or nonfiction. In other words, you could interview puppets or you could interview real children. Just remember to get their parents' signatures."

"When is the deadline?"

"It's all in the folder," he said.

Lyra thanked him for giving her this opportunity and walked to the door with her head spinning. What was the matter with her? She couldn't take this on. Her life wasn't her own right now. There were two large, creepy men trying to grab her, and God only knew why. She certainly didn't. Keeping the worry and fear in the back of her mind was becoming more and more difficult, especially with Sam at her side to remind her.

Pretending she wasn't in danger was foolish. She should run and hide, not do a children's film.

She was definitely out of her mind.

TWELVE

Lyra and Sam stopped at a restaurant just off Oak Avenue called Macy's. It was a popular place with the university crowd because the food was fantastic and the prices were surprisingly reasonable. It was always packed, no matter the hour, but they were fortunate and got the last available table. They were seated in the back by the kitchen door, which Sam liked because he could face the front window and see not only everyone in the restaurant but also the people and the cars moving past.

After they ordered lunch, Lyra asked, "How long does Alec expect you to stay with me?"

"I'm not sure," he answered. "I'll talk to him tonight. But probably in another couple of days he or the detectives working the case will find someone else to take over."

"Working the case? I don't think they have much to work with. The men wore masks and didn't happen to mention why they were after me."

"Those two left something behind, and their DNA will nail them."

"If they're in the system."

"Yeah?" He flashed a smile.

"I watch television. There are fifty or sixty CSI shows on now," she exaggerated.

"Detective O'Malley is in charge of your case, and he knows what he's doing."

"You've talked to him?"

"Yes."

Sam's cell phone vibrated. He saw who it was and apologized to Lyra before he answered. Although he was sitting across from her, she couldn't make out what he was saying. She finally caught a word or two and realized he wasn't speaking English.

Checking her iPhone, Lyra saw there were forty messages. Several of her friends on campus, including Carl and Eli, wanted to know what country Sam was from and how he was able to become an FBI agent. She deleted most of the messages and saved others for a later reply.

The waiter brought them iced tea and water. She thanked him, took a sip of water, and looked out the window. It occurred to her that she knew next to nothing about the man sitting across from her. When he had appeared at her apartment door that morning, she had recognized his name. He was the agent who had saved Sidney's brother. Now she was trying to recall what else her roommate had told her about him. All she could remember Sidney saying upon her return to Los Angeles after visiting Alec was that Sam Kincaid was from Scotland, that he had dual citizenship, and that he was incredibly heroic.

And that was all she knew . . . except that every time she looked at him her heart raced. No man had ever gotten that kind of reaction from her before. This physical attraction was growing, and it was disgustingly animalistic.

She would be relieved when he left because what she was feeling was simple lust, and she didn't want to make a fool of herself by throwing herself at him. The longer he stayed with her, the stronger the possibility that such a thing could happen.

Keep it on a professional level, she told herself.

Uh oh. She suddenly realized she wasn't looking out the window. She was staring at him. At his mouth, to be exact. Sam ended his call and turned toward her. Fortunately, the waiter brought their food, and she pretended to be ravenous.

"How good is your memory?" he asked.

"Pretty good."

"Tell me what you did last week. Day by day," he said.

She went through her schedule, and only after she'd finished recounting her days and nights did she realize how boring it all sounded.

"What about men?"

"What about them?" She twirled her straw in her tea.

"Dates? Sleepovers? You know what I'm asking."

"No dates. No sleepovers."

He looked dubious.

"What? You don't believe me?" she asked.

"I believe you could have any man you want."

"Why would you think—"

"You're a very beautiful woman," he said very matter-of-factly. "And you're smart, interesting . . ."

He was complimenting her, but it sounded as though he was reciting words from a lawn mower manual. His monotone suggested he wasn't the least bit interested in her attributes. It was a real kick to her ego.

"I'm not going to go out with just anyone, and the last couple of weeks have been grueling with work. I haven't had time to date."

She wasn't sure how he'd done it, but he had managed to put her on the defensive, and she felt embarrassed about her lack of a social life. When was the last time she had looked forward to a date? She couldn't remember.

Pushing his plate to the side, Sam leaned forward. "We're up to Friday," he reminded her.

"Let's see," she said, biting her lower lip and looking up at the ceiling. "I went to class, hurried back to the apartment, packed an overnight bag, dropped some film at the library, and headed home—"

"You flew to Texas?"

"No, I drove to San Diego. I live with my grandmother."

"I thought you lived in Texas."

"I do."

"Lyra." His impatience was apparent.

"How do you know about Texas?"

"I read your file."

She shot forward and nearly knocked her glass over. "My file? I have a file?" She was moving from surprise to outrage. "There's a file on me?"

He was amused by her reaction. "You're not going to go all Mahler on me, are you? Lecture me on Big Brother?"

"Of course not."

"I'm an FBI agent. I can get anything I want." He grinned as he made the boast. "I got a copy of the police report, and the detective in charge gave me copies of his notes and interviews. Alec added some personal data for me as well."

"Such as?"

"Legally, you're squeaky clean. You've never been arrested, never even had a speeding ticket or parking ticket."

He took a sip of his tea and watched the couple at the next table leave the restaurant before continuing. "You graduated summa cum laude from the university. Your brothers, Owen and Cooper, and your grandmother Prescott attended your graduation. Neither of your parents came."

"Which made it a festive event. What else?"

"There weren't any boyfriends there," he said. "It was expected that you would become engaged to John Forest—"

"No, it wasn't expected. I never had any intention of marrying him."

"From what I was told, you broke it off with Forest quite abruptly and wouldn't tell anyone why."

"It wasn't *abruptly,* and it was a mutual decision. We wanted different things."

"Yeah? What did you want?" he asked out of curiosity.

Not to be bored to death, she thought but didn't say. In all the time she had known John, she had never heard him laugh really hard, the kind of laugh that brought tears to your eyes and took your breath away. He was always so serious. Who wanted to live like that?

"Lyra?"

"Passion," she blurted. "I wanted passion and laughter."

He didn't even raise an eyebrow. He went back to sounding like he was reading the lawn mower manual. "Your parents tried to have your grandmother declared incompetent, and you stopped it."

Sam made it sound as though it wasn't a big deal, but the reality was far more complicated. Lyra had spent every penny she had on legal fees because her parents had their attorney freeze Gigi's assets and Lyra's trust fund. For the duration of the trial, neither of them could even buy a cup of decent coffee.

"I didn't stop them," she told him. "My grandmother did. She proved without a doubt she is of sound mind. And how is any of this relevant to the break-in?"

Sam was looking out the front window, and he answered almost absentmindedly. "Everything's relevant."

"Now it's my turn," she said.

He glanced at her. "Your turn to what?"

"Ask questions. Do you live in Washington, D.C.?"

"Yes."

"You flew all this way—"

"No. I was in Seattle."

"Why?"

"To give a lecture."

The waiter laid their bill in a black folder on the table, and Sam put his American Express card inside and handed it back.

"Where do you go next? Home?"

"No."

"No, what?"

"I was coming here to give a lecture. Alec knew that and called me to ask for a favor . . . and before you ask . . . you're the favor."

"After you give your lecture, are you going home then?"

"No."

Was he being evasive on purpose, or was he frustrating her just for the fun of it?

"No, what, you impossible man?"

He flashed a smile. "I go to San Diego, talk to some cadets, and then I'm done."

"Now, was that so difficult?"

The waiter handed him the folder. Sam signed, picked up his card, and said, "Are you ready to leave?"

Ignoring his question, she asked, "And then you go back to D.C.?"

"For a few days, then on to Scotland."

"One more question and I'll stop," she promised. "Any serious relationships? You asked me about John Forest," she hurriedly reminded him.

"There was a specific reason for that question," he said.

"And there's a specific reason for my question."

"Yeah? What?"

"I'm curious."

He paused for several seconds. "No."

She sighed. "No, what?"

"No serious relationships."

"Have you ever been in love?"

"Yes."

"What happened?"

"I married her."

THIRTEEN

Married? Oh my God, he was married.

Lyra was mortified. Had she been flirting with him? She thought about it and decided no, she hadn't, but still, her attitude would certainly have been different if she had been privy to that important information. She might have said one *hubba-hubba* to herself, and that would have been it. Lyra had never gone after a married man, and she wasn't going to start now. Not that it mattered. First of all, she didn't know how to go after any man, and second, Sam had made it perfectly clear with his one-word stay-out-of-my-business answers that he wasn't interested in her, even if he weren't married.

She wasn't going to ask another personal question. Sam had let her know—and he hadn't been subtle about it—that he wanted to keep his private life private, and she would respect that. If he wanted to tell her anything more, he would. But she would not ask.

"Children?"

"No," he answered.

Stop asking, she told herself. Just stop. "How long?"

"How long what?"

"Married."

"Three years."

Dear God, why couldn't she stop with all the questions?

Had his cell phone not rung, she would have kept right on interrogating him. Perhaps to discourage her, he looked out the window while he listened to the caller. He was only on the phone for a minute, and when he finished the conversation, he was still staring at the street.

"Look out the window," he told her.

Lyra turned around.

"Do you see the man across the street?" Sam asked. "He's leaning against a post, and he's holding a newspaper in front of his face."

Lyra leaned to the side to see around the other diners. The man in question had the newspaper plastered against the lower half of his face just below his eyes. Peeking over the top, he was obviously not reading.

"I see him, but I can't see his whole face."

"You will. Just wait a minute. He keeps lowering the paper to get a better look inside the restaurant. Okay, there he is."

"I see him." The man was standing in the sun, and his face was clearly visible. "Oh, my, are those scars?" She squinted against the sunlight's glare. "And is that his real hair? What's he doing? Is he trying to see us?"

"I think that's his plan."

"He's spying on us?"

"Uh-huh."

Lyra tilted her head and leaned closer to Sam to get a better look. The way the man's head kept popping up over the newspaper reminded her of the arcade game Whack-a-Mole.

"He's not very good, is he?" she said.

Sam smiled. "No, he's not."

A car sat a few feet away from the man. It was the only one parked on the busy street, which had NO PARKING signs every fifteen feet. He was so preoccupied watching the restaurant, he didn't notice the tow truck that had pulled up behind the car.

Lyra watched as the incident unfolded. "You know what? He looks familiar, but I can't think where I might have seen him. Maybe on campus," she decided. "He doesn't look much like a student, though."

The tow truck driver had finished making the connections to the car and was getting back into the cab of his truck when the man behind the newspaper glanced in that direction and realized what was happening. Looking dumbfounded, he dropped the newspaper and started running toward the car, shouting and waving his hands.

"Do you think he has anything to do with those men who broke into my apartment?" she asked.

Sam went to the window to watch. The tow truck came to a stoplight, then drove off. The car owner chased down the street after it.

Sam shrugged. "I don't know. That guy doesn't look like he could pull off much of anything."

Lyra gathered her things and started toward the front door, but Sam grabbed her hand and pulled her behind him through the kitchen and out the back door.

"Are we going back to my apartment?" she asked.

"Yes, but we won't stay long. Pack what you need, and we're out of there."

"What about my car?"

"It stays."

"It's crazy for me to move. If those men come back, they'll find me on campus. It would be easy for them to get my schedule. So why bother moving from one place to another? They could just follow me home from class."

"Your apartment isn't safe," he said. "There's only one way in and out, and the door is flimsy."

"The super is replacing it. It might already be done."

"Replacing it with another flimsy, hollow door that anyone could kick in. As soon as the door's open, you're a target. Anyone on the street could see you. There's no real security," he continued. "No peephole in the door, no cameras filming the parking lot . . ."

"There's an electronic gate," she reminded him. The gate was why she chose the tiny apartment in the first place, that and the fact that it was on the border of the campus. She and Sidney could walk anywhere.

"Did the gate keep them out?"

"No, but . . ." She stopped arguing. Anyone who wanted in could get in.

"After this is over, you could make the apartment safer before you move back in. Better locks, cameras, intercom . . . there's a lot more that can be done."

"Moving back depends on how long it will take the detectives to catch those men. I'm finishing the program pretty soon, and I'll be officially done with the university. Same with Sidney."

"Do you have a job lined up?"

"No."

"Any ideas where you want to live? Maybe close to your ranch in Texas?"

"No," Lyra answered. There had been a job offer from that TV station in Texas, but she knew she really didn't want that.

"San Diego then?"

"I don't know."

His questions were bringing back her panic. Here she was almost finished with her graduate work, and she still didn't know exactly what direction her career would take. Oh, and there were two horrible men who wanted God-only-knew-what from her. They'd turned her apartment upside down looking for something. If she didn't have whatever it was, they would kill her, she decided, and if she did have it, they'd take it and then kill her. Either way, it was a lose-lose situation for her.

"I think I should stay in the apartment, and the detectives could set up a trap and catch these men. Sidney should move to a safer place, of course. That's a good plan, don't you think?"

"No."

"No? No explanation? Just no?"

"That's right. No."

All the way across campus Sam scanned their surroundings looking for possible threats. He never once looked at her. Until she said, "You should wear your wedding ring."

"What?"

"Your wedding ring. You should wear it." She put her hand up. "That's all I'm going to say."

He looked to be at a loss for words. Embarrassed because she had turned the conversation from professional to personal, she blurted, "I'm just saying . . . you should, that's all."

"Why?"

"Why wear a wedding ring? Because you're married," she pointed out.

"No, I'm not."

She was beginning to really dislike this man. Yes, he was being professional, and seemed to be good at his job, and from what she had heard about him, he was heroic and a good friend, but, in her opinion, he was also nuts.

She had a feeling he would get along great with Gigi.

"Three years, remember? Married three years?"

He nodded. "Yes, that's right."

"But you're not married."

"No, I'm not."

Okay, she was done. He didn't want to tell her the truth or share anything personal with her, and she had to accept that.

Married. Not married. She no longer cared.

Lyra figured he was divorced and didn't like to talk about it, which was fine with her. She would quit trying to be sociable.

When they finally arrived back at the apartment, Sidney was sitting on the sofa organizing and stacking papers she'd collected from the floor. Max was fishing papers from under the sofa and handing them to her.

"Are you okay?" Sidney asked. "You look irritated."

Lyra sat down beside her. "I'm fine. How about you?"

"Good," she answered. "I cleaned up the mess in my bedroom and packed, and now I'm tackling the living room."

"I'll do the kitchen and my room," Lyra said. She was full of nervous energy and wanted to burn some.

She worked on her bedroom first. The two thugs had torn everything apart. They'd broken most of her treasures. The old clock she'd had since high school and her old-fashioned phone were in pieces. They'd even trashed her ocean sound machine.

Muttering to herself, she went into the kitchen to get a trash bag and carried it back to her bedroom. Once it was filled, she put the bag by the front door. Sam, she noticed, was on the phone, and Sidney was still sitting on the sofa. Max was sprawled next to her. His hands crossed on his chest and his legs stretched out, he appeared to be sleeping.

Sidney looked at Lyra, tilted her head toward Max, and rolled her eyes. Max was good-looking but nothing like Sam, Lyra thought.

Lyra went back to work. She must have made twenty trips between the kitchen and her bedroom and bathroom before all three rooms were clean.

Then she packed an overnight bag with enough clothes to last a week, carried the small suitcase into the living room, and dropped it next to Sidney's. Remembering her laptop, she slipped that into her backpack and put it next to her overnight bag, and she was finished. All she needed to do now was take a quick shower and change her clothes.

Sam finished his call, opened the door, and stepped outside.

"What are you doing?" Max asked without opening his eyes.

"New door's here," Sam said.

It wasn't the flimsy door Lyra expected. It was a top-of-the-line model, according to the man installing it. It had a peephole and not one but two dead bolts. Just what Sam would have wanted, and a sure sign that he had something to do with it.

"Is the super okay with the new door?" Sidney asked.

Sam answered. "I didn't ask him. A kid could have broken through that old door." He winked at Lyra. "After all this is done with, this should keep you safe."

Lyra blushed and suddenly remembered to tell Sidney about the children's film Mahler just assigned her. They moved into Lyra's bedroom to discuss the opportunity at length.

"Do you really think you can get it all done in time?" Sidney asked.

"I already finished the toxic dumping documentary and handed it in."

"Congratulations. You did a fantastic job, and I'm sure everyone will be blown away by it."

"I love that you're so optimistic."

"What about that garden in the middle of the dump? Are you giving up on that?"

"I don't want to," she said. "The professor doesn't want me to drop it either. He thinks it's an interesting idea, and he seems to think I can do the children's short first and then the garden documentary."

"If anyone can do it, you can," Sidney encouraged.

Lyra let out a long sigh. "I hope so. The break-in, and the threat of someone still out there waiting, and the bodyguards . . . it's all so much to deal with. It's going to be difficult to stay focused."

Sidney sat on the bed. "Let's change the subject to something more pleasant," she said. "What do you think of Sam?"

"I think he can't wait to get away from me."

"Wrong. No way. Since you walked in, the guy hasn't taken his eyes off you."

"That's his job," she said.

"Inside our apartment where you're perfectly safe? He watches you, Lyra, and no wonder, he's no different from any other man."

She shook her head. "He's very standoffish. He doesn't talk about himself at all."

"And?"

She sighed. "Don't you think he's the most gorgeous man you've ever seen?"

"He's not bad," she drawled. "Max is no oaf either."

Sam appeared in the door. "Time to go. You, too, Sidney."

"Why can't we stay together?" Sidney asked.

"Anyone who gets near Lyra is in danger."

"Lovely," Lyra whispered. "Now I'm a lightning rod."

She put her arm around Sidney's shoulder as they walked into the living room to gather up their bags. The fear she had felt at first was now turning to anger. Sidney had been attacked; their apartment had been destroyed, and no one knew why. Who were these men and what did they want? Lyra was determined to find out.

FOURTEEN

MILO CHASED THE TOW TRUCK HALF A BLOCK, caught up with it at a stoplight, and tried to bribe the driver into letting him have his car back. He offered him two hundred dollars at first and kept increasing the amount, until the light changed and the driver stepped on the gas and drove off.

Cursing a blue streak didn't help. The tow truck was already out of sight. Milo was thankful that no one from the company had witnessed his stupidity. He should have known better than to park his car on one of the busiest streets in Los Angeles.

Watching his car being towed away was the culmination of a disastrous weekend.

The unfortunate chain of events had started last Friday at the Rooney yard sale.

Before the police arrived, Milo quickly left the Rooney house, drove home, and unloaded all the treasures he'd gotten at the sale, including Babs's huge diamond ring. Then he got back in the car and drove to the office to talk to Mr. Merriam.

The boss was in a frenzy. The door to his office

was closed, which meant he didn't want to be disturbed. As Milo hesitantly approached, he could hear Mr. Merriam ranting and raving. Milo took the risk of knocking.

"What do you want?" Mr. Merriam bellowed.

"I want to tell you about a sale I attended," he called out so the second shift at the collection agency wouldn't think anything was out of the ordinary.

"Come on in then."

Milo expected to see other men in the office with the boss, but Mr. Merriam was alone. Had he been shouting at the walls?

Mr. Merriam went to his desk and plopped down in his swivel chair.

"I'm doomed, Milo. If I don't get it back . . . if someone else finds it . . ." With the back of his sleeve he wiped the sweat from his forehead, then motioned for Milo to sit. "I'll go away for the rest of my life . . . no parole for me, not after what I've done."

Milo had never seen his boss like this. He looked as though he was going to cry.

"Sir, if you could just trust me and tell me what it is—I mean, what Rooney took." He quickly raised his hand to ward off Mr. Merriam's reaction. "I need to know what I'm looking for. A diamond maybe? Or a famous painting or an accounting book with numbers?"

Mr. Merriam frowned while he thought it over. Then he nodded. "Yes, you need to know. Like you said, how can you look for it if you don't know what it is? It's a DVD," he whispered.

"Rooney could have taken it out of its case and hidden it anywhere."

"Like maybe in a book?"

"Yes, it would be easy to hide a disk in a book. Why?"

"There was a good-looking girl at the yard sale who filled up her car with nothing but books and a few DVDs. Maybe some CDs, too. Babs had dumped them in the middle of her front yard, and she kept bringing out more and more. The girl would have taken every one of those books if she'd had the room. All the other shoppers were carrying out chairs and lamps and kitchen stuff. None of them even glanced at the books."

Mr. Merriam straightened up. "How long had the sale been going on when you got there?"

"I'm pretty sure it'd just started."

"That's good, that's good. The DVD could still be in the house, in a wall maybe, or under a floorboard. It could be anywhere. Or that girl could have it and not know what it is . . . until she watches it," he added with a shiver. "We've got to get it back."

"I'll get it for you," Milo promised.

"Was the girl there when Babs killed her husband?"

"No, she had just left. And after Babs shot him and made sure he was dead, she walked inside and shot herself. That's what it said on the news. Most people at the yard sale stood around and watched, but I didn't wait for the police to show up."

"I'm going to have Charlie Brody and Lou Stack get into Rooney's house tonight. I want them to bring me every DVD they can find. It's a big house," he lamented. "The damn thing could be anywhere, but I'm not taking any chances. If they can't find it after a couple of tries, they'll blow the place up. I don't want there to be anything left to sift through. Charlie has connections, and he says he can get explosives that will do the job."

Shocked by what he had just heard, Milo stammered, "You . . . you already told Charlie and Stack what you were looking for?" *But not me,* he silently added. *I had to practically beg you to tell me.*

Mr. Merriam didn't notice how rigid Milo had become. "Sure I did. They needed to know."

"Yes, of course they did."

Milo was angry and feeling horribly insecure. He'd thought he was Mr. Merriam's number one, but it seemed his boss had more faith in the two bone breakers, Charlie and Stack. Apparently, Merriam didn't care that they were sloppy and unprofessional.

"It sounds like they've got it under control."

Milo stood to leave, but Mr. Merriam waved him back down. "Hold on now. Let's go back to your pretty girl. She just wanted books? No jewelry or furs . . . I know Babs had a couple of furs . . ."

"Just books and DVDs. Babs had made a big pile of them, and I heard her tell the woman she was going to burn what she didn't take. None of the other shoppers were interested in a bunch of old books."

Merriam shook his head. "I don't know how you're ever going to find her."

Milo was ready to impress. "I know how."

"What's that?" Merriam popped up from his chair and braced his hands, his fat stomach resting on the desktop.

"I said I know how to find her." He couldn't keep the cockiness out of his voice.

"How?"

"I wrote down her license plate number."

Mr. Merriam looked flabbergasted. "What made you do that?"

Milo couldn't admit the truth, that the beautiful young woman had gotten into his heart, and that she would belong to him one day. His Bond girl. If he told his boss he had found his soulmate, Merriam would probably laugh at him. No, he couldn't tell him the truth.

"I thought there might be something hidden in one of the books. You hadn't told me what Rooney had on you, so I thought I'd be on the safe side . . . it just seemed like the thing to do."

"Good for you, Milo, good for you. I don't know what I'd do without you. Give me the number of that plate. I'll get her name and address." He reached for his cell phone and found a phone number in his list of contacts. "It pays to have connections," he told Milo as he waited for an answer.

A few minutes later Mr. Merriam was writing down the woman's name and address.

"Lyra Prescott." He rattled off the address, which

Milo hurried to write down, and said, "She lives in San Diego or just north of it by the zip code. Thanks, Milo," he added almost as an afterthought. "I'll send Charlie and Stack down there right away."

"That would be a waste of time," Milo blurted out, his lies coming fast and furious. "The woman was going out of town with her friend for a long weekend." His mind raced to come up with a convincing story. "They were flying out of Los Angeles, and her car might be in the long-term or short-term parking. Why don't you let me take care of this? Charlie and Stack have a big job going through Rooney's house."

"All right. She's all yours."

Milo was feeling good when he left the office, but by the time he got home, his insecurities had come roaring back. Mr. Merriam wasn't a patient man, and Milo knew it would be only a matter of time before the boss called on the bone crushers to lend a hand.

He consoled himself with the knowledge that he knew more about Lyra Prescott than the crushers did. They hadn't seen the university sticker in her vehicle's back window. Her address might be San Diego, but Milo was betting she lived in L.A. while she went to school. Saturday morning he would drive to San Diego. He'd break into her home and find something with the L.A. address. If the house wasn't empty, he'd figure out another way to get what he wanted.

He needed a disguise. And he wouldn't drive his own car either. He'd rent one.

Friday evening he purchased what he needed for the disguise, and early Saturday morning took a bus to the rental agency. He used a fictitious name and a phony identification when renting the car, and because he knew there would be cameras monitoring the office and the lot, he wore his new disguise.

There were, however, a few glitches along the way. He should have tried on the black wig before buying it. It had way too much synthetic hair, especially the thick, straight bangs. He was afraid to thin it by cutting some of the hair out. He'd paid good money and didn't want it ruined, even though the bangs made him look like Moe from the Three Stooges. He also wore a black beard—glued to his face so it wouldn't slip—and dark sunglasses, which were almost covered by the long bangs. The man working the counter at the car rental office kept staring at Milo's new hair and barely paid attention to his ID.

As Milo drove off the lot, he glanced in the rearview mirror. His disguise had turned out pretty good. No one looking at the surveillance video would recognize him.

He was halfway to San Diego when his face started to itch, and scratching only made it worse. He must be allergic, he decided, but the irritation wasn't unbearable. For now, he could take it. As soon as he was back home, he'd remove the phony beard.

Once in San Diego, he found the address, then circled the block a couple of times before finally parking a few houses away. Acting as though he was nothing more than a neighbor out for a stroll, he passed the house and turned the corner, spotting Lyra's SUV through the garage window. He couldn't believe his luck. The books and DVDs from Rooney's yard sale could be right in front of him. It didn't take a minute to get inside the garage, but the sun streaming through the open door soon revealed that the SUV was empty. She must have taken the books and DVDs into the house.

Milo slipped out of the garage and was sneaking around the side of the house when he saw her standing on the porch looking out at the ocean. She turned toward the door and called, "Gigi, I can't stay for Sunday dinner tomorrow. I have to get back to L.A. to finish some work."

An old lady came onto the porch, kissed Lyra on the cheek, and gave her an affectionate hug. "I understand, dear. I'm just glad to see my grand-daughter whenever I can."

He was right after all. Lyra Prescott did have a place in Los Angeles. Milo smugly congratulated himself on his detective skills.

He sneaked back to his car and drove around the corner. Would she leave the books here or take them back with her tomorrow? He would wait and see. If Lyra left without them, then he'd break into the house when the old granny wasn't home.

He parked on the side street adjacent to the garage and hunkered down to wait. Throughout the evening, a stream of visitors came and went, the last one departing around ten o'clock. Milo figured if Lyra hadn't left for L.A. by eleven, she was in for the night.

All the lights were out by midnight.

Milo found a motel about a mile away. After checking in to his room, he pulled off the wig, tossed it on the table, and went to work on the beard. His face was itching like crazy, but no matter how much he pulled, the beard wasn't going anywhere. Maybe he shouldn't have used superglue. Each time he managed to rip out a clump of hair, he took skin off with it. After an hour of tugging, he looked in the mirror to see bald spots between the thick patches. Where he'd ripped off the beard, the skin was bruised and bloodred. His face looked as though he'd been afflicted with a horrible rash. Exhausted, he collapsed into bed.

Sunday morning he decided to shave off the beard, but that was a mistake. The shaving cream stuck to the tufts of hair and only made them sticky. His next attempt was to get in the shower and scrub them away. Another mistake. The beard absorbed the water and expanded. Thinking maybe alcohol would loosen it, he applied his aftershave. When he stopped screaming from the pain, he jumped back in the shower to let the water soothe his reddened skin.

Once his hands had stopped shaking, he put on his wig, added the sunglasses, and drove back to Lyra's house. He sat in his car the rest of the morning and grew impatient when she didn't come out. Finally, he spotted her and her grandmother carrying shopping bags and walking down the sidewalk toward their house. They'd been gone that entire time! He couldn't believe he'd missed his chance to get in and out when no one was there.

"Stupid," he said, slapping his own face. Hitting an especially raw spot, he yelped.

Minutes later, Lyra came outside again carrying an overnight bag. She pulled her car out of the garage and left. She hadn't been carrying books or DVDs. They were still inside the house. He'd score big points with Mr. Merriam if he brought him the books and DVDs, but Milo wanted to follow Lyra and find out where she lived in L.A. He'd come back Monday to get the books and DVDs, and wouldn't mention the delay to his boss.

It was still light when Lyra pulled into the apartment complex. Milo drove past her and went around the block. He approached the iron gate again and could see her getting her things out of her car. He couldn't take the chance that she'd see him, so he pulled away. It would be easy for him to get the apartment number tomorrow. If he had the nerve, he might just knock on her door and introduce himself.

Milo glanced in the rearview mirror and saw the clumps of hair stuck to his cheeks and chin. He looked like the Wolfman. Introductions would have to wait.

Five miles away from the apartment complex, Milo spotted one of his favorite drive-through restaurants. He pulled in and ordered two double hamburgers, fries, and a gallon-sized drink. The cup holder was too small for his soda, so he balanced it on his lap and found a parking spot.

After he finished his meal, he decided to drive back over to Lyra's apartment to make sure her car hadn't moved. He might even park across the street from the gate and watch for a while. Maybe he would get lucky and she would come outside.

Turning the corner onto her street, Milo had to swerve out of the way of a police car. The stupid cop should have put his siren on if he was in such a hurry, Milo thought. He looked ahead and saw two police cars enter Lyra's apartment complex. They were followed a minute later by an ambulance. The drivers in the two cars ahead of him had pulled to the curb idling their engines while trying to see what was going on. Milo stopped behind the second car to watch with them. A policeman was guarding the open gate so no one could get inside, and he was telling an old man what had happened. Milo caught most of what he was saying: two men had broken into an apartment, tied up a woman, and torn the place apart.

Charlie and Stack? It had to be those two. Milo was furious. Who else would have done this? Mr. Merriam hadn't trusted Milo and sent in his new favorite go-to team.

Hold on now. He was jumping to conclusions without concrete facts. It might not be Lyra's apartment that was broken into. It could have been someone else's. That thought had only just registered when he saw her, his Bond girl. Standing beside her were two plainclothes cops with guns. Milo guessed they were questioning her. She looked tired and worried, but was still as beautiful as ever.

The policeman at the gate noticed all the gawkers and motioned everyone to move along. As

Milo drove away he turned his head so that the policeman wouldn't get a good look at him.

All the way home, he fretted about Charlie and Stack. How had they gotten to Lyra's before him? Had they already found the books and DVDs? He decided he wouldn't talk to Mr. Merriam for a couple of days. Let him realize the bone crushers weren't the way to go. Of course that would only work if Charlie and Stack hadn't found the books and the DVDs. There were so many unanswered questions. Milo needed to clear his head. He'd come up with a plan tomorrow.

He made a detour to a drugstore, enduring the other customers' stares as he purchased cream that he hoped would soothe his face when he tore off the rest of the beard. He also bought lotion to help dissolve the glue. Unfortunately, the solvent didn't work. By the time he had finished ripping off the last of the synthetic hair, his face looked as though he had just undergone an industrial-strength chemical peel. At two a.m. he finally fell into bed, and drifted into a fitful sleep, dreaming of giant, hairy beasts gnawing at his face with razor-sharp teeth.

The following morning, Milo slept until nine o'clock. He got dressed, put on the wig, reached for his baseball cap and his surveillance binoculars, and headed over to Lyra's apartment. Seeing her car still there, he made a U-turn and went to the drive-through for breakfast. When he came back, he parked close to the corner facing the apartment and slumped down in his seat to wait.

He was thinking about going back to the drive-through for a snack when he spotted them in the distance: a man and a woman walking toward the apartment complex. The woman looked like Lyra, but she was too far away to know for sure. He reached for the binoculars on the car seat and raised them to his eyes. It was Lyra. And there was a man with her—a big man, he qualified as they got closer. A good-looking guy with muscles, Milo noticed. Was he her boyfriend? The way he looked at her suggested as much. Then he saw the gun at his side. Ah, a bodyguard. Smart girl. She'd hired a bodyguard. The guy looked hard, and Milo found himself hoping that Charlie Brody and Lou Stack came back. They wouldn't stand a chance against this dude.

His throwaway cell phone rang. Mr. Merriam was the only one who knew the number. Milo debated answering, but curiosity got the better of him.

"Yes?"

"You got those DVDs yet?" Merriam asked.

His spirits lifted. Charlie and Stack hadn't found them in Lyra's apartment.

"No, but I'm getting close," he promised.

"I'm sweating bullets, here, Milo, bullets. Find that disk."

Milo heard the desperation in his voice. In the past, he would have been sympathetic. Not now, though. Not since Charlie and Stack had been elevated above him.

He tucked the phone back in his pocket and slouched lower. The couple was getting closer, and he could see Lyra looking up at the man and smiling. Then suddenly, a block away, they changed course. Instead of continuing on to the apartment, they turned the corner and headed in a different direction.

Milo wasn't sure what to do. He didn't care so much about the disk in her apartment now. He wanted to know if Lyra was involved with the bodyguard. He felt a surge of jealousy over the possibility. She was *his* Bond girl, not anyone else's.

An hour later, he was chasing his rental car down the street.

FIFTEEN

SAM AND LYRA LEFT THE APARTMENT AND drove toward her new home away from home. Once Sam was certain they weren't being followed, he stopped at a grocery store to get supplies. Lyra went in with him and immediately headed for the candy aisle. She carried a basket and filled it with chocolate-covered nuts, chocolate candy bars, and chocolate mints.

"Are you planning to eat that for breakfast, lunch, and dinner?" he asked.

"Pretty much."

She handed him the basket, grabbed another one and filled it with milk, juice, apples, and healthy cereal. She couldn't resist adding a box of chocolate-covered doughnuts.

When she got to the checkout counter, she saw he'd added bottled water and soft drinks.

She placed the milk, juice, and apples on the counter for the clerk to scan, and then turned to Sam. "Happy now?" she asked.

"I'm always happy," he said with his sexy accent. He grabbed their grocery bags with one hand

and put his other hand on her back, gently nudging her forward. His hand lingered for only the barest of seconds, but she felt a shiver down her spine.

"How far away is this safe house?" she asked as they crossed the parking lot.

"Not far," he answered.

A half hour later, Lyra was completely disoriented. He seemed to be driving around in circles. She was surprised when he finally turned into a new housing development. Identical duplexes lined both sides of the street for as far as the eye could see. He pulled into the drive of one of them, dug through the glove compartment until he found a garage door opener, and pushed the button.

Lyra looked around and said, "They're all exactly the same. How can anyone find his own home?"

"Maybe they count garages," he suggested. "Or I suppose . . . just maybe . . . they could look at the address."

"Very funny," she countered.

The duplex was two stories and furnished. Everything—the walls, the carpet, the furniture—was beige.

While Sam took their luggage upstairs, Lyra carried the bags of groceries to the kitchen. She opened the refrigerator and was surprised to see someone had already stocked it. The cupboards were also filled with cans of soup, pasta, and all sorts of staples. She added their groceries, then went to explore the rest of the house. There were two bedrooms upstairs, one on either side of a short hallway. Sam had put her things in the master bedroom, which had a lovely king-sized bed.

Lyra was testing the mattress when Sam appeared in the doorway. "This okay for you?"

"It's wonderful. I can actually walk from the bed to the bathroom without stubbing my toes. But I think you should sleep here."

He leaned against the door frame. "Yeah? You think?"

It wasn't what he said or how he said it that affected her. It was the way he was looking at her, as though he was noticing her for the first time.

"Yes, I do."

He smiled. "With or without you in the bed?" Her startled expression made him laugh. "How can any woman blush that quickly? Your face is bright red."

"So we're flirting now?"

With a wry grin, he shrugged.

"You are the most confusing man," she said.

"Good to know," he laughed.

"I invited you to sleep in this bed . . . without me," she clarified, "because I was being thoughtful. You're much bigger than I am, and you need more room. I'll sleep in the other bed."

"My bedroom is identical to this one."

"So you have a king-sized bed?"

"Yes, but thanks for the offer."

He went downstairs. She followed. "The refrigerator is packed, and so are the cupboards."

"Yes, I know."

"You didn't need to stop at the store?"

"No."

"Then why did you?"

"Chocolate."

"How did you know I like chocolate?"

"It's in your file."

"No," she said incredulously.

"Actually, Sidney mentioned it," he confessed.

He had placed his laptop on the dining room table and sat down to work. Without looking up, he asked, "Have you thought of any ideas for that children's film Mahler wants you to do?"

"A few," she answered. "I also . . ." She stopped mid-sentence. "Oh gosh, I forgot. I should have changed the card."

"What card?" he asked.

"The camera I have at the park. I'm trying to get a sequence of photos of a little garden at the park, and I haven't changed the memory card in the camera for several days."

"I thought you were going to do the children's film."

"I can work on more than one project," she said. "Tomorrow I have to go there, okay?"

"Okay," he agreed.

Sam turned back to his computer screen, so Lyra went up to her bedroom. She sat on the bed with her back against the headboard, balanced her laptop on her knees, and started working out ideas for the children's film. She really got into the process, and it was after eight o'clock when she finished two possible outlines.

Sam was still typing on his computer when she came downstairs.

"I'll fix dinner," she offered. She went into the

kitchen to survey their provisions and decided on red sauce and meatballs and a salad. After dinner, she offered him a candy bar for dessert, which he declined.

Sam insisted on cleaning the kitchen, so Lyra went back upstairs to turn in for the night. After a long, relaxing shower, she wrapped a towel around her and opened her suitcase on her bed. She took out a pair of long cotton pajamas her grandmother had given her. The top had a row of buttons to the neck, and the pants were long and loose. She laid them on the left side of the bed, then took out a pink nightgown that her grandmother would thoroughly disapprove of. It was silky and had spaghetti straps. She laid it on the right side of the bed. One assured nothing was going to happen; the other offered possibility. A couple of fantasies popped into her head. If Sam saw her in the cotton pajamas he'd think she was on the fast track to spinsterhood. But what would he think if he saw her in the silky nightgown? Would he be tempted? She let her mind enter her fantasy world for a second.

"I vote for the one on the right."

Lyra quickly grabbed the towel so it wouldn't slip and spun around, expecting to see Sam standing in the open doorway. He wasn't there. His door was already closing.

"Good night," he said.

Lyra dropped down on the bed. Did he know what she'd been thinking?

She slipped into the silky nightgown, then turned on the television and got into bed. The eleven o'clock news had just begun, and the big story was an explosion in an exclusive neighborhood. A newscaster was standing in front of the rubble describing what was quite apparent behind him. A picture of the house before it was destroyed flashed on the screen next. Lyra threw the covers off and sat up. "Is that . . . ?"

Then the pictures of the owners flashed on-screen.

"Sam!"

The door to his bedroom flew open, and he came running. "What is it?" he asked, eyes darting in every direction.

She pointed at the TV. "The yard sale."

SIXTEEN

"**W**HAT DID YOU SAY?" SAM STARED UNCOM-prehendingly at the television.

"The yard sale," she repeated. "You know. People put out stuff they don't want any longer, and other people buy it at a reduced price. Sit down and watch this, please."

Sam pushed aside a pillow and sat on the bed facing the TV.

Lyra got up on her knees and leaned forward to reach the remote so she could turn up the volume.

Ah, man. She had the sexiest backside he'd ever seen. No way in hell could he look away.

"I was there, Sam."

"What?"

"There," she said, pointing to the television. The photo of the Rooneys stayed on the screen. "That's the woman who was throwing out all those wonderful books. Some were first editions," she added with a nod as she sat back. "Actually, she was throwing everything out, and she wouldn't take money for any of it."

Lyra turned from the television to look at him. He was watching her with a puzzled expression.

"What is it?" she asked.

He shook his head and turned to the screen. The newscaster continued with his report about the murder/suicide, then cut to a police detective who explained that the explosion and subsequent fire were being investigated as arson. The report ended with eyewitness accounts. There didn't seem to be any lack of witnesses wanting to tell their stories on television. The newscaster introduced a woman who had seen the murder.

"I saw her do it, all right. I went back inside the house to get another lamp, and when I was crossing the yard to put it in the car, the woman's husband pulled into the drive and started screaming. Of course, he didn't know she was hiding a gun . . ."

"Were you there when she killed her husband?" Sam asked Lyra.

She didn't answer immediately. She'd realized that Sam was sitting on her short robe. Her nightgown wasn't obscene, but it did have a rather low neckline. Better cover up, she decided. She tugged on the hem of the robe until he moved. She tried to act nonchalant as she put it on.

"Lyra?"

"Yes?"

"Did you see her kill him?" he asked again.

"No, I must have just left. Now that I think about it, I guess I knew she was unbalanced. She had a wild look in her eyes. At the time, I thought she was just angry with her husband. I tried to explain that some of the books were valuable, but she didn't care. She said she was going to burn what I didn't take. I'll tell you this, I wouldn't have argued with her if I'd known she had a gun in her pocket."

Lyra pulled her hair back and let it fall around her shoulders. Propping a pillow next to him, she leaned against it, stretching her legs out and crossing one ankle over the other.

She was killing him. "Ah, come on," Sam practically groaned. Unbelievably long, gorgeous legs, perfectly shaped . . .

Lyra misunderstood. "I know. Can you believe it? First, she gets rid of everything her husband owns, then she waits for him to come home and see what she's done. That's one vindictive wife," she added. "But she's not done with her diabolical plan. She whips out the gun, shoots him, then, according to witnesses, calmly walks into the house and shoots herself. I'd say that was a crazy woman."

A commercial interrupted the newscast. Lyra looked at Sam. She was sitting so close to him it was difficult to think. Staring into his beautiful eyes while she asked a coherent question was impossible, and so she turned back to the television and feigned extreme interest in a dancing cereal commercial until she remembered what it was she wanted to ask.

"The house . . ." she began.

"Yes?"

"Who would blow it up? Why would they blow it up? You heard the newscaster. The Rooneys didn't have any children and no relatives to speak of. That's kind of sad, isn't it?"

"It's probably a good thing they didn't have children."

She nodded. "True. It would be difficult for them, what with a crazy mother."

Sam went back to her question. "Maybe whoever blew up the house wanted to cover something up. When did you see her?"

"Just last Friday. I was on my way out of town and stopped at her yard sale." Without realizing what she was doing, Lyra leaned into his side. "What a weekend," she sighed. "I narrowly missed being the witness to a murder and then my apartment was broken into."

"Could there be a connection?" Sam asked.

She thought about it. "I don't see how. Who would know I stopped at the yard sale? I never told anyone."

"I'm going to find out how Rooney made his money."

"Bet it wasn't legit. Why did they stay married? She was obviously miserable. Why didn't she walk away?"

"Maybe she liked the lifestyle? Or even loved him? Who knows? There could be a hundred different reasons."

"Ever get into a fight with your wife?" Lyra didn't mean to pry, but her curiosity about Sam grew stronger with every minute she was with him.

He didn't close up on her this time. "No. Disagreements, sure, but no big fights."

She was about to ask him another question, but being this close to him, she completely lost her train of thought. Sam turned his attention back to the TV, but Lyra couldn't take her eyes off his face.

Sam had told her that he was married three years. He wasn't the type to blow off a commitment, so what had happened? He was too . . . solid, too responsible. How could any woman in her right mind ever leave him? The man was sexy and adorable and strong and obviously smart and heroic. No woman would leave him . . . willingly. And that meant . . . Lyra felt an ache in her heart, suddenly realizing why Sam was so reticent to talk about his marriage. His wife had died.

SEVENTEEN

EARLY IN HIS CAREER, SAM HAD LEARNED TO keep his professional life and his personal life separate. He had done a good job of it, too . . . until Lyra came along. He'd known he was in trouble about ten minutes after he met her. There was just something about her. Just looking at her took his breath away, but more surprising, her passion for everything in life felt like a light turning on inside of him.

She probably thought he was rude when he abruptly stood up and walked out of her bedroom, but she had been looking up at him with those sexy green eyes. The urge to take her in his arms and kiss her had been so intense, he'd had to summon all his willpower to look away. She was wearing a robe over her nightgown, but he'd seen enough of the silky fabric skimming over the curves of her incredible body to know what was underneath.

He closed the door of his room behind him and dropped down on the bed in a cold sweat. Keeping his distance was becoming difficult. He needed to get away from her as soon as possible, before he did something he would regret.

He had more than enough on his plate right now. His future was undecided. A part of him wanted to go home to the Highlands and take one of the jobs that had been offered to him there, but he also wanted to continue the work he was doing in Washington, D.C. For the last couple of years, he'd been completely immersed in his career, never really stopping long enough to take stock of his life. When his wife, Beth, died of complications after minor surgery, it had nearly destroyed him. He couldn't go through that kind of pain again. Wouldn't.

Lyra was the type of woman that men wanted to marry, and Sam wasn't interested in long-term relationships.

He got into bed. The more he thought about Lyra, the more frustrated he became. Sleep wasn't happening. He stacked his hands behind his head and decided to concentrate on the Rooneys and the break-in at Lyra's apartment. Was there a connection, or was it a coincidence?

An hour later, he heard Lyra's door open. She obviously couldn't sleep either. After a few minutes passed, he heard noise from the kitchen. Sam watched the clock. When she didn't return to her bedroom, he decided to see what she was doing. He pulled on his jeans, automatically slipped his gun into the waistband, and went out into the hallway.

Lyra was creeping up the stairs. He waited until she was on the landing and turning toward her room before he said, "Couldn't sleep?"

Startled, she bumped into the wall as she whirled around.

He stepped closer. "What have you got there?"

"A candy bar," she admitted with a tinge of guilt.

Lyra didn't move. It was an awkward situation, but she could handle it. Yes, they were standing a foot apart in a dark hallway, and yes, he was half-naked and she wore only a thin nightgown and an open robe, but she could pretend to be blasé, and he would never know how nervous she was. First, she would have to stop staring at his chest. Then maybe she could catch her breath. The man's body was amazing. His bare chest looked as hard as steel and his biceps bulged. He was in incredible shape, but then he was an FBI agent, so she supposed he had to stay fit. There was a scar on his left shoulder and another one just above his rib cage. Lyra had an overwhelming urge to wrap her arms around his neck and feel his hard chest against her. Okay, the blasé plan wasn't working. *Put your damn shirt on,* she thought.

"Would you like a bite?" she asked nervously.

"Maybe just a taste," he answered. He didn't take his eyes off hers as he took another step closer.

Lyra was totally unprepared for what happened next. She held out the candy bar, but he ignored it. She could feel the heat radiating from him. He tilted her chin up slowly, leaned down, and stroked her lips with his tongue. It was the most erotic sensation she had ever felt. Her stomach turned to Jell-O. She was weak all over.

Before she could show any reaction, his mouth

covered hers, and his tongue slipped inside to rub against hers. Lyra was melting into him when he abruptly pulled back.

"Night," he said, then disappeared.

Lyra stood there staring at his bedroom door for at least a minute trying to figure out what had just happened, finally coming to the realization that she didn't want the chocolate any longer. She wanted him.

EIGHTEEN

AFTER A RESTLESS NIGHT, SAM STOOD IN THE shower letting the hot water pour over him. Maybe he should be taking a cold shower, he thought. That might bring him to his senses.

He put the palms of his hands against the tile in front of him and bowed his head. What was he doing? Kissing Lyra like that only made him want her more. Not good.

He couldn't understand his own behavior. He had never had such a strong initial reaction to any woman before, not even his wife, but with Lyra it was different. It had been an almost instantaneous attraction, and it wasn't going away. In fact, it was getting stronger, this need to touch her. What worried him most was that he knew it wasn't lust. Okay, it was lust, but also something more.

Getting to sleep last night had been a bitch because he couldn't stop thinking about her soft full lips and how she had felt against him.

While Sam shaved, he considered his situation. He wouldn't be in this mess if it weren't for Alec Buchanan. As soon as he got dressed, he was going to call Alec and give him a deadline to find someone else. Twenty-four hours was more than generous, he thought.

Fortunately, it was up to Sam to set the day and time for his lecture to the cadets in Los Angeles. He had a two-week window, but he should give the officer in charge at least a couple of days notice. He'd schedule the lecture for Friday, then rent a car and drive to San Diego for his final lecture on Monday. If he was lucky, he could catch the red-eye to D.C. that evening . . . and his life would be back to the way it used to be.

Plan in play, he thought, as he started down the stairs. He turned around and went back up. Lyra's alarm clock was buzzing, and her bedroom door was partially open. He knocked and looked in.

"Ah, that's just not fair," he groaned.

Her nightgown was hanging off the foot of the bed, and she was sound asleep, lying on her stomach with her arms above her head, a sheet barely covering her derriere. She didn't have on a stitch of clothing.

She slept in the nude. He didn't need to know that. His fantasies were never going to go away now. Damn.

Sam didn't go into her bedroom to wake her. Too risky. Letting the alarm continue to buzz, he went down to the kitchen to call Alec.

"How's it going?" his friend asked.

"You've got to get me out of here." Sam winced. He sounded desperate.

"How come? What's going on?"

How come? She sleeps in the nude. That's what's

going on. "I said I would help you out, but I can't do this indefinitely."

"Wait a second," Alec said. He was walking into his office and stopped to give instructions to someone. Coming back to his phone, he said, "When do you give your lecture?"

"I'm thinking I'll do it Friday, get it over with. Alec, tell me about this case. Have you found out anything?"

"No," he answered. "Detective O'Malley says they don't have a single lead. They're still working on it, still digging."

"Lyra needs a bodyguard until someone finds out what the hell is going on." His anger came through loud and clear. He told Alec about the yard sale Lyra had gone to and what he had learned about the Rooneys. "Run him through the system. I've got a feeling he's got a long record. And find another bodyguard for Lyra by tomorrow, okay?"

He disconnected the call and made himself breakfast. Lyra came down dressed for the day. She looked rested, which meant she'd slept.

"Morning," she said as she poured cereal into a bowl.

Sam was sitting across from her eating his second bowl of organic granola.

He started the argument. "Do you know how much sugar is in that bowl?"

She took a big bite, chewed it slowly, and said, "No, but I'm guessing there's a lot."

"You might as well eat a couple of hot fudge sundaes."

"I can't. No ice cream and no fudge. I should have gotten some at the store."

"Lyra, it's not healthy."

"You're eating gravel. Some things in life are just not worth it. Eating gravel is one of them."

She finished her cereal while Sam told her about his conversation with Alec.

"So the detectives don't have any leads? Nothing?"

"Not yet," he said. "And tomorrow you're getting a new bodyguard."

Lyra had become an expert at hiding her emotions. Not letting her parents know what she was thinking or feeling had once been the only way she could get through the day.

"Okay," she said nonchalantly. She got up, rinsed her bowl and spoon, and put them in the dishwasher. When she turned to leave, he blocked her.

"Listen . . ." he began.

"Yes?"

"About that kiss . . ." he said.

Lyra stared into his eyes and waited. She saw how uncomfortable he was.

"It was a really nice kiss, but . . ." He stopped. There was a moment of awkward silence.

What was he trying to tell her?

"I think you're a wonderful woman. It's just that . . ." he continued.

Uh oh. Now she understood. He was going to tell her the kiss was a mistake.

Oh no you don't, she thought.

Lyra moved closer. Her face inches away from

his, she gently placed her hand on his cheek. "I think I know what you're trying to say. Even though you kissed me, you're not going to marry me?" She tried to sound sympathetic when she said, "Don't worry, Sam. I could never marry you."

With a gentle pat to his cheek, she turned and walked out of the kitchen. She didn't start smiling until she was out of sight.

NINETEEN

"WHAT THE . . . ?"

Sam heard Lyra's laugh and shook his head. She was messing with him. Their kiss obviously hadn't fazed her, and if she wasn't going to make a big deal about it, then neither would he.

Sam had been trained to read people, and it didn't take him any time at all to figure out Lyra. She wasn't into casual sex. He doubted she had ever gone into a bar with the intention of hooking up for the night. She just wasn't the type. She had to have an emotional connection with a man before she let him touch her.

At that moment his cell phone rang—it was Alec—and Sam welcomed the distraction.

"A new bodyguard will be there early tomorrow morning," Alec said. "His name is Brick Winter."

"Is he FBI?"

"No," Alec answered. "He's with Mead Security Company out there in L.A. Detective O'Malley recommended him, and I checked him out. He's good. He knows what he's doing."

"Have you got a file on him?"

"Yes. Why?"

"Email it to me. I want to check him out, too. I'm not about to leave Lyra with just anyone."

"Sam, the guy does this for a living. He's been in Iraq, Special Forces, two tours. What's bothering you?"

"I want to be convinced she'll be in safe hands." Sam didn't realize how transparent his words were.

"What do you think of her? She's a sweetheart, isn't she?" Alec asked, a smile in his voice.

"What do you mean 'What do I think of her?' She's a job. That's all."

"She's gorgeous, isn't she?"

"I haven't noticed."

Alec laughed. "So you like her?"

"Just email me the damn file." Sam ended the call.

So you like her? What kind of question was that? Alec sounded like a teenage girl.

Sam's concern made perfect sense—to him. If he was going to bail on Lyra, the least he could do was make certain he left her in good hands. Assuming that Brick was going to work out, Sam thought he should probably call and schedule his lecture to the cadets, but something held him back. He'd call tomorrow, he told himself, as soon as he had talked to—and evaluated—Brick.

Lyra was coming down the stairs with her laptop and her cell phone. She had changed her clothes and was wearing a short skirt that showed off her tanned, shapely legs, and a white T-shirt that showed off her other assets.

"I've just talked to O'Malley," she said. "I told

him about the yard sale. He wants to look through those boxes of books and DVDs, and I explained they won't get to the ranch for a couple of days. I also told him I can't imagine anyone knows I have them."

"What's on the schedule today?"

"I haven't made up my mind what I want to do for the short film and I thought I'd do some research today, but then I got a text from Sidney. She ran into Professor Mahler, and he wants to see me in his office. So I guess we're headed back to campus. But after that, I need to stop at Paraiso Park and switch out the memory card. Do you have any leather boots . . . thick boots?"

"Not with me."

"Then you'll have to wait in the car. You can't get around in that run-down park or climb its hills in those loafers."

"You're not going up there without me."

"Okay, then. We'll stop and buy some boots."

"When do you want to leave?"

"Five minutes?"

It was twenty minutes before she was ready. He put her boots and backpack in the trunk and was walking around to the passenger door when she asked him if he wanted her to drive. Instead of answering, he just smiled as he opened the passenger door for her.

They found a sporting goods store off the highway and, at Lyra's insistence, Sam bought a pair of sturdy hiking boots. She looked them over and approved. Hopefully, none of the stray needles on the hill would get through the thick soles.

"This brand is more expensive, but they're worth it," she told him.

"How many times do you expect we're going up that hill before I leave tomorrow?"

"Just once."

With this reminder that he was leaving, Sam thought he saw sadness in Lyra's eyes. It was there, then gone in a flash.

"Lyra—"

"Here you are, sir." The salesman handed Sam his credit card and shopping bag with his boots.

She waited for Sam by the store's front entrance. Two college-age clerks rushed to open the door for her and ended up in a tug of war over the door handle.

Sam came up behind her, put his arm around her shoulders, and said to the clerks, "You want to get out of the way?"

The eager young men looked deflated when they saw her in his embrace. "You're with her?" one asked.

"Out of the way," Sam said.

"The guy's got a gun," the other clerk whispered.

As though someone had just yelled "free pizza and beer," both clerks raced back to the counter.

Sam dropped his purchase in the trunk of the car, and they were once again on their way. Lyra texted the professor's teaching assistant and asked when Mahler would be available.

After reading his reply, she said, "The T.A. is almost as obnoxious as Mahler."

Sam looked preoccupied, and she didn't think

he'd heard her until he asked, "You want to tell me why?"

"Listen to this text: Eleven-thirty in professor's office. Be prompt or else."

Sam smiled. "What's the 'or else'?"

"Or else I won't be in his office at eleven-thirty," she shrugged.

"I don't like going back to campus. The men who are after you must know by now that you're not staying in your apartment. And because they don't know where you're staying, most likely they hope to find you on campus."

"The campus is huge," she pointed out.

He gave her an exasperated look. "If they're any good, they'll have your class schedule by now. That should narrow it down for them."

"So if I don't show up back on campus, how long will they wait before they move on?"

"You're dreaming."

She sighed. "I know."

"I doubt they'll waste too much time strolling around campus. They'll find other ways to draw you out."

She didn't want to hear about them just now, but he thought she should. "They could use your family or friends to get to you. They've probably figured out you'll do anything to help your friends. Look what you did when Sidney was in trouble. That took courage to go into your apartment—with what, pepper spray?"

"I couldn't wait any longer."

"I know."

"I wish I knew what it was they wanted. I've

told the police everything about my life since the day I was born and nothing explains this."

They both fell silent. Every once in a while she would sneak a peek at his profile. He was so strong and confident. She didn't want him to leave. She would never admit it, though.

She didn't realize she was staring until he said, "What are you thinking about now?"

"You."

Frowning, he glanced at her. "Yeah?"

"I was wondering if I would ever see you again once you leave."

"If I had to guess, I'd say probably not."

"That's not good enough. I need to know."

"Why?"

"If I knew I would run into you again sometime in the future, then tonight would be a quiet evening. Watch a little television and go to our separate bedrooms."

He was intrigued. "And if you'd never see me again?"

"I can assure you it wouldn't be a quiet evening."

TWENTY

"**W**E'RE GOING TO HAVE A QUIET EVENING."
Sam sounded irritated.

"So you don't want to go out to dinner then?"
she asked innocently.

"That's not what you're suggesting."

She would have tried to come up with a few more
suggestive hints, but was prevented from doing so
by his frown. She decided to stop provoking him.
He would be gone in the morning, and she'd be
glad about it. Damned glad, as her brothers would
say. It had hurt her that he had such regret over a
kiss. One little kiss. Granted, it had been amazing,
and his mouth had been firm and demanding, and
oh my God, his tongue . . .

Apparently, she was the only one who had
liked it.

She folded her arms and stared straight ahead as
she brooded. Sam sure knew how to make a girl
feel special.

They both were silent for a few miles. Lyra
looked out the window and tried to figure out

where they were. Los Angeles had always been difficult for her to navigate.

"Do you miss Scotland?" she asked.

The question took him by surprise. "Yes, I do."

"What's it like where you're from?"

"The Highlands are magnificent," he said. "When you hike through the glens, you're surrounded by the most spectacular rolling mountains. Many of the valleys have long narrow lochs that are so deep, they look like pools of onyx. And in the forests, you'll find the clearest streams on Earth. The fishing there is the best, especially in the cool mornings when the mist is rising from the water."

"It sounds so beautiful. Why did you ever leave?"

"I moved with my parents when I was young."

"To the United States?"

"No, not at first. My father has dual citizenship, American and Scottish. Most of his family is in Scotland, but he was raised here. After university he went to work for the State Department, and he met my mother when he was stationed at the consulate in Edinburgh. A couple of years later, my parents left the diplomatic service, and moved to the family estate outside Cairnmar, a small village in the Highlands where most of the Kincaid clan still lives."

"Is that where you were born?"

"No, I was born in the United States. My mother and father had come back for a visit, and, from what I've been told, I arrived on the scene a few weeks earlier than expected. Shortly afterward, we returned to Cairnmar, and I lived there until I was ten. That's when my father was called to work for the government again, and we were transferred to Paris. After that we lived in Algeria, then Tokyo, and a half dozen other places before I was out of high school. By that time, we were living in the United States, so I went to university here. After law school, I joined the FBI."

"Are your parents still alive?" She realized she was grilling him again. She couldn't explain why she was so interested. Maybe it was because he had been given every detail of her life before he met her, and she wanted to even the playing field.

"Yes," he answered. "A few years ago, my mother and father moved back to Cairnmar, and I try to go home to see them as often as I can."

"Would you ever want to live there again?"

"I've thought about it. I love this country, but I guess I'll always be a little homesick for the Highlands."

They were just pulling off the highway when the rain started. Sprinkles quickly turned into a torrential downpour. By the time they reached the campus, the grass was under water and the dirt had turned to mud.

The rain stopped as swiftly as it had begun. Sam found a parking spot at the end of the lot and backed in so Lyra wouldn't have to step in the mud to get to the pavement.

As Lyra was reaching for her backpack in the trunk, she asked, "Do you want to change into hiking boots now?"

"I'll wait."

Sam tried to take the backpack from her, but she slipped one strap over her shoulder and said, "I'm used to it."

That was the last time he looked at her until they were inside the building. He was occupied watching the people walking along the sidewalks, sitting on benches, standing in windows. He analyzed every possible sniper position, while he kept her tight against him.

"I don't like this," he muttered as they crossed the quad, which offered little protection. The trees grew close to the buildings, and the rest of the space was a big open expanse. He felt as though they were targets in a shooting gallery. "We have to find another way in and out of this place."

"Don't worry about it. You won't be back here." She hadn't meant her remark to be a jab, but it sounded like one, so she quickly said, "The new bodyguard can worry about it."

Sam didn't respond. His face was set in stone as he continued to scan. He didn't relax his guard once they were in the classroom building either, making Lyra walk close to the wall as he led the way. It seemed that every man who walked past knew her name. Sam heard "Hi, Lyra" at least twenty times.

Professor Mahler's door was open a crack, and Lyra knocked on it.

"Come in, come in," he called impatiently.

The professor sat at his desk with stacks of papers in front of him. He was signing his name to what appeared to be legal documents. When he looked up and saw Sam standing behind Lyra, his lips clamped together in a pinched expression. He moved two stacks of papers aside and pulled out one of his desk drawers.

"I forgot to have you sign a form for the competition. If it isn't postmarked by the end of the day, you won't be able to submit your children's short to the board."

Like the proverbial absentminded professor, he rifled through the drawer and went through three stacks of papers before finding the entry form and envelope.

"I see your friend is still at your side . . . with his firearm," he said with noticeable disgust in his voice.

Sam gave no response, but Lyra felt the need to defend him. "He is required to carry a weapon."

"Yes. Big Brother FBI would have such rules. I hope he isn't going to be a distraction for you. If you think he might be, I'll give this opportunity to another student."

"He won't be a distraction," she assured. "In fact, he's leaving tomorrow."

Mahler's pinched lips relaxed, and he handed the form to Lyra. "I may be doing you a disservice by letting you submit. You only have two weeks to come up with an idea—a stellar idea," he corrected. "You must be honest with yourself, Lyra. If you don't think it has a chance to win or place, then don't submit it. It would reflect poorly on me."

"Professor, aren't you going to approve it before I submit it?"

"No time for that. You'll need every minute of the next two weeks. Now fill out that form and get it in the mail today."

"Yes, I will."

As she was walking out the door, the professor called out, "Fill in every line. You don't want to be disqualified for something as minor as not writing down your phone number. Shut the door behind you."

Lyra saw the scowl on Sam's face and said, "Isn't Professor Mahler a sweetie?"

"I've got another name for him."

Lyra took a seat in an empty classroom and filled out the application. She stopped in an office two doors down to get postage and the smiling secretary kindly offered to mail it for her.

"Hi, Lyra." A young man carrying a large box passed them in the hall.

"Hi, Jeff."

And so it started again. This time Sam decided to count, and five men tried to engage her in conversation before Lyra and he got to the building's exit. Their familiarity bothered him, but he wasn't ready to admit why. Other than being friendly, Lyra didn't seem interested in any of them.

"How come there's no man in your life?"

"Who says there isn't?"

"I've read your file, remember? It was thorough."

"In other words, Sidney told you there wasn't anyone."

Thunder rumbled in the distance. "Come on. Let's go."

They crossed the quad as quickly as Lyra could move without running. She was long-legged, but her stride wasn't nearly as long as his.

A strong storm was brewing. The sky grew darker and darker as the black clouds rolled in.

When they reached the car, Lyra hurried to the passenger side and waited for Sam to unlock the doors. He was about to push the button on the remote when he saw the footprints in the mud next to the door. He followed the footprints around to the passenger side.

"Ah, hell," Sam muttered. "Lyra, get away from the car."

Sam got down on one knee and looked underneath. He saw the red light blinking and backed away. "Let's go," he said.

"Where?" she asked, bewildered by his strange behavior. He had his arm around her and was pulling her away from the car while he reached for the phone in his pocket and punched in a number.

"Sam, who are you calling?" She was tripping to keep up with him.

"Bomb squad."

TWENTY-ONE

To her credit, Lyra took the news about the bomb squad in stride, probably because she was having difficulty wrapping her head around the notion that someone had planted an explosive device under their car. She was informed it was connected by wires to the ignition, and if Sam hadn't noticed the muddy footprints, they would both be part of the campus now. She might have ended up on top of one building and Sam on another.

The thoughts were too gruesome. Lyra forced them from her mind.

Sam wouldn't let her stay around to watch the bomb squad—not that she wanted to—nor would he let her talk to the detectives out in the open. He wanted her away from the crowd and the chaos. No cars were allowed to enter or leave the parking lot. Dozens of onlookers, some angry they couldn't get to their cars and others curious to see what had brought so many police to the campus, stood behind barricades.

Sam took Lyra into a tiny coffee bar a safe distance away. She sat on a bench while he got her a cup of hot tea. She didn't realize she was shaking until she tried to hold the cup. Sam took it away from her before she burned herself and put it on the table, then sat down next to her and put his arm around her shoulders.

"Your first bomb?" he asked casually.

She laughed at the ridiculous question.

"That's better," he said. "You're safe now, Lyra. Don't be scared. I'm not going to let anything happen to you."

He was stroking her arm as he pulled her closer. His body was hard and warm.

"You misunderstand, Sam. I'm not scared. I'm angry, very angry. I want answers. I hate being helpless."

She tried to stand but he wouldn't let her. "Take a couple of deep breaths."

O'Malley and another detective joined them and took turns asking Lyra questions while they drank coffee. Every once in a while one or both of them would look at Sam to judge his reaction.

Lyra tried to get some answers of her own, especially about the motive behind the threat, but the detectives were evasive and would only say that they were working on it.

On what? she wanted to ask. Did they have any leads at all? Or were they just humoring her until the culprits gave themselves up?

"I'd like to leave, Sam," she said wearily after an hour's interrogation.

O'Malley stood. "We'll get in touch with you soon. Hopefully with some good information."

Sam waited until they had left and then said, "I know how frustrating this is for you."

"When can we get out of here?"

"The new car will be here in a minute."

"What's wrong with the car you're driving? They took the bomb away."

"That car is a crime scene now."

"Of course," she said, feeling foolish. She had watched enough crime shows to know that. Maybe she wasn't as in control as she thought.

Sam's cell phone rang a minute later.

"Car's here," he told her.

"We have to get our boots out of the trunk before we leave."

"Sorry, can't," he said. "They're part of—"

"The crime scene," she recited.

"Right."

As she stood to leave, she put her hand on Sam's arm. "I'm so glad you didn't get hurt."

Sam couldn't believe what he did next. He bent down and kissed her. It was quick and over before she could react, but the warmth and softness of her lips made him want more. What was he doing?

"Let's go," he said gruffly. "Do you still want to drive to that park?"

"Yes."

"Okay," he agreed. "We'll go, but only after I make certain we aren't being followed. That could take awhile."

"Fine with me," she said. "But we also have to go back to the sporting goods store to get another pair of boots."

"No, that isn't necessary."

"Oh, we're going," she snapped. "I'm not walking up that hill without boots, and neither are you unless you want hepatitis, encephalitis, dumbitis . . ."

His smile stopped her rant. That adorable smile could melt hearts—and probably did, she thought.

The car was black, shiny, and what the FBI driver called a dream.

"Let me run it down for you," the eager young man said. "It's got bulletproof glass and armor in the doors. The hood and trunk lids are reinforced, and the wings over the tires make it tough to shoot out one of them. Shooter would have to come at them from below, which is impossible . . . unless you drive over him, I guess.

"It's built like a tank, but don't worry, with an 850 engine it's got more power than a race car. I don't think a bomb could take this baby apart," he exaggerated.

He opened the passenger door for Lyra and winked at her when she thanked him.

"You're gonna be real safe inside this ride, Miss," he drawled as he draped himself over the door.

Sam walked around to the driver's side and was about to get in when he heard Lyra ask, "Is there a gun in the glove compartment that I could borrow?"

"I don't think so, but here's my card. My name's Ed. If you need anything . . ."

He shut the door before she could say, "I need a gun."

Sam opened the glove compartment to make sure there wasn't a weapon.

"I want a gun," she insisted. "Any kind will do."

"No."

"All right. I'll get my own."

His jaw was clenched. "No, you won't."

She smiled. "Okay."

He didn't like her smile one little bit. "You're not getting a damn gun. You'd kill yourself."

Oh, please. "Sam, you read my file—if there really is a file on me."

"There is, and I've read it."

"Then you know that I was born and raised on a ranch in Texas." In other words, there wasn't a gun she couldn't take apart, clean, put back together, and shoot with impressive accuracy. Her brothers had taught her how to shoot, and whenever she returned to the ranch, she practiced.

"You never know when a gun might come in handy. That's what my brothers would tell me," she explained. "To kill rattlesnakes, of course."

"There aren't any snakes here."

"Oh, yes, there are. The men who planted that explosive are definitely snakes."

He couldn't argue with her there.

"Buckle up, Lyra," Sam said as he turned the key in the ignition.

The car was a gem to drive. The engine purred, and barely touching the gas pedal sent them flying. Sam took them on five different highways, a dozen overpasses, and a maze of side streets, and when he was convinced no one was tailing them, he found another sporting goods store and pulled in.

Fortunately, the store carried the same brand of

boots and had their sizes as well. Lyra picked out socks for both of them and put them on the counter. Ignoring her protest, Sam paid the bill, and they walked out wearing their new boots. Lyra knew she looked ridiculous wearing a skirt with hiking boots, but they were necessary attire for where they were going.

"Are you hungry?" he asked, once he had pulled onto the street. "While you were changing shoes, the clerk told me about a good sandwich place just down the street."

"Oh, no, we can't eat before we climb the hill. We should stop and get some bottled water for after, but no food. You wouldn't be able to keep it down."

"Sure I would."

Forty-five minutes later, he was gagging like a man who had mixed his beer with whiskey and wine. The stench made his eyes water, and he kept muttering what Lyra assumed were curses in a different language. Every once in awhile, she'd hear "Ah, man . . . brutal . . ."

Lyra was embarrassed to admit she was getting used to the toxic odor of all the illegally dumped garbage. When they reached the top of the hill and looked on the other side, she pointed to the garden below. "Isn't it fascinating?"

Sam didn't want to stand around discussing it. "Hurry up," he said, "so we can get out of here."

Then he gagged again, and she laughed. "Still hungry?"

"Lyra, get it done."

He was turning green. "All right."

The camera was right where she had placed it, and it took only a minute to switch out the memory card.

There weren't any mishaps getting back down the hill.

"I've never seen anything like this," Sam said.

He dug the keys out of his pocket, popped the trunk, and both of them leaned against the car to change their shoes. Lyra opened her backpack and took out a small metal file box, carefully slipped the newest memory card in its folder, and placed it in front of all the others.

She was zipping the backpack shut when Sam drew her attention. Staring intently at the one road that led in and out of the park, he tilted his head, listening. Suddenly he said, "Lyra, get in the car. Someone's coming."

Though she didn't hear anything, she didn't question him. She slammed the trunk shut and ran to get in the car. She had barely snapped her seat belt in place when Sam backed their car out.

A dark gray car coming into the park careened around the corner, picked up speed on the straight road, and headed directly at them.

"Hold tight," Sam ordered.

"Maybe they're here to . . ." she began, thinking they might have trash in their trunk to throw away.

A shot rang out from the passenger's side of the gray car.

". . . shoot us," she finished.

The car nearly sideswiped theirs as it sped past in the opposite direction.

Sam was already on the phone to the FBI telling the location of the park and giving a description of the car shooting at them.

Lyra twisted in her seat to look out the back window. She knew there were at least two men in the car, the driver and the passenger who shot at them, but were there more? Tinted windows prevented her from seeing.

She waited for Sam to finish talking to the agent and said, "Sam, swing around so I can get the license plate number."

"I'm getting you out of here."

"You can't pass up this opportunity. There's only one way in and out, and if you could trap them . . ."

"No. I'm not risking your life."

"At the very least, shoot their tires out. Or let me."

"Are you out of your frickin' mind?"

"Here they come."

Almost out of sight as it reached the curve in the road, the gray car suddenly spun around, fishtailing as it sped toward them.

"You do remember you're driving a tank," Lyra said.

Sam tossed her the phone. "Okay. One pass, but that's all. I'll try to keep them in the park as long as possible."

The men in the gray car fired repeatedly, but the bullets missed their target.

In another life, Sam could have been a race car driver. One second they were racing into the wind, and the next they were spinning to get behind the gray car. Lyra was ready with her cell phone and snapped a picture of the plate.

At the sound of sirens, the attackers slammed their car into reverse, all but stripping the gears as they lurched around Sam, disappearing up the hill.

He didn't follow. He could see lights flashing on two cars coming into the park. Pulling over, he waited for the squad cars to pass, then drove toward the entrance.

"Don't you want to wait and see—" Lyra began.

Sam didn't let her finish. "I'm getting you out of here, and that, sweetheart, is the last time I'm going to tell you."

TWENTY-TWO

MILO WAS HAVING YET ANOTHER WORST DAY OF his life.

His problems started in the morning when he decided to go to the university and prowl around. He hadn't seen Lyra in a couple of days, and he thought he might spot her on campus. In order to blend in and not draw attention to himself, he trimmed the bangs on his pageboy wig and slathered half a tube of tanning lotion on his face and arms to even out his skin tone. The color was a nice bronze. He thought it looked pretty good on his face, and it didn't sting his raw skin much at all. He probably did go a little overboard whitening his teeth. Nevertheless, he gave it a try because he reasoned that the college students, being young, would have white teeth . . . and he wanted to blend in.

When he left his house, he was convinced he looked ten years younger.

Later he realized he should have read the instructions on the tanning bottle because his face and arms were getting darker, and the orange tinge was getting more noticeable. Within an hour, he had turned from a cool bronze to a freakish tangerine.

Milo wandered around campus oblivious to the stares he was getting. He went inside one building and saw students filing into an auditorium but didn't go inside for fear someone would ask him what he was doing there. He didn't have any identification, but if anyone asked, he was prepared with a good lie, that he was looking for his cousin.

Once outside again, he found a bench and waited, hoping Lyra would walk by. Hundreds of coeds passed in front of him, but no Lyra. The bench was uncomfortable, so he decided to try more of the buildings. He meandered up and down hallways, peeking in open doors, but still no sign of her. He was getting bored and had decided it was time to give up for the day when his attention was caught by a bulletin board outside one of the classrooms. His heart leapt when he saw her name. It said "Lyra Prescott, Parks." And next to that, in parentheses, it said "Paraiso Park." What did that mean?

A weird-looking student with thick glasses walked up to the board. He didn't even glance in Milo's direction as he studied another notice.

Milo tapped the board and asked, "What's this list for?"

The student's eyes widened when he turned his head toward Milo. "What?"

"What's this list for?"

It took the student a while to peel his eyes away from Milo's face. "Those are projects. That one," he said, pointing to a name, "is writing about malls. The script—" He turned, but no one was there.

Milo was hurrying down the hallway. Paraiso Park. That's where Lyra would be. She was probably walking around the park and writing down her thoughts for her school paper. Bet she goes there often, he thought.

He wondered what kind of paper she was writing. The project sounded boring. What could anyone write about a park? Now, a mall, that would be easy. She could write about all the shops and the food court. Just listing all the different kinds of food could take up two full pages. But what could be interesting about a park?

Hold on. Maybe it was the kind of park with Ferris wheels, and a merry-go-round, and a train. That'd be okay. Milo liked trains. If that's where she was spending her time, then things were looking up.

He needed another rental car. He didn't go to any of the major companies, but instead chose a fly-by-night outfit. He used a different fake ID and credit card but thought maybe the clerk suspected something because of the way he kept staring at him.

"I'm over twenty-five," Milo said, knowing that most car rentals had a minimum age requirement. Maybe the man was hesitant to assist him because he looked so much younger.

The clerk nodded and finally started typing on his computer. "We've only got a couple of cars left, and they're older models," he said. "There's a convention in town."

*   *   *

MILO DROVE OUT OF the lot in a scratched-up, faded, blue piece of junk. The engine sputtered when he first started it, but then it warmed up and chugged along. Since it didn't have a GPS, he stopped at a gas station for a city map. He finally located the obscure park and asked a couple of people at the station for directions.

Milo was shocked as he neared his destination. The park was in a bad part of town. Real estate agents might lure their clients to this neighborhood with the pitch that it was more of a transitional area, but they wouldn't mention it was transitioning into a ghetto. Every corner had a deserted building with gang signs painted on the walls, and the few stores that were still in business had bars on their doors and windows. Milo was glad he hadn't gotten a better rental car because it would probably be stripped while he was inside the park, and then how would he get home? Fortunately, no one would want to take anything from the beat-up jalopy he was driving.

Milo finally located the park entrance and drove down a long straight road for about half a mile. The road curved and curved again before it reached a huge hill. Much to his disappointment, there weren't any Ferris wheels or trains. He drove all the way around the hill. He could smell a foul odor, but with the car windows up and the air-conditioning on, he thought it was coming from the engine.

There was no sign of Lyra, or any other human being for that matter, but Milo decided it could be worth his while to wait. She might show up. He turned around and headed back toward the park entrance, looking for a good place to hide his car. He thought about using branches as camouflage, but that would take too much time and effort. The abandoned park shelters didn't offer enough cover. There was a pile of rubbish big enough for the car to hide behind, but he was afraid some of the sharp objects lying around the heap would cause a flat tire. He finally decided to leave his car behind a burned-out building across the street from the park entrance.

Once the car was hidden, he went back to the park to find a hiding place for himself. He wanted a good vantage point from which to watch her, and if he was close enough and she was alone, he might even try to engage her in conversation. This time he'd be prepared. He'd felt a strong connection between them when she'd smiled at him at the yard sale, and he was certain she'd felt it, too.

IT WAS A WARM MORNING, and with each step the odor grew stronger. Milo had almost reached the base of the hill, and was standing on the road mopping his brow, when he heard a car coming. Where to hide? Where to hide? He couldn't hide on the hill unless he could get quickly to the top. He whirled in a circle. The car would soon reach the first curve and he'd be exposed. There were dead bushes to his left, and in a panic, he dove into the dried shrubbery.

The stench was horrible. His face was buried in something foul. He used his shirtsleeve to wipe it off, then pulled his shirt over his face, all the way to his brow.

Was that Lyra driving into the park? He could endure just about anything as long as he got to look at her again. The car stopped, and he heard doors opening and closing. Milo lay in a gully wrapped in garbage and covered with dead shrubs and branches. He thought he heard a man's voice, but he couldn't be sure, and he couldn't take the chance of raising his head, fearing he'd get caught.

He suddenly remembered the gun he'd stowed in the glove compartment. How could he protect his love without a gun? He hadn't been thinking. Stupid, he told himself. *Stupid*.

There wasn't a sound for several minutes, then he heard a man's voice in the distance, coming closer to the car. Someone was with him. Milo thought he heard a woman's voice. They stood for a couple of minutes talking before they got back in the car. Milo couldn't stand not knowing if Lyra was in the car with some man. He darted a quick look. The passenger side faced him, and there she was, staring out the windshield. His heart sang. If Lyra turned just a little, she would look straight at him.

Screeching tires signaled another car roaring in their direction. Milo started to rise up to take a look, but then heard gunshots and flattened out in the garbage again. Someone was shooting at Lyra's car. Charlie! It had to be Charlie and his sidekick, Stack. Those stupid thugs. No class at all, those two. How did they find out about Lyra's Paraiso

Park project? Probably the same way he had, Milo thought.

The gunfire got louder and closer. A bullet smacked into a rotten banana peel close by, and he ducked. He'd kill them if they hurt her. He heard gunshots, screeching tires, and roaring engines. It all finally stopped after the sirens blared past him.

Milo raised his head. Seeing no one, he darted from the garbage heap and raced down the road to his car. As he drove away from the abandoned building, he held tight to the steering wheel to keep his hands from shaking. Lyra had barely escaped being shot by her attackers, and he felt an overwhelming sense of guilt. He had put his love in terrible danger. This was all his fault. He never should have told Mr. Merriam about her.

Tears flooded his eyes. Letting her go was the only way Milo could save her.

TWENTY-THREE

THE GOOD NEWS WAS THAT THE TWO MEN TRYing to kill Sam and Lyra were now in handcuffs. The bad news was that they weren't the two men who had broken into her apartment.

Sam drove her to the police station where the men were being processed. She stood in a tiny room behind a one-way mirror and waited while Sam stepped out into the hall to talk to two other agents. Ed, the man who had delivered the car, saw her and came in.

"I looked at the car, and not a single bullet touched it. The perps were either lousy shots or Agent Kincaid was too fast for them." Shaking his head, he repeated, "Not a single bullet."

Sam walked up behind Lyra and put his hands on her shoulders. "They're bringing them up. Ready?"

"Yes," she answered. "Have they said anything?"

"Yes. They want lawyers."

Two men were led into the interrogation room. They hadn't even taken their seats when Lyra said, "They aren't the same men who were in my apartment."

"You're sure?" Sam asked. "You told me they were wearing masks."

She looked through the glass again. "They were," she said, "but these men are much shorter and stockier. The man I hit with the pepper spray had coal black eyes, and he was over six feet. He was almost as tall as you are," she added. "The other one was tall, too, but thin. Those two," she nodded at the men sitting at the table facing her, "they're much shorter, and the color of their eyes . . . they're not the same men."

"Max is on his way here with Sidney. She was with them long enough to recognize their voices."

"Who are they? Did they have identification?"

"Wouldn't matter. They're both in the system. They're members of the Flynn gang."

"I've never heard of them."

"They're enforcers for a local crime boss, Michael Flynn."

"What would they want with me? What did I do to cause all this?" She folded her arms and took a step toward the window. "I'd like to go in there and ask them."

"They want nothing from you. You're just a job."

She stepped back and looked at him. "A job?"

"They're hired guns, Lyra."

"Then thank God they're locked up."

He nodded. He didn't tell her that whoever had sent these goons would only send more. He glanced at the clock and said, "Lyra, it's almost five, and I'm starving. Let's go."

Lyra wanted to wait until Sidney arrived, but her stomach was grumbling, too. Neither she nor Sam had had anything to eat since breakfast. They'd been too busy getting rid of explosives, dodging bullets, and giving statements at the police station to think about food.

A woman opened the door and stuck her head in. "Agent Kincaid? There's a call for you."

"Stay here. I'll be right back."

"I'm preparing dinner," Lyra told him.

"You can cook?"

"Not really, but I'm going to prepare dinner."

Lyra waited until he'd left, then pulled out her phone and called Noel's restaurant.

"Hi, Tim, it's Lyra. I'd like carryout, please."

"Same credit card, love?" the voice on the other end said.

"Yes," she answered and ordered a couple of Noel's specialties. "I'll be there in thirty to pick it up."

Sam returned. "Ready?" he said.

"I think I could be a good policewoman, except for one thing. I might get in trouble shooting too many suspects . . . but only the ones I knew were guilty."

He opened the door for her. "I wouldn't put that down on an application."

Sam once again checked they weren't being followed before heading back to the duplex.

"We have to make a quick detour."

She gave him directions. "There it is, on the corner. Pull into the side lot, please."

She made a call and said, "We're here."

They didn't have to wait long. A heavyset man wearing a chef's jacket carried out two large shopping bags.

"Pop the trunk . . . ooh, no, don't," Lyra said. "Our smelly boots are in there. Backseat will have to do."

She got out of the car and opened the back door. Tim placed the bags inside, shut the door, and kissed Lyra on both cheeks before hurrying back inside.

"French, huh?" Sam asked.

"No."

"Then why'd he kiss you on both cheeks?"

She smiled. "He likes me."

"You shouldn't let him kiss you like that," he said.

She rolled her eyes. "Tim's my friend."

"Half of California's your friend," he countered.

"Did you ever find out who Rooney worked for?" she asked suddenly, remembering the yard sale.

"Yes."

"And?"

"A guy named Merriam," he answered. "Rooney did some laundering for him. We've been watching Merriam for a while."

"What does he do?"

"Owns a big collection agency."

When they pulled into the garage, Sam said, "Food smells good."

Lyra carried both bags inside while Sam put their boots by the garage wall to air out. He carried in her backpack.

"This is preparing dinner, huh?" he asked her, grinning.

"I'm warming it up," she said, arching an eyebrow as she lifted one container out of the sack. "Thus, I'm preparing dinner."

"Need any help?"

"No thanks, I think I can manage."

"I'm going to make some calls."

He went upstairs, which meant he didn't want her to hear any of the conversation. Maybe he was talking to a girlfriend. Odd, she never thought to ask Sam if he had one. It no longer mattered. He'd be gone in the morning. And she was glad about it, she reminded herself.

Sidney called while Lyra was setting the table, and they had a long talk about the two men in lockup. Lyra gave her all the details of the shooting at the park, and Sidney asked a hundred questions.

"How did Flynn's thugs find you? Were they following you?"

"No. There was no way anyone could have followed us. Sam made sure of that."

"So how did they know you were at the park? Maybe you weren't their target. Maybe it was a random drive-by."

"This was no drive-by, Sidney. They were there deliberately to shoot us. When they drove by us the first time and missed, they turned around and tried again."

"That means they knew you would be there. Who else knew about your film project?"

"Almost anyone could have found out about it.

Most of the students in my class, the techs at the lab . . . countless people. Our project titles were even posted on a bulletin board outside the classroom—anyone could have seen it. Oh, and we went to Mia's party last week, remember? I told a number of people about my film. Then, of course, there's everyone at City Hall, the reference librarians at the public library, the archivists at—"

"Okay," Sidney said to stop her. "I get it. Everybody could have known. But not everybody knew the time and day you would show up."

"That's true. They had to be waiting nearby."

"The police said they are hit men?"

"They're not very good ones," Lyra said. "They couldn't even hit our car."

"Don't take this lightly. They're not talking, but Max says it won't be long before they know who they're working for."

"That's good."

"I wanted to stay and watch the interrogation, but Max said we had to leave. He's very . . . assertive."

"You like him?"

"Not enough to . . . you know. What about Sam?"

"He's leaving first thing in the morning, so I'm making him a farewell dinner."

"Luigi's or Noel's?"

Lyra laughed. "Noel's."

"You still need a bodyguard."

"I'm getting a new one in the morning."

"Why is Sam leaving?"

"He has other commitments. He doesn't do this

type of work. He's only helping out as a favor to Alec."

"You sound funny . . . strained. I can hear it in your voice."

"I'm just tired. Dinner's going to get cold. I'll talk to you tomorrow."

"Stay safe."

"You, too."

When Lyra had dinner on the table, she ran upstairs to get Sam.

She knocked on the door. "Sam?"

"Yes?"

She made the mistake of opening the door and peeking in. Sam had just stepped out of the shower and was barely wrapped in a towel that hung low on his hips. His chest and legs glistened with drops of water.

"Dinner's ready." She sounded hoarse.

She tripped hurrying down the stairs and surely would have broken something vital if she hadn't grabbed the handrail. The thud of her feet on the steps sounded as though an elephant had lost its footing. Cause and effect were at play here. If she hadn't seen him barely covered, she wouldn't have tripped. But she *had* seen him, and it was going to take her a long while to get that image out of her head. Just looking at Sam made her throat dry.

How could any man be that perfect?

She was taking the rolls out of the oven when Sam walked in wearing a white T-shirt that hugged his muscles, faded blue jeans, and soft leather loafers.

The kitchen was small. Lyra closed the oven

door and held the hot pan over her head, pressing her back against the refrigerator so Sam could get past.

"Steak or chicken?" she asked.

"Which do you want?"

"Chicken."

They made small talk through dinner, sharing stories of their families and their homes. After hearing about all the exotic places Sam had lived, Lyra felt that her life was rather mediocre and humdrum, but Sam seemed just as interested in her stories of the ranch and her grandmother and her dreams of becoming a filmmaker as she did in his stories.

He never once mentioned his wife, and Lyra was afraid to ask about her for fear of intruding. She remembered what Gigi had said when Lyra asked if she'd ever remarry: there's only one true love. Maybe Sam felt the same about his wife.

Lyra picked at her salad, cut a small portion of the chicken breast, and left the rest on the platter between them. Sam finished his dinner and polished off the chicken and vegetables.

"That was a great dinner," he told her.

"I wanted to make a farewell dinner for you to say thank you, and had there been time, I would have prepared one of my grandmother's dishes. She's the real cook in the family. It's too bad she didn't cook for you."

"Maybe someday she will."

"I doubt it, unless she decides to visit D.C."

"Or Scotland," he said.

Lyra stood and took their plates to the sink. He

followed with the empty platter and said, "I don't know how you did it."

She turned around and leaned against the sink. "Did what?"

"Went up and down that godforsaken hill every day. The stench . . . I'd be in the shower three times a day."

"Actually, it was two showers a day," she corrected. "And I'm about to take my second one. I always feel like the smell is in my hair."

He bent forward. "You smell great."

She started to load the dishwasher, but Sam stopped her. "Let me do that."

There wasn't any argument from her. It was probably psychological, but the mention of the hill made her desperate to feel clean.

Twenty minutes later her hair was washed and dried and she was feeling much better. Except for feeling abandoned. She told herself things would be better when he was gone. Sam was an unneeded distraction. Nevertheless, this was their last night, and she knew he felt something for her . . . he'd kissed her.

She put on her cotton pajamas and robe, propped herself up with pillows on the bed, and turned on the television.

He knocked on her door. "You decent?"

"Sort of."

He opened the door and walked in. "I thought you might be working."

"Not tonight."

"Do you have an extra disk of your documentary on the park? Or is it back at the apartment?"

"I keep extra disks in my backpack, and I've got the memory cards. I have my film on my laptop, too. Why?"

"I want to watch it."

"You saw it at the lab, didn't you?"

"I did, but I had other things on my mind, so I didn't get a close look."

"Okay." She started to get up, but he told her to stay put; he'd bring her laptop and backpack to her. Lyra suddenly felt vulnerable, wanting to call out excuses, such as the film will be boring, or she could have done a much better job narrating, or she should have picked up the pace . . .

Sam handed her the laptop. "You want to watch it with me?" he asked.

He didn't give her time to make up her mind. "Scoot over," he said and sat down beside her. Kicking off his loafers, he swung his legs up and stretched out.

"You're going to be bored," she warned. She handed him a pillow for his back.

"I won't be bored."

"It isn't very long."

Lyra scooted closer, opened the video on her laptop, and moved it to his lap.

"I think—"

"Stop worrying."

"Just tell me why you want to watch it again."

"The hill made an impression on me," he said. "I saw that you got the license plate numbers of those bastards who used the park as their own personal landfill. Now I'd like to see if you got any faces."

"Oh, I did," she told him. "Almost all of them

turned around at some point, and if I freeze the shots, you can get a really good look at them."

"Yeah?" He turned his head and smiled at her. He was so close he could see the green flecks in her eyes. Emeralds, he thought. As bright as emeralds.

"How did you manage that?"

"It's all in the angle of the camera."

"Ready?" he asked.

She nodded, and he started the film.

Neither one of them spoke while the documentary was playing. Lyra was watching with a critical eye. She cringed over the huskiness of her voice. Why didn't she have two cameras going at the same time, one facing east, the other west? And why hadn't she noticed the spots where the narration dragged?

Sam thought the film was excellent and told her so.

"How come you were so nervous watching it?" he asked.

"I was nervous because *you* were watching it," she admitted.

He laughed. "I thought having others watch it was rather the point. To expose something horrible that was happening so that something could be done about it?"

"Yes, but I wouldn't be sitting beside any of them listening to their comments."

He closed the laptop and put it on the table next to the bed. He thought silently for a while, then said, "Of all the people who could have known you were doing your project on that particular park, are there any who questioned you about it, anyone who seemed particularly interested?"

"No," she answered.

"Could the men who broke into your apartment have known about it?"

"They could have. I had files and notebooks all over the apartment. They might have seen the name of the park. Sidney said they were tearing through all my papers, and there were photos of the hill before and after it was desecrated."

"They might have been following you during your trips back and forth."

The thought of being watched gave her a chill. "There were a couple of times I thought someone else might have been there," she said, "but I just thought it was my imagination. I was nervous because the park is in such an isolated area."

"I would like to send this film to the FBI office here and to my office in D.C."

"Will anything get done to clean up the hill?"

"Oh, hell yes, if it gets in the right hands."

She was pleased. "Good."

He finished sending the file and said, "That should do it." Handing her the laptop, he slipped on his shoes to leave, but when he looked down at her, a knot formed in the pit of his stomach. The last thing he wanted to do was walk out that door.

He had almost made it when she called out. "Sam?"

He turned. "What?" he asked impatiently.

"I just want you to know how much I've appreciated your help."

Almost dismissively, he said. "It was nothing. I was here because Alec asked me."

"I know, but—"

"I would have done it for anyone."

"I'm just saying—"

"Damn it, Lyra, I've got to get out of here."

His flash of temper ignited her own. "Then go. I know you're dying to get away from me."

He crossed the room and stood over her.

"Go," she said again. "I certainly won't miss you."

"Yeah?" he said as he pulled her into his arms.

TWENTY-FOUR

SAM OBVIOUSLY BELIEVED IN LONG GOOD-BYES. He took Lyra's face in his hands, and his mouth came down on top of hers, taking absolute possession, his tongue thrusting inside to rub against hers. He wanted to know all of her, to kiss every inch of her, to possess her completely. The kiss deepened, becoming carnal as his tongue moved in and out of her mouth. Lyra wrapped her arms around his neck and dug her fingers into his hair. She clung to him, tasting him, losing all thought until she was trembling with passion.

When he lifted his head, his eyes swept over her face and he slowly brushed his thumb across her full lips.

"You're going to miss me, sweetheart," he said as he kissed the side of her neck.

"Not going to happen," Lyra panted. She could barely get the words out. He was nibbling her earlobe, and she couldn't concentrate. She sighed as he continued to play, kissing a path from her earlobe to the sensitive spot at the base of her neck.

"Your skin is so soft," he whispered. His warm, sweet breath sent shivers through her. When his tongue tickled her skin, she felt goose bumps.

His hands slipped under her pajama top and stroked the small of her back, then moved around her waist. His fingers brushed across her breasts as he captured her mouth again with his. When he pulled away, his breathing was as unsteady as hers. She thought she was still in control until she looked down and saw that he had unbuttoned her top.

"Your heart's racing," he said as he placed his hand over it. "I can feel it pounding."

Sam needed to feel her against him. He stepped back and pulled his T-shirt over his head, tossed it on the floor, and started to unbutton his jeans. She stopped him by pushing his hands away. Staring deeply into his eyes, she slid her fingers inside the waistband and slowly unbuttoned each button, the backs of her fingers causing havoc. Her painstaking slowness was deliberate and drove him wild.

"Too slow," he said gruffly.

He pulled a condom from his back pocket, dropped it on the bedside table, and then stripped.

He wasn't the least bit shy. Looking at his beautifully sculpted body, Lyra understood why. He was built like a Greek warrior, a ripple of muscle from his chest to his legs. She could feel his strength, his power.

"Your turn," he told her.

She wasn't embarrassed, but she was feeling vulnerable, wanting him to like her body as much as

she did his. She removed her top and tossed it on
the bed, then untied the ribbon at the waist of her
pajama bottoms. The fabric puddled at her feet.
Completely naked now, she stepped out of them
and turned to face him, waiting for his reaction.
She could feel the heat in her cheeks and thought
she might be blushing.

The muscle in Sam's jaw twitched as desire
knifed through him. He let out a long, ragged
breath. "Ah, Lyra . . . you're beautiful." His voice
shook with emotion.

He reached for her and pulled her against him.
Her soft breasts rubbed against his chest, and the
sensation coursing through him made his need all
the more profound.

Lyra rubbed her cheek against his chest. The
sprinkle of blond hair tickled her skin as she in-
haled his intoxicating scent. Leaning up, she kissed
him just below the jaw, then kissed the pulse at
the base of his neck.

Sam couldn't remain still. He tilted her chin up
and kissed her hungrily while he lifted her onto
the bed and covered her body with his. Careful
not to crush her with his weight, he braced himself on his arms.

Looking into her eyes, he whispered, "Tell me
what you like."

"This," she answered as she rubbed her lips over
his. "I like this."

She kissed him thoroughly, exploring his mouth
with her tongue. She gripped his shoulders. His
body felt like hot steel against her. Each kiss was
hotter than the one before.

Sam tried to slow the pace. If she was trying to drive him crazy, she was doing a damn good job.

"I like this," Sam said. He slowly moved down her body until he reached her breasts. He kissed the valley between them and skimmed each breast with his tongue. He knew she liked what he was doing because she moved restlessly against him and arched her back. He moved lower, circled her navel with kisses, and lower still until she cried out and her nails dug into his shoulders. He rolled over, pulled her on top of him, and kissed her almost savagely.

"I want you," he growled.

"Not yet," she answered, barely recognizing her own voice.

She wanted him to lose his control before she did. She tugged on his ear with her teeth, smiling when she felt him tense against her. Moving lower, she caressed his hard stomach and moved lower still, touching, kissing. He grabbed her and pushed her onto her back. His movements were rough, but her passion matched his. When he nudged her legs apart, she locked her hands behind his neck and trembled in anticipation.

He knelt between her thighs and the feel of her was his undoing. He slowly rubbed against her but stopped when he heard her indrawn breath. Rolling to his side, he reached toward the bedside table.

She was trying to catch her breath when he came back to her and wrapped her in his arms. God, she felt good. She moved beneath him and he couldn't wait any longer. He thrust deep. He tried to take it slow, to draw out the pleasure, but she was so tight, he didn't last long. He moved back and thrust again. Her legs wrapped around him, and his thrusts became quicker, harder, less controlled. Sam had not felt such raw passion with any other woman. It threatened to consume him. He couldn't stop, couldn't control his pace as he slammed into her again and again.

Lyra was as out of control as he was. When she climaxed, her entire body tightened around him, and she cried out in ecstasy. Was he hurting her? Lyra answered by digging her nails into his back and arching against him.

Her climax triggered his. Waves of pleasure washed over him. He'd never experienced anything like this. She took every bit of his strength, and he collapsed on top of her, his head nuzzled in the crook of her neck. His breathing was harsh, and it took a long while to calm his racing heart.

Their bodies glistened with perspiration, and their hearts pounded against their chests in unison.

He finally found enough energy to roll off her. Without a word he got up and went into the bathroom. She heard water running and thought he was taking a shower, but a couple of minutes later, he came back to bed.

Lyra had turned onto her stomach but hadn't covered up, and that pleased him considerably. He liked the fact that she was comfortable with her body and with him.

He tapped her shoulder. "Lyra?"

She lifted her head. "Yes?"

"Would you like a performance evaluation?"

She opened her mouth to say something, then closed it. "A what?" she asked.

"A performance evaluation. You want to know how you did, don't you?"

He had rendered her speechless. She leaned up on an elbow, narrowed her eyes, and frowned at him. Was he kidding? Then she saw the flicker of laughter in his eyes. Okay, two can play at this game, she thought.

"Yes, please. I would love an evaluation. How did I do? And is there room for improvement?"

He stretched out beside her, folded a pillow behind his head, and said, "I've got to give you high marks for enthusiasm."

"Thank you."

"And the effort was there."

"Is that so?"

"Absolutely," he said. "Your technique was definitely above par."

He was having a good time. His grin was slow and totally unrepentant.

"Meaning I can improve?" she asked.

"I'll help you with that."

"That'd be nice," she said, smiling. "Now it's my turn to judge your performance."

He clasped his hands together as if to brace himself and said, "Okay, I'm ready."

She rolled on top of him. "Not bad for a warm-up."

TWENTY-FIVE

He wore her out. Lyra fell into a deep sleep around two in the morning but woke up a little after five with Sam kissing the side of her neck.

He had to be superhuman. She had lost count of the number of times he had reached for her. Three? Four? She supposed she should be honest with herself. She had reached for him, too. Still . . . didn't he need any sleep?

"Sam?" she purred.

"Hmmm?"

"What are you doing?"

"Trying to wake you for good-bye sex."

"Didn't we already have good-bye sex?"

She turned in his arms so she could look at him and tell him she thought he might be insatiable, but his warm body, his sleepy eyes, and his sexy mouth changed her mind. She kissed him instead. Maybe she was insatiable, too.

Their lovemaking wasn't leisurely, but wild and consuming. He was tender with her, yet she could sense the hunger in him. Lyra felt as though she was coming undone. The sensations were terrifying but at the same time wonderful. She clung to him and knew she was safe.

Sam's climax was shattering and exhilarating. His voice was deep and raspy as he called her name and held her hips tight against him. When he found the strength, he lifted up and kissed her brow. She ran her fingertips along his unshaven face.

He touched her soft cheek. "Did I scratch you?"

Her eyes were closing, and she didn't answer his question. "Night," she said.

She was sound asleep less than a minute later.

SAM RELUCTANTLY GOT OUT of bed and went into the bathroom to shower and get dressed. He wasn't certain how early his replacement would be at the door, and he wanted to be ready.

He shaved and packed his bag, pulled on his khaki slacks, and strapped his gun and holster onto his side. Still shoeless and bare-chested, he crossed the hall for the third time to check on Lyra, even though he knew his actions were ridiculous. She was perfectly fine. Everything about her was fine . . . and amazing.

She was going to be okay. Alec had assured him that the new bodyguard—Brick Winter—would keep her safe. Brick Winter. What kind of name was Brick? Sam should have checked him out personally. Alec had vouched for him, but Sam bet if he'd looked he would have found something wrong. And how could anyone take a guy named Brick seriously? Maybe in Hollywood, but not in the real world.

Sam went back into Lyra's room to get his shoes and the clothes he'd left on the floor. He had just stuffed everything in his bag when he heard a knock at the door. Still barefoot, he unsnapped the strap over his gun and went downstairs. He looked through the peephole, saw the identification, and opened the door.

He swore to God a frickin' movie star stood on the welcome mat. As a rule Sam didn't notice what men looked like, but this Brick was built like his name. In a fight, Sam would have to work hard to defeat him. He'd do it, though. Damn right.

Sam sized up his replacement in a split second. He didn't know where he'd ever seen anyone quite so handsome. A movie poster perhaps? These weren't the usual features of a guy who worked as a bodyguard. His profile was too chiseled, too flawless. Where were the scars, the leathery skin, the bags under the eyes from the late nights on watch? He had to be an actor or a model. Maybe he was just doing this part-time until he got a part in the next big action adventure flick.

Brick extended his hand and flashed a smile with his perfect white teeth, and that was all the convincing Sam needed. There was no way Lyra could be safe with anyone like him.

Sam shook Brick's hand, then gave him a firm pat on the shoulder as he turned him around and told him there had been a mistake; Lyra didn't need him after all. Thanking him for his trouble, Sam sent the bewildered Brick on his way.

Yawning, Sam went into the kitchen and poured himself a glass of orange juice and gulped it down.

Sex with Lyra had dehydrated him. He smiled, thinking about that. He could stay one more day, maybe even catch the men who were after her. Then he wouldn't have to worry about her when he went back to D.C.

Yeah, that was a plan.

He took a cold bottle of water upstairs and set it on the nightstand for Lyra, then stripped out of his slacks and slipped into bed beside her. Her back was to him, so he pulled her up against him, draped one arm over her waist, and fell asleep for another couple of hours.

IT WAS CLOSE TO ten o'clock when Lyra finally awoke. She reached for Sam's side of the bed, but it was empty, yet she could feel the warmth where he had lain. She closed her eyes and listened. There was no noise coming from the rest of the house. Sam was gone. No surprise there. He had told her he would be gone in the morning. That's what all the wonderful good-bye sex was about.

She fought off melancholy, and then sank into a deep sadness, followed by painful regret, and finally indignant anger. How dare he leave? Okay, maybe he had to, but he could have told her . . . what? He'd come back? That would have been a lie, and Sam had been up front from the very beginning.

A long shower didn't make her feel any better. By the time she'd blown her hair dry, she'd made up her mind to move forward. If he could leave her that easily, then she hadn't meant anything more to him than a night of sex.

"Glad to be rid of him," she muttered. As she applied lip gloss, she looked in the mirror and added, "Damn glad."

Too bad she couldn't believe her own lie.

Time to go downstairs and meet the new bodyguard. She shoved her laptop in her backpack, unplugged her cell phone from the charger, and went downstairs. Dropping her backpack by the sofa, she crossed to the kitchen.

"Hello," she called.

She came around the corner and stopped cold. Sam was leaning against the counter drinking from the milk carton. Her mouth dropped open. "You're here."

The way he looked at her made all the memories of what happened last night rush into her thoughts. Her heart was racing. She wanted to throw her arms around him and tell him how happy she was to see him, but she couldn't let him see her vulnerability.

She reached for the carton in his hand and casually took a swig of the milk. "You were supposed to be gone this morning," she said.

"Replacement didn't work out," he told her with a shrug. He took the carton away from her and set it on the counter, then pulled her into his arms and kissed her.

A phone rang.

Sam pulled back and said, "Mine or yours?"

"Mine," Lyra said with a sigh.

She went into the living room, fished her phone out of her bag, and looked at the caller ID. "Oh, no," she groaned.

"What's wrong?" Sam called from the kitchen.

"It's Father Henry," she answered. "My grandmother must be at it again."

Sam watched Lyra's expression turn from one of irritation to one of fear as she listened to what the priest was telling her. When the conversation was over, she dropped her phone in her bag and said, "I need to go to San Diego."

"When?"

"Now."

"Okay. Tell me why. What's happened?"

Lyra threaded her fingers through her hair. "I need to pack and get going."

When she tried to get past him, he stopped her. "Tell me," he repeated calmly.

"I thought Father was calling about the holy water."

"The what?"

"The holy water from the font in the church. Gigi—my grandmother—steals a little every now and then."

"I see," he said, though he honestly didn't have a clue.

"This time it wasn't about the holy water, though she did take a little for her petunias."

What was Lyra talking about? Sam figured he'd get a fuller explanation when they were in the car. She was too upset to be coherent. All he needed now were the basic facts.

"What was the priest's main concern if it wasn't the water?"

"He was having lunch with Gigi. He loves her cooking, so she'd invited him over for lunch."

"I see."

"He told me he was sitting on the porch swing enjoying his iced tea when a car drove by very slowly. He noticed the man in the passenger seat was looking intently at Gigi's house. A couple of minutes later, it drove by again. Father tried to get the license plate number, but there was mud smeared all over it. He thought they might have done that on purpose. Alarmed, he went inside and stood by the window to watch. And sure enough, the car came by again. This time one of the guys in the car got out and looked in Gigi's mailbox. Father rushed outside and shouted at him to leave the mailbox alone; it was private property. The man yelled back that he was looking for the Prescott house. He said the Prescott woman was going to be sorry she messed with them. They drove away when Father shouted that he was calling the police."

"Did he call them?" Sam asked.

"No, he called me. He promised to always call me first."

Sam wanted to find out why she had gotten the priest to make such a promise, but he would wait until she was calmer to ask. Lyra's hands were shaking now.

"You do know you're not going anywhere without me."

"I assumed Alec was sending another bodyguard."

"Tomorrow. I'm staying until tomorrow. Then you'll get a new one."

"Even if I'm at my grandmother's house?"

"Yes, even then."

"Are you upset that you had to stay?"

"I don't get upset," he scoffed. "It's just a minor change in schedule, that's all."

Lyra ran upstairs. Since she had a closet full of clothes at home with Gigi, she didn't have to pack much.

Sam had his bag and was waiting for her in the living room when she came back down. She hurried into the kitchen and tossed a few candy bars into the zippered compartment on the side of her overnight case. Finally pausing for breath, she said, "Okay. Let's go."

Traffic was slow, and the drive to San Diego seemed to take forever. Lyra's impatience to see her grandmother grew with every mile. When they were about an hour out of Los Angeles, her cell rang. The call came from her grandmother's phone, so Lyra hurriedly answered.

"Lyra, dear, it's Gigi," her grandmother said.

"Are you okay?" Lyra asked.

"I'm fine," she assured her. "Father Henry had to get back to the church, but Harlan Fishwater is here doing some work. Father Henry made him promise to stay until you arrived. I really don't think that's necessary. I'm perfectly capable of taking care of myself."

"Gigi, I'm on my way and will be there soon. Promise me you won't send Harlan away until I get there."

"All right, I promise. But don't hurry. There's nothing to worry about. I told you, I'm fine."

Gigi hung up the phone, and Lyra slumped back

against the car seat. While relieved that her grandmother was so calm, she couldn't help but worry about her.

She looked at Sam. "Gigi said not to hurry. She can take care of herself."

"Sounds like a strong woman," Sam said.

"Yes, she is," Lyra agreed.

She thought for a minute, then said, "Sam, the man shouting at Father Henry said that the Prescott woman was going to be sorry she messed with them. He had to mean me, right? The two men who broke into my apartment were looking for something. They think I took whatever it was to Gigi's."

"It adds up," he admitted.

"Obviously they're looking for something of value," she continued. "At least to them."

"You said you didn't have anything of value for them to take," he reminded her.

Lyra sat up straight, as though a light had suddenly been turned on in her head. "But I did," she said. "The books."

"The books from the yard sale?"

"Yes, they were very valuable. I don't know how much they were worth, but a signed first edition of a classic sells for thousands of dollars. It makes sense now. They want the books back."

"Why would they think your grandmother has them?" he asked.

"After the yard sale, I drove to San Diego." She paused as the realization hit her. "Oh my God. They followed me."

TWENTY-SIX

"TELL ME ABOUT YOUR FAMILY," SAM SAID AS HE weaved their car through traffic.

"Wasn't all that in my file? And by the way, how long has there been a file on me?"

"Since the break-in at your apartment."

"Oh."

He laughed. "You sound disappointed."

"You should get in the other lane."

They were getting close to the turnoff for Gigi's house, and Lyra was finally beginning to relax. It wouldn't be long before she could see for herself that her grandmother was okay.

"We've already talked about my family. Two brothers, a grandmother who raised us . . . what more do you want to know?"

"When did your parents officially become 'those people'?"

"When they tried to have my grandmother declared incompetent. You see, the two of them had gone through an extremely generous trust fund my grandfather left for his only son, and now they're stuck having to live on a budget. That cramps their style."

"What about the ranch?"

"My grandfather gave it to my brothers and me before he died."

"Then what kind of work does your father do?" he asked.

"He doesn't. He golfs and has meetings. They're very social people."

"They're your parents, and you love them no matter what." Sam phrased this matter-of-factly, yet a question was implied.

"Not when they're hurting my grandmother . . . for money of all things."

"How do your brothers feel about all of this?"

Lyra smiled. "Gigi raised them, too. There's no way they'll let her be *put* somewhere. It's nice to have them on my side. Turn right at the light," she instructed. "Since you're an only child, I'll bet you're close to your parents."

"I am."

"Were you ever lonely as a child?"

"At times. What about you? The only girl . . ."

"I was close to my brothers. I drove them crazy following them around when I was young." She looked out the window, for a moment missing the Texas ranch.

"My wife, Beth, had sisters and brothers."

This was the first time Sam had mentioned his wife's name, and Lyra looked for a hint of sadness in his eyes, but as he drove he was smiling at the memory of her family.

"Did they like you?" Lyra asked.

"Her sisters did. It took longer with the brothers. We were young, maybe too young to get married, but we had three years together."

She folded her hands in her lap. "It doesn't matter how old or young you were. She was your love."

He laughed. "You're a romantic, Lyra."

He was right, but she didn't think that was a bad thing. What was wrong with wanting to find the perfect love?

"About your brothers . . ." Sam said.

"Yes?"

"They'll be calling you real soon."

"Why?"

"Two FBI agents should be knocking on their door anytime now. They're going to confiscate the boxes you shipped."

"Please tell me the agents aren't going to tell Owen and Cooper about the break-in."

"Probably not."

"Probably?" She raised her voice. "You don't know my brothers. They'd go berserk if they found out."

"Perhaps they have reason to worry."

"They might ask Gigi to come stay at the ranch for a while. That'd be good," she conjectured. "Speaking of Gigi . . . there are a few things you should know."

"Like what?"

"Like you're a Democrat. I don't care if you really are or not. When you're with my grandmother, you're a dyed-in-the-wool Democrat."

"And why is that?" Taking his eyes from the road, he glanced at her.

"It's just easier."

"What else?"

"Don't talk about sex."

He burst into laughter that made tears come to his eyes. "I'm going to wreck the car. Why in God's name would you think I would talk to your grandmother about sex?"

"Just don't. Gigi isn't a prude, but just don't. She walked into my bedroom one night—"

"And you weren't alone."

"Of course I was alone!" she cried out. "I was at my grandmother's house."

"Then what happened?"

"She found out I don't like to wear anything when I sleep."

"Hey, Gigi and I have something in common. I found that out, too. Now, there's something we could talk about."

She ignored his smart-ass remark. "Ever since that night, Gigi buys me old-fashioned pajamas every chance she gets."

Sam turned serious. "I will be talking to her about you."

"I know. I'll talk to her, too. We don't keep secrets. I just really hate making her worry, and I hate that I put her in danger."

"You aren't responsible for any of this."

He saw the worry creeping into her eyes. "So after Gigi and I talk about the serious stuff, I'm allowed to discuss the weather. Anything else?"

"Food. She's a great cook. You'll gain five pounds by tomorrow," she promised.

"I know what I'll talk about," he said with a teasing grin.

"What's that?" she asked warily.

"Long good-byes." He reached over and ran his hand up her thigh. "How about I tell her about *really* long good-byes?"

Lyra playfully slapped his hand away. "Speaking of long good-byes . . . when does the new body-guard take over?"

"I'll talk to Alec and let you know." To change the subject, he quickly asked, "Are we getting close?"

"We're here. The one on the end is my grand-mother's house. Park in the back."

Gigi opened the kitchen door and stood on the stoop waiting to greet them. She started talking as they approached from the car. "You know I'm al-ways happy to see you, Lyra, but I'm also vexed that you think I can't take care of myself. There was no need for you to drop everything and drive here. I'm perfectly capable of taking care of my-self."

Lyra kissed her on the cheek. "I know that," she said, "but something has happened and I wanted to talk to you about it."

Sam walked up with the bags and Lyra made the introductions. "Grandmother, I would like you to meet FBI agent Sam Kincaid. Sam, this is Gigi."

He dropped his bag and shook her hand. "It's nice to meet you."

"FBI agent? And with a brogue. Scottish?"

He smiled. "Yes, ma'am."

"Where are my manners? Come in, come in."

She stepped out of the way and held the door for them. "Agent Kincaid, will you be spending the night?"

"Yes."

Gigi didn't bat an eye. "Lyra, will you show Agent Kincaid to the guest room?"

"Please call me Sam."

"Of course," she said. "Just one question."

Lyra knew she had a hundred questions but they would probably wait until after dinner. Then Sam would get the grilling of his life.

"Yes?"

"Are you on the job now?"

He nodded. "I am."

"And you're working with Lyra?"

"That's right."

"I'll make a fresh pitcher of tea."

Lyra led Sam upstairs. They could hear pounding and Lyra assumed Gigi's handyman was at work on some project. Lyra entered a soft blue bedroom. She feared the queen-sized bed might be small for Sam, but the mattress was good. She explained that they would share a bathroom.

The floors in the old house creaked when he crossed the hall to put Lyra's things in her room. The walls were painted a pale yellow. It was a feminine room with its white comforter, white curtains, and tray of perfumes on the dresser. Sam set her bags on a chair and followed her to the door. When she turned around to tell him something, she bumped into him. He grabbed her arms to steady her and neither of them moved, their bodies touching. All she had to do was look up at him, and he couldn't resist. He took her face between his hands and gently kissed her.

She had to kiss him back. Lyra was wrapping her arms around him when Gigi called up, "Lyra, dear, let me know if it's too hot up there."

He pulled away from her. "It could get hotter."

"No, it couldn't. Come on, I'll show you the rest of the house."

Gigi's home was what Lyra called a "straight through." The front door opened into the living room, which opened into the dining room, which opened to the kitchen. There was a small room behind the kitchen that Gigi had converted into a study.

"Gigi's room is down this hall, across from the bathroom," she pointed out. The pounding was getting louder.

Gigi had put on an apron and was wiping her hands on a dish towel. "Come have a glass of iced tea."

Harlan came up from the basement, said hello to Lyra, and was introduced to Sam.

"Would you like some tea, Harlan?"

"No thanks. I've got to pick up the kids. It's getting on."

"Yes, it is," Gigi said. "I'll see you in the morning."

"Remember, I'll be late. I've got to pick up supplies for the new shelves."

Sam walked to the door with the handyman and

stood talking to him on the porch for several minutes.

"Agent Kincaid is quite handsome," Gigi said peering through the open door. "Don't you agree?"

"Yes, I do."

"I'm not waiting until after dinner to hear what's going on, Lyra. If something has happened, I need to know about it."

Lyra waited for Sam to return before broaching the subject. Gigi sat across the table from the two of them.

"Where should I start?" Lyra asked Sam.

"The yard sale," he answered.

As Lyra recounted the events of the last few days, her grandmother sat silently, listening intently. When Lyra was finished, Gigi folded her hands on the table and thought for a minute.

"It's a blessing neither you nor Sidney was seriously hurt." She paused another few seconds before saying, "And you believe those two men who showed up here earlier today were looking for the things you packed and sent to the ranch?"

"That's certainly a possibility," Sam answered. "I've already talked to the field office in L.A., and they've got a couple of men on this. They'll notify the police here so they'll be aware of the situation."

Lyra explained, "Sam's a good friend of Alec Buchanan. He's acting as my bodyguard for the time being."

Gigi patted Sam's hand. "Well, I'm sure Lyra is in good hands."

Lyra was relieved that Gigi was remaining so calm. "Shall we take our drinks out on the front porch? It's a bit stuffy in here," Lyra suggested.

"You two go ahead. I'll turn the air up," Gigi said.

Sam sat next to Lyra on the swing, his arm draped across the back. Every now and then his hand brushed her neck.

Gigi joined them. "I'm so ashamed you're seeing my garden like this. It's in such disarray. For the life of me, I can't understand why nothing will grow. Two years in a row now! I used to have such a lovely garden, didn't I, Lyra? Now it doesn't even respond to holy water."

Sam got up from the porch swing and walked down the steps with Gigi. He bent, pulled a leaf off one plant, and held it up to examine. On one knee, he dug a couple of inches into the soil. "What are you spraying on the plants?" he asked.

"Holy water, of course . . ." Gigi said as though everyone did it.

"Besides the holy water."

"Last year, I tried all sorts of fertilizer and pesticides, but this year only water."

He took Gigi's arm as they went back to the porch.

"What's happened to my green thumb?" she asked.

Lyra was sympathetic. "Maybe next year . . ."

Sam couldn't believe two smart women wouldn't know what was happening.

"It's poison," he said.

Gigi sat down and turned to Sam. "I'm sorry, Sam. What did you say?"

"It's poison," he repeated.

Gigi shot out of her chair like a bottle rocket. "Someone is poisoning my flowers?"

"Actually, it's not the flowers themselves. It's the soil."

Lyra nudged him. "Are you certain?"

"Ah, come on. Look at it. Someone's put some kind of herbicide in the soil."

"Lyra?" Gigi said, huffing with rage.

"Yes, Gigi." Lyra had only seen that look in Gigi's eyes a couple of times in her life, and she knew what was coming.

"Go get my thirty-eight."

TWENTY-SEVEN

IF LYRA HADN'T BEEN THERE TO CALM GIGI down, Sam was convinced the irate woman would have grabbed her gun and marched across the yard to her neighbor's house. He doubted she'd actually pull the trigger, but he was certain she'd have no qualms in using the weapon as a deterrent.

"How can you be sure Mrs. Castman is responsible for the dead flowers?" Lyra asked.

Gigi stopped her furious pacing long enough to answer. "Of course it was her! Who else would be so diabolical? I knew there was something strange going on when she was so sympathetic about my garden."

Imitating her neighbor's condescending voice, Gigi crooned, " 'Oh, I'm *so sorry* you're having trouble with your petunias this year . . . Maybe the nursery sold you a bad batch . . . It's *a shame* you worked so hard and have so little to show for it. . . . I'm *sure* you'll do better next year.' I'll bet those bottles of water she carried from the church were just a hoax to throw me off. I have half a mind to go over there and rip out every single flower she planted."

When she took the first steps off the porch, Sam rushed to her side. He slipped his arm through hers and patted her hand. "You know, Gigi, there might be another way to handle this. You do want Mrs. Castman to admit she's responsible, don't you?"

Gigi stopped and thought about it. "Yes, I suppose she'd never admit what she's done if I destroyed her garden the way she's destroyed mine." She looked tearfully at her dry and wilting flowers. "I'm afraid nothing's going to bring them back now."

"That's right," Sam agreed.

Gigi straightened her shoulders and looked at Sam with vengeance in her eyes. "What can we do?"

"I think this calls for a little undercover work," he said.

"Like FBI undercover work?"

"Exactly," he said as he led her back to the porch.

Gigi was incredibly pleased to have an FBI agent on the case. They sat and talked until dusk, watching the sun slip beneath the ocean's horizon.

Neither Sam nor Lyra was particularly hungry, but later, when Gigi called them into the kitchen and set fresh baked bread and bowls of chowder in front of them, they were suddenly starved.

"It's been a long day," Gigi said. "I'm going to turn in."

After clearing the dishes, Lyra stretched her

arms over her head and yawned. "I think I'll go to bed as well." She kissed Sam on the cheek and went upstairs.

Sam's phone signaled a text. It was his third from Alec asking about the bodyguard that Sam had dismissed. He decided to stop putting off the conversation and went out on the porch to return the call.

"What the hell, Sam?" Alec began.

"You called?"

"What was wrong with Brick?"

"He wasn't right."

"And just how wasn't he right?" Alec's exasperation came through loud and clear.

"I didn't feel comfortable leaving Lyra with him."

"I see." Alec drew out the words as though he'd just made an intriguing discovery.

"See what?" Sam asked irritably. He didn't give Alec time to speculate. "We're in San Diego now. I don't know when Lyra will go back to L.A."

"I heard about the explosive under the car," Alec said, his voice serious now. "And the shooters coming at you in the park. I understand they're locked up."

"They're not talking."

"They're not getting bail, either."

They talked about the case for some time, each posing theories on the who and the why, and then Alec said, "Don't you have things to do? Like giving speeches and getting back to D.C.?"

"Yes, I do, but I can stay one, maybe two more nights. I'll call you when I need someone to take over. Probably the day after tomorrow."

"What about Brick taking—"

"Hell no," Sam said quickly. "I don't think he's qualified."

"Are you kidding me? He was in Special Forces," he reminded Sam.

"Got to go, Alec. Talk to you soon."

Alec was still talking when Sam disconnected the call.

He made sure all the doors were locked and went upstairs to get ready for bed.

He was coming out of the bathroom when Lyra opened her bedroom door. "I forgot to tell you where the towels are."

"I found them."

"Good night then."

She stepped back to close the door, but he was walking toward her. His chest was bare, and he wore only his khaki pants, but it didn't seem to matter whether he was fully clothed or wore nothing at all: he took her breath away. Backing her into her room, he quietly shut the door behind him.

She shook her head. "We can't sleep together in Gigi's house."

"We can be quiet."

He pulled her into his arms and slid his hand behind her neck, gently twisting her hair in his fist. He forced her chin up as his mouth covered hers. His tongue swept inside and rubbed against hers.

Her resistance was dissolving, but she found enough strength to say, "No, we shouldn't . . ."

"Okay, we won't."

He was nibbling on her neck, sending shivers all

the way to her toes. She put her palms against his chest, but his kisses became more demanding and more arousing. She couldn't be certain who removed her pajamas. She thought she had done it, but Sam might have helped.

His mouth slanted over hers again and again, and he groaned when her soft breasts rubbed against him. When his caresses became more intimate, she tugged on his hair and begged him to stop tormenting her.

"Take me to bed," she demanded.

Twice he had to quiet her with his mouth as she climaxed. His own release was so powerful, his entire body tightened against her. He wanted to shout her name, but he groaned against her neck instead.

Long minutes passed as they clung to each other. Then Sam gently kissed her brow, whispered good night, and left her.

Lyra heard water running. Deep inside, she felt a longing. She knew he would go back to the guest room, but she wished he would sleep with her.

It suddenly dawned on her that these were the thoughts of someone who was needy. Not good, she told herself. Not good at all. She didn't want to go to sleep worrying about such things, so instead, she focused on the positive. She thought about his smile and how it made her want to sigh, and the way he watched out for her, and how calm he was in the face of disaster.

She was drifting off to sleep when Sam slipped into bed beside her. She opened her eyes slightly. His gun was on the bedside table, which meant he was there for the night. Feeling his arms around her, she fell asleep with a smile.

LYRA WOKE UP to pounding. For a second she thought it was an earthquake; the house felt as though it was moving. She bolted up in bed and looked around for Sam, but he wasn't there. She cleared her head enough to realize the pounding had a rhythm to it. Someone was downstairs making all the noise.

Oh, no. What was Gigi having Harlan do now? She had enough shelves to open a shoe store. He couldn't be building more, could he?

If Lyra and Gigi were home alone, she would have gone downstairs in her robe, but Gigi would have heart failure if Lyra wasn't dressed for the day with two men in the house. Muttering to herself, she took a shower and got dressed in a navy skirt and white blouse. She was just starting down as Sam was coming up to get her. He had a goofy grin on his face.

Immediately suspicious, she said, "What?"

He shook his head. "Come see."

Lyra followed the pounding and found Harlan smashing a giant hole in Gigi's bedroom wall. He'd hung a clear plastic drape to keep the dust and drywall inside his work area. Spotting Lyra, he lifted his mask and waved, then went back to work.

Lyra stood as though in a stupor for a few seconds before abruptly turning and going into the kitchen. She was pouring herself a glass of orange juice when Gigi walked in.

"Good morning. You slept late today. It's almost nine."

Sam was standing in the doorway, leaning against the frame. Lyra pulled out a chair and sat, but she didn't stay there long.

"Is Harlan building more shelves?" she asked.

"No, dear. It's my panic room."

Lyra nearly knocked the glass of juice over when she shot up. "What? A what?"

"A panic room. Surely you know what those are."

Lyra dropped into her chair and looked up at Sam.

He folded his arms across his chest and said, "I tried to explain to your grandmother that she might be overreacting to the news she heard yesterday . . ."

You think? she wanted to say.

She looked across the table at Gigi waiting anxiously for her opinion. "I think it's a great idea," Lyra said.

Gigi nodded. "There you are, Sam. She agrees with me." Smiling, she went to see how Harlan was doing.

Sam pulled out a chair, straddled it, and stacked his hands across the back. He leaned in and stated, "A panic room."

"Yes, I know. And why not? Yes, this house is small, but Gigi's bedroom is good-sized, and she has a closet she doesn't need, so why not build a panic room? It will make her feel safer."

He rubbed the back of his neck and started to

laugh. "In a little while, I've got to go next door and terrorize an old lady into confessing that she's killing Gigi's flowers. Don't know why I was so surprised by a panic room. I should have taken it all in stride after hearing about the holy water."

Gigi poked her head in the doorway. "Do you want some toast, Lyra? Sam?"

"No thanks."

"Sam, dear, did you tell Lyra the news?"

"I was just about to."

Gigi disappeared down the hall, and he turned back to Lyra. "There's more news?" she asked. "What else is Harlan building?"

"Your brothers called Gigi. They want her to come home. I assume that's the ranch. Your brothers heard about the break-in . . . everything, actually."

"How did they hear? Who told them?"

Before she could become outraged, Sam said, "Two FBI agents appeared at their doorstep and took the boxes, remember?"

"Did they have to tell my brothers?"

"If they wanted the boxes, yeah, they did. They couldn't just stroll out of there with your property without a reason."

"I should have called them."

"Gigi said they'll be calling here again."

"I can handle them," Lyra assured Sam. She knew she was facing a long argument. They were her older brothers, and they couldn't come to grips with the fact that she had grown up and could make her own decisions.

"There's a little more news," Sam said as Gigi returned carrying an empty coffee cup. An uncomfortable glance passed between them.

Uh-oh. "What is it?"

Gigi answered. "Your parents have heard that there's trouble."

Her shoulders slumped. "How did they find out?"

"Your father called the ranch while the FBI agents were there, and the housekeeper told him. He and your mother are coming here this afternoon."

Gigi and Sam waited for Lyra to react. She said nothing, but the blood was rising in her face and her jaw was clenched. Slowly she pushed her chair back and stood. As she was walking out of the kitchen, Sam asked, "Where are you going?"

She didn't look back when she answered. "To tell Harlan he should hurry up with that panic room."

TWENTY-EIGHT

MRS. EDITH CASTMAN FOLDED LIKE A HOUSE of cards.

She was outside tending her flowers, so Sam didn't have to knock on her door and identify himself as an FBI agent. Instead, he casually strolled into her yard, his gun conveniently covered by his navy blue sweatshirt. He complimented her flowers, told her he was a bit of a gardener himself, but certainly not as good as she was, and he would love some tips.

She looked at him suspiciously. "You a foreigner?"

"Yes."

"You're not here to take a job away from an American, are you?"

"No, I'm not."

She took off her glasses and wiped the lenses with her apron. The wrinkles that extended from her nostrils to her chin were deep craters, and her mouth seemed to be permanently downturned. It took only a second for Sam to size her up: Mrs. Castman was an unhappy woman.

The flowers, she explained, were her pride and joy because they never talked back.

Having no wish to hear a more detailed explanation, he nodded, pretending to understand.

"Not everyone can grow flowers like I do," she bragged. "Just look at those burned-up flowers next door. Never even came to bloom."

"They do look pretty bad," he agreed.

"They're not bad; they're dead." She snickered and lowered her voice. "The woman living there poured holy water on her flowers because she thought that's what I did."

Mrs. Castman wasn't just unhappy, Sam decided. She was mean-spirited, the kind of woman who enjoyed watching other people suffer.

"Wow, look at those!" he said, pointing to some purple flowers. He wanted to draw her back to her garden. "I've never seen anything so full of blooms. You have an amazing touch. I'd give anything if I could get results half as beautiful in my garden."

"Are you going back to your foreign country?"

"Yes."

"Then I'll show you what I use to grow my flowers. I wouldn't tell you if you were staying around here. I can't have you competing."

Harlan was putting sheets of drywall in the back of his truck when Mrs. Castman and Sam walked into her backyard. He wasn't there by accident. Sam had asked him to hang around as a witness in case the situation came down to Sam's word against hers.

"That young man is inside that woman's house all the time," she said under her breath as she nodded toward Harlan. "I know something's going on, but I keep my mouth shut. I'm just thankful I won't have to live next door much longer. I'm moving back to Pennsylvania in the fall. I've already sold my house to a young couple. You can be sure I didn't mention the carrying-on next door when they were looking at my house."

Sam knew Gigi would be happy to learn that Mrs. Castman would be moving. He followed her through her tiny backyard and waited while she opened her garage door. The light streamed in and Mrs. Castman set the watering can she was carrying on a bench. The odor of soil and fertilizer hung in the stagnant air. Gardening tools were strewn on an old table. Bags of fertilizer lay on the concrete floor, and bottles of liquid fertilizer and pesticides were lined up on the shelves on the wall.

"I use a special mixture of fertilizers," she confided as she reached for one of the bottles. "It's my secret formula," she added with a fiendish grin that reminded Sam of an old silent movie about a mad scientist.

As she poured liquid from several bottles into a bucket, Sam stepped to the side. In plain sight was a black bottle with the words "Perma-Kill" on it.

He picked up the bottle, held it toward her, and asked quite pleasantly, "Did you use this herbicide on your neighbor's flowers, or did you just mix it into the soil?"

Mrs. Castman's hand went to her throat. "What? What are you talking about?"

She reached for the bottle, but Sam held it away from her as he read the warning on it. "Caution.

If Perma-Kill is absorbed by the soil, it can kill all vegetation for up to a year." He looked back at the woman's shocked face. "So you had to reapply this to Mrs. Prescott's garden each year, did you?"

"You have no right to poke through my things!" she shouted.

"It's in plain sight," Sam countered, "and you invited me in. Isn't that right, Harlan?"

At that moment, Harlan stepped around the corner and stood in the open doorway.

"But I . . ." she stammered. "I didn't . . ."

"Oh, but I think you did, Mrs. Castman. There could be witnesses, you know," Sam said, suggesting that he already knew of some. He pulled out his badge. "You have the right. . . ."

"Wait, wait. What do you mean, I have the right? Are you a policeman?"

"FBI."

She took a deep indrawn breath, and Sam could almost see her mind racing as her eyes darted back and forth. "I didn't break any laws. Did that woman say I did? Did she call you? Don't you have better things to do than arrest a poor, elderly woman who only wants—"

"You want to know how many laws you've broken? Let's start with trespassing and vandalism and—"

"All right. All right. I didn't mean anything by it."

"By what?" he asked, hoping she'd admit what she had done.

"I noticed her flowers were dry, so I . . . They

would have died anyway . . . I don't want to go to jail," she cried. "What can I do to make this up?"

Sam pretended to think about the problem. "I should take you in," he said. "Your neighbor's yard will have to be torn up, and all that contaminated dirt will have to be hauled away. Then there's the cost of hauling in new dirt and flowers for planting—"

"I'll pay," she rushed on. "I'll do the right thing here. I'll have it all replaced."

He nodded. "Okay, but I'm warning you, you step one foot in your neighbor's yard and you're going to jail."

As Mrs. Castman hurried into her house to make the call to the nursery, Sam walked back to Gigi's. Harlan stood by the kitchen door waiting.

"Thanks, Harlan."

"I didn't do anything to help."

"Mrs. Castman knows you heard her admit what she did. If she causes any more trouble, you call the police."

"She's a mean old lady," Harlan said.

Sam didn't disagree.

Harlan was heading back to work in Gigi's bedroom when Sam said, "If any of Lyra's family asks what you're doing in there . . ."

"I'll tell them I'm building a closet."

Sam smiled. "Did Lyra—"

"No," Harlan interrupted. "I've met them."

Lyra was in the living room, sitting on the sofa with her feet up on an ottoman. Her laptop balanced on her knees, she was typing furiously and mumbling something to herself.

"Are you okay?" Sam asked.

She looked up from her work. "I'm trying to work on the script for my children's film. I've started a dozen outlines, but I'm not happy with any of them. I just don't know where I want to go with it."

"You'll come up with something great," he assured her.

"Thanks," she answered, appreciating his confidence.

Gigi came up from the basement carrying clean hand towels. As she crossed the living room to get to the linen closet, she saw Sam.

"Did you talk to Mrs. Castman?"

"I did."

"And did she confess?"

"Yes," he answered.

"Good," she said with a nod. "Now I'm going over there and give her a piece of my mind." She laid the towels on the arm of the sofa and marched to the door.

Sam rushed to cut her off before she stepped outside. "I know how angry you are . . . and you have every right to be. She vandalized your property and ruined all your hard work. But she's promised to repair the damage and give you new flowers."

"That's the very least she can do," Gigi said angrily.

"I know, I know," he said to calm her. With Gigi's stubborn streak and Mrs. Castman's mean streak, Sam envisioned the start of an all-out war between the two. "What you really want is vindication, isn't it? For everyone to know that you really are a good gardener?" He paused to let her think about it, then continued, "Mrs. Castman is going to have to hire people to work on your yard."

The light was dawning in Gigi's eyes. "That's right. They'll all find out why she has to replace my flowers. I know she'll use Hatfield's nursery. They're the only ones in town, and everyone there likes to talk." She smiled and patted his cheek. "Thank you, Sam."

Gigi picked up the towels, and there was a lightness in her step as she walked down the hall.

Lyra had been watching Sam with her grandmother and was in awe. She'd never seen anyone charm her the way he did.

Sam turned and saw her smiling at him. "What?"

"Thank you," she said.

He smiled back. "I like Gigi."

TWENTY-NINE

CHRISTOPHER AND JUDITH PRESCOTT WERE NOT likable people, but Sam didn't expect they would be.

Like actors sweeping onto a stage, they swept into the house. Neither of them greeted their daughter. Sam stood in the doorway to the kitchen observing the reunion. If he had to sum up Lyra's parents, he would have said that they were polished, pompous, and pretentious.

Lyra's mother was attractive. There wasn't a single wrinkle on her face, and Sam figured dermatologists and plastic surgeons deserved all the credit. Her father was tall, lean, and had a deep golfer's tan. Both of them had blond streaks in their hair—one got them from a salon, and the other from the sun.

Lyra didn't look anything like them. Her bone structure and her beauty came from her grandmother, who to this day was a lovely woman.

Lyra's father finally looked at his daughter. "Lyra."

"Father."

"Where's your grandmother?"

"Upstairs," she said. "She's on the phone. She'll be down when she's finished."

"And who is this gentleman?" her mother asked. "Try to remember your manners and introduce us."

Lyra walked over to Sam and stood beside him while she made the introductions. Lyra had always thought of her father as a tall man, but Sam dwarfed him as the two men shook hands.

"FBI," her father remarked. "And you're here with Lyra to protect her? That must be very stressful."

Lyra's mother went into the kitchen for a bottle of water. "No Perrier?" she called. No one answered her. She poured herself a glass of tea and carried it into the living room. "Darling, would you like a drink?"

"You know Mother doesn't keep alcohol," Christopher reminded her.

"I know. I meant iced tea."

"No, not now. What's taking her so long? Lyra, go check on her. She might not know we're here."

"I know you're here," Gigi said as she entered the room.

"It's not like you to keep guests waiting, Mother," her son said as he kissed her on the cheek.

"Christopher, you are not a guest. You are my son. Hello, Judith."

Judith placed a peck on her cheek as well.

Sam could tell that, despite everything, Gigi was happy to see both of them. She took a seat in an easy chair and listened as they caught her up on their busy lives. Every so often, Lyra's parents would politely draw him into the conversation and ask his opinion or inquire about his background, but for the most part they focused on themselves. He was amazed at how they could be so personable and outgoing, and at the same time be so completely self-involved. Not once did they show concern for Lyra or ask about her life.

"Have you moved into your new house in La Jolla?" Gigi asked them.

"No, but the moving vans will be arriving next week. Because of finances, Mother Prescott," Judith said with a touch of anguish in her voice, "we've had to sell our home in New York."

"The penthouse?"

"Yes," she said, bowing her head.

Lyra sat next to Sam on the sofa and leaned into him. She fought the urge to laugh. Her mother made the sale of a penthouse sound like a death in the family.

"Where have you been staying?" Gigi asked her son.

"The apartment in Houston."

"We want you to come back with us," Judith said.

"That's right," Christopher agreed. "I want you to pack your bags, and we'll leave first thing in the morning."

"We're staying at the Coronado tonight," Judith explained.

"I am not going anywhere with you. Christopher, I thought this was all settled in court. You are not taking over my life."

"Don't you see how very worried we are?"

"About what?"

"You," he said, his voice dripping with sincerity. "I'm not blaming Lyra . . ."

Lyra sighed and whispered, "Here we go. *But* . . . "

"But she's put you in danger," said Christopher.

"It's not that Lyra is selfish," Judith interjected. She didn't even glance at Lyra as she continued. "She doesn't have a selfish bone in her body."

"But . . ." Lyra whispered.

"But she just wasn't thinking," Judith finished.

"Those men coming here to threaten . . ." Christopher shook his head, a concerned look on his well-tanned face. "I can't have that, Mother."

"You don't have to worry," Gigi said. She daintily folded her hands in her lap. "I have an FBI agent here for tonight, and tomorrow I'm leaving for the ranch. That was Cooper on the phone. He wants me to come home until Agent Kincaid catches those men, which I'm sure he will," she added with a smile at Sam. "Besides, I miss my friends and would like to see them again. This house won't be empty," she assured them. "Harlan will be here working every day. He's building a—"

Lyra blurted, "Another gorgeous closet with shelves."

Gigi frowned at her. "But Lyra—"

"Gigi, shouldn't you get ready for the spaghetti dinner?"

"Oh my, look at the time. Harlan will be here any minute." She jumped up and patted her son's shoulder before he could stand.

"You're going out?" he asked.

"With a handyman?" Judith chimed in.

"He's a contractor," Gigi explained. "He and his family will be picking me up soon to go to dinner at St. Agnes's. I really must change my dress. Don't stay away so long, you two."

"Should you be going anywhere when there's been a threat against you?"

"There's been no threat against me," she insisted. "Besides, I'll be with Harlan's family and with dozens of other people at the church. I'll be just fine."

"But Mother . . ."

"Good-bye now. Enjoy your stay at the Coronado."

Christopher stood. "My own mother can't spend an hour with me?"

Lyra's back stiffened. How dare her father accuse Gigi of not spending time with him. How many hours had he spent with *her?* She sat forward, ready to retaliate, but Sam put his hand on her arm.

"Are you going to the church dinner, too, Lyra?" Judith asked. "You and Mr. Kincaid are more than welcome to have dinner with us at the hotel."

"I think she should stay away from Gigi," her father said. "I believe she's put her grandmother in enough danger."

"I think I should keep my distance from you, too," Lyra said.

"Chris, she's right," Judith agreed. "It might be dangerous. We don't have bodyguards like Mr. Kincaid here."

Christopher turned to Sam. "I'm sure you understand. My mother isn't getting any younger, and we worry about her. I wish we could convince her she'd be better off with us."

Sam shrugged. "She seems to be a pretty strong woman to me."

By the time her parents left, Lyra was ready to scream. She was closing the door on them when her mother said, "We aren't about to give up. We care so deeply about Gigi and know that she would be much happier living with us. I don't know why you keep fighting us on this. All we want to do is take care of her."

"No," Lyra said angrily. "You want her to take care of you."

THIRTY

LYRA WAS EMBARRASSED BY HER PARENTS' BE-havior, and she was ashamed. She couldn't change who they were, and she accepted that, but she wished Sam hadn't been there to witness their superficial concern about Gigi's welfare. They were hypocrites, and their greed sickened her.

Sons and daughters were supposed to love their parents, and that was where the shame came in. After so many manipulations for more and more money, Lyra couldn't love them. And they certainly didn't love her. Lyra found it difficult to look at Sam after her parents left, but she held her head up high as she walked past him toward the kitchen to find some chocolate.

Seeing her discomfort, Sam distracted her. "Have you talked to your brothers yet?"

The question jarred her. "What? Oh, yes, I talked to Cooper. He and Owen think I should come to the ranch and stay there until, and I'm quoting, 'this thing blows over.'"

"They're worried about you."

"I know," she said. "I was nice when I declined their invitation to come stay."

He smiled. "Good for you. I've got some news, too."

He took her hand and pulled her down onto the sofa next to him. The window was open, and a cool ocean breeze brushed the curtains aside. It felt good to sit and let the tension that had filled the room minutes before drift away.

"I'm listening," she said.

"I got a call from the agents in Texas who picked up your boxes. They've gone through every book, every DVD, and CD. There's nothing there."

"The books are worth a lot of money."

"Yeah, I know. They're getting them appraised."

"If I figured out a way to get the books back to these people who want them, maybe then . . ."

He shook his head. "It's not the books they're after. Think about it. Could those books be so valuable that they're worth killing for? No, these people must want something else."

Lyra thought about it for a minute and then in frustration said, "You're right. Killing for a bunch of books, even though they might be worth thousands, doesn't make sense. So that brings us back to square one. What do they want?"

"We won't give up until we know," he assured her.

He gently nudged her head down onto his shoulder, and they sat silently for several minutes.

"How long will Gigi be gone?" Sam asked.

"I don't know. She'll probably be back by nine

or nine-thirty. Harlan and his wife will want to get their children to bed."

"How many do they have?"

"Five."

"So Gigi's helping him out by giving him work, is that it?"

Lyra raised up and looked at him. "You could tell, huh? He's been out of work for a while. Harlan had a good job with a construction company, but it went out of business. It won't be long before he finds another one. In the meantime . . ."

"He's building a panic room."

"I still think it's a good idea," she said.

Laying her head on his shoulder again, she asked, "Sam, how long will you be here, and when will I get another bodyguard?"

"Not until we get back to L.A.," he said. "We'll start back after we take Gigi to the airport."

"And see her safely on the plane," she added.

"Let's go upstairs."

"Oh, no. Not a good idea."

He lifted her onto his lap, wrapped her in his arms, and kissed her passionately. She couldn't resist; he tasted so wonderful.

"Let's go upstairs," he repeated before kissing her again.

Lyra had any number of reasons why they shouldn't, but in the end, they went upstairs.

Sam wouldn't let her be shy with him, and she gave herself to him completely.

He loved seeing her naked, loved the way she curled into him after she climaxed. He loved the way her eyes became all misty and her lips looked full and red from his kisses. But he hated leaving her bed.

Lyra was dressed and back downstairs just in time to open the door for Gigi.

"The dinner was lovely, just lovely," her grandmother said as she entered. "Father Henry was pleased with the turnout."

"That's nice," Lyra said

Her grandmother moved closer, frowning. "What's happened to your face? It looks chapped."

Lyra touched her cheek. "Really?"

She knew why her face was chapped: Sam's whiskers. The culprit stood just behind Gigi, grinning.

"Lyra, I promised Father Henry you would stop by with a check for him tomorrow before you drive back to Los Angeles."

"Yes, I will," she promised. "How much should I give him?"

"A hundred thousand should do for now."

There was no hesitation on Lyra's part. No questions, no explanations required.

"And Harlan . . ." Gigi continued.

"Do you want me to pay him in advance since you'll be at the ranch?" Lyra asked.

Gigi nodded and told her how much to pay Harlan. "That should include the supplies he'll be needing to finish the job. He's going to have to hurry and have it done in three weeks because he'll be working full-time again."

Lyra was thrilled. "He got a job?"

"He's starting his own company, and his first

job is an addition to the parish school. It's terribly crowded," she added. "When you see Father tomorrow, have a look around."

Lyra turned to Sam. "Both the church and the school at St. Agnes need a lot of work."

"It's a poor parish," Gigi added. "The people struggle." She kissed Lyra on the cheek and motioned for Sam to bend down so she could kiss him as well. "I'm going to bed now."

"Gigi, I'd appreciate it if you would sleep in the guest room," Sam said. "I'll sleep on the sofa."

Lyra thought that was a good idea. "I know Harlan sealed his work area off, but dust gets through, and you shouldn't be sleeping in your bedroom."

"But Sam, you won't be comfortable on the sofa," she protested.

"Of course I will," he assured her. "I can sleep anywhere."

"I've already changed the sheets," Lyra said to her grandmother, which was a complete lie. Since Sam had never slept in the guest bed, his sheets were still fresh. Luckily, all Gigi's sheets were white.

Lyra waited until her grandmother had gone upstairs before she moved closer to Sam and whispered, "No more messing around."

"Okay." He pulled her to him and kissed her.

She pushed him away. "What are you doing?"

"Messing around."

"So you do the opposite of what I ask, huh? Maybe I should use reverse psychology on you."

"That sounds good. Try it."

The sparkle in his eyes made her heart speed up. "All right. Sam, I think we should fool around."

"You got it." He kissed her again, hotter this time, longer.

She was trembling when she pulled away from him. "Blankets are in the linen closet across from Gigi's bedroom." It was nearly impossible for her to walk away from him, but she summoned the willpower.

Only later, when she was in bed and trying to fall asleep, did she realize how much she cared for him. She'd been successful blocking those feelings, but now they were glaringly obvious. Of course she cared for him. He was putting his life on the line to protect her. She punched her pillows and stuffed them behind her head in an attempt to get comfortable. She tried to clear her mind, to no avail. Thoughts of Sam kept creeping back in.

He was the calm in the middle of any storm, and she responded in kind. It just wasn't possible to freak out when he was so relaxed, so confident, so in charge. She remembered when he found the explosive under her car, and he casually told her he was calling the bomb squad. He didn't seem fazed, so why should she be? He led her away as if there were no worry at all. And when they were being shot at in the park, he was so steady.

His dry sense of humor made her laugh. And physically, she thought he was the sexiest man alive. She'd never responded to any other man the way she responded to him. All he had to do was look at her with that twinkle in his eyes, and she melted.

Still no sleep. She had to stop thinking about him. She tried to clear her mind and relax. That lasted about a minute, and then her thoughts went right back to Sam. She couldn't ignore the reason for her insomnia any longer. Lyra was in love with him.

Great. Just great! Lyra was furious with herself. She should know better. Sam would never marry again. Look how long it had taken him to even say his wife's name. No, marriage was never going to happen.

She could never move in with a man she wasn't married to. That would kill Gigi. Not that Sam would ask her. And what kind of woman with any self-respect would chase a man all the way to D.C. knowing there would never be a commitment? Thoughts like these usually came a year after meeting a man. Not this quickly.

Why was she worrying about any of this anyway? Nothing would come of it. So what if Lyra loved him? With her predatory parents circling Gigi like sharks, it was up to her to keep them away. They had dragged her into court once, and Lyra knew, given the chance, they'd do it again. Her brothers would help, but the main responsibility fell to her. As long as Gigi was alive, Lyra would protect her and take care of her.

Lyra pulled the blanket up to her chin and let out a sigh. She had worked it all out in her mind: Sam was a good man, but he wasn't interested in a committed relationship, and neither was she. With that settled, she finally fell into a fitful sleep.

THE FOLLOWING MORNING, they packed their bags, left Harlan working on the panic room, and drove to the airport. Sam and Lyra watched from the security checkpoint until Gigi disappeared down the ramp.

After leaving the airport, they headed to St. Agnes with a check. Wearing a black cassock, Father Henry was in the schoolyard watching the children at recess. It was apparent the kids loved him. He stood with his hands behind his back while child after child implored him, "Watch me, Father. Watch me."

Lyra was drawn to a group of first graders, boys and girls playing some sort of jumping game. She left Sam and Father Henry and walked across the yard to find out what they were doing. All of them wanted to explain the game they had made up. Each voice contradicted the one before, and by the time they had finished their interpretation of the rules, Lyra didn't think even they knew what the game was. So they showed her. And they made up a few new rules as they ran and hopped around the markings on the playground, but what fascinated Lyra the most was the fun they were having as they created their own game.

It suddenly struck her what her project should be and what she should call it: The Art of Play.

There were no handheld gadgets or tiny computer games that would keep them sitting for hours. No electronic screens. No motorized toys. No fancy anything. Nothing but their imaginations. And the fun they were having made quite a statement.

Two little girls held her hands and walked her back to Father Henry, chattering the entire way.

Sam watched Lyra with the children as they vied

for her attention. She responded as though what each of them had to say was the most amazing thing she'd ever heard. There was such joy in her face. Such warmth. How could they resist her?

How could he?

THIRTY-ONE

MILO WAS FURIOUS WITH MR. MERRIAM. LYRA had almost been killed by her attackers, and Milo had no doubt who they were: Merriam's two puppets, Charlie Brody and Lou Stack. He stormed into Mr. Merriam's office, marched up to his desk, and was about to give him his resignation when Mr. Merriam handed him an envelope full of hundred-dollar bills.

"What's this?" Milo asked, losing some of his steam.

"With all the craziness lately, I forgot to pay you your monthly retainer . . . you know, the mess with Rooney."

"Oh, yeah. Thanks." Milo had also forgotten about the money he was owed. "It was a crazy time," he agreed as he stuffed the envelope into his jacket.

Mr. Merriam always paid him in cash, so there was no record that Milo worked for him. Milo used to believe his boss didn't think he was good enough to be on the company payroll, and that he was a little ashamed of the work Milo did for him,

but then he figured out that Mr. Merriam was helping him. Getting wads of cash, Milo would never
have to declare income or pay taxes. It was a real
sweet deal. His boss was actually being thoughtful . . . at least Mr. Merriam had been thoughtful
up until now.

"Do you have any news for me?" his boss asked.

"Not yet."

Mr. Merriam didn't hide his disappointment.
"That disk is gonna be the death of me. I've got
Charlie and Stack digging through Rooney's office.
He owned his office building, and according to
Charlie, Rooney had crap everywhere. So far they
haven't come up with a thing. Looks like I'm
gonna have to torch that building, too. What about
that girl from the yard sale? And how certain are
you that no one else took any DVDs and books?
Any one of a hundred people could have taken it.
I'm doomed, Milo, done for."

"No," Milo said, feeling a little sympathetic.
"Babs Rooney had just started the sale—or the
giveaway, I guess you'd call it—and the people
there were after the big stuff. Maybe they would
have gotten around to the junk eventually, but no
one was giving that heap of old books a second
look—not when they were seeing flat screen TVs
being carried out."

"I guess I've got to assume the disk was either
burned up in Rooney's house, or that girl took it
and hasn't looked at it yet. If she had, I'd already
be behind bars. I think it's time I cleaned out my
office."

"Another fire?" Milo asked. "I don't think that's

a good idea. Three fires? Rooney's house, then his office building, and here? Sir, don't you think the police might be able to find a connection if there are three fires?"

"No, no fire here. I've got to get rid of a few things. I can destroy most of it, but I've got a safe that came from an office where there was an unfortunate accident. The owner fell out a window twenty stories up. There was an open safe just sitting there, and since I needed a safe, I took advantage of the situation. Unfortunately, I didn't know at the time that the owner had his name engraved on it. I've got to find somewhere to dump it."

"How could anyone lift it?"

"It's not like the one in Rooney's office. Two men can carry it. Strong men," he added.

"Aren't you worried it could get stolen?"

His boss scoffed at the notion. "I've got a reputation, an excellent reputation, thanks to you, Milo. Anyone who messes with me knows I'll send you or Charlie or Stack after them."

Milo knew Mr. Merriam meant it as a compliment, but lumping him in with Charlie and Stack, two unproven newcomers, was an insult.

"You should take the safe to Paraiso Park. I'm sure Charlie and Stack told you about it," Milo said sarcastically.

Mr. Merriam shook his head. "What's Paraiso Park?"

Milo studied his boss's face. He looked puzzled. Was it possible he didn't know about Paraiso Park and the shooting?

He waited for Mr. Merriam to say something, but he continued to stare at him as though he was crazy. Milo came to the conclusion that his response was sincere. Mr. Merriam didn't know about the park. And that meant that Charlie and Stack didn't tell the boss that they had followed Lyra there and shot at her. If they had killed her, she couldn't tell them where she'd put the books and DVDs, and that would have made the boss go ballistic. Milo knew he could blow the whistle on them right now, but he thought better of it. If he revealed that Charlie and Stack had gotten out of control and were shooting at Lyra, then Mr. Merriam would know he was at the park, too. How would he explain that one?

Now that he'd brought up the subject of Paraiso Park, he might as well use it to his advantage. He told Mr. Merriam how it had become a dumping ground. "You could have Charlie and Stack bury the safe . . . maybe in the back somewhere."

Mr. Merriam rocked in his chair and drummed his sausage-sized fingers on the desk.

"Hmmm. Think the city will come in and clean it up?"

"No, sir, I don't, but say they did. What would it matter? If you wiped your prints off it, who cares if it gets found, right?"

"That's right," he agreed. "Now what about that girl? She's a loose end I want tied up."

"I'm working on it," he said. "But, sir, I've got to say something. I'm . . . disappointed . . . yeah, disappointed that you didn't have enough faith in me to get the job done. Bringing Charlie and Stack onto the case is upsetting to me. You know, breaking into her apartment and all. I feel I've shown my abilities and. . . ." Milo had prepared his speech, and he nervously stumbled through it.

Mr. Merriam looked perplexed. "What are you talking about?"

Was he really playing dumb? Milo felt his temper rising again. Before he could repeat what he had just said, Mr. Merriam's phone rang.

"I've gotta take this."

Milo nodded. He would wait.

Mr. Merriam answered his phone, said "Hold on," and looked at Milo. "This is a private call."

Milo dragged his feet as he left so he could find out who was on the phone with the boss. Mr. Merriam called to him, "I think you need more help, Milo. I'll talk to Charlie and get back to you."

Milo didn't acknowledge his boss's insult. Why would he think he needed help? And how had Charlie and Stack weaseled their way into Mr. Merriam's inner sanctum? When he got into his car, he pounded his fists on the steering wheel until tears came into his eyes.

He had known that he would have to end it with Lyra, his beautiful Bond girl, but his conversation with Mr. Merriam had just clinched it. If he had a relationship with her, Charlie and Stack would find out. As long as Mr. Merriam thought she had his precious DVD, she was in danger. It was up to Milo to keep her safe.

Milo was more than willing to sacrifice his own future for her, but maybe there was another way out of this. He needed a plan.

Then it came to him. It was brilliant in its simplicity. Milo would tell a lie.

MR. MERRIAM PHONED HIM the following afternoon.

"Charlie and Stack are here in my office, and they're going to lend you a hand—"

"I found them!" Milo blurted before Mr. Merriam could utter another word.

"What? You what?"

"I found them . . . the boxes with the books and DVDs and a few CDs."

"Hold on. Charlie, Stack, Milo found them. You don't need to help him. Yes, Milo found them," he repeated, giddy with excitement.

When Mr. Merriam had repeated the news to Charlie and Stack, Milo assumed he did so because they didn't believe him. Didn't those two goons think he was smart enough to find them on his own?

"Good job," Mr. Merriam told Milo. "I can always count on you."

Phone to his ear, Milo was fuming. So now Charlie and Stack got to sit around in the boss's office. What was next? Lunches together? Milo couldn't help but be jealous. He should be sitting in that office having lunch. Not those two losers. He held his tongue and didn't tell Mr. Merriam how he felt, reminding himself that Lyra was more important, and he was doing this for her. Getting on the boss's bad side might mess up his plan.

"I looked through every book in case the DVD was stuck in one of them, and I looked at every

DVD, and they're all like the labels say, just movies and stuff. I'm thinking your DVD got burned up in Rooney's house."

"I hope you're right. Where did you find them?"

Milo wasn't prepared for that question. "Where did I find them?" he repeated to stall for time. "In her grandmother's garage." Just in case Charlie and Stack had gone into that garage and looked for themselves, he blurted, "I was thorough in my search. They weren't where anyone else could find them."

"Excellent work," Mr. Merriam said. "Bring them to the office tomorrow morning. I've got an appointment tonight, or I'd have you bring them now."

"Bring what?"

"The books and DVDs." Mr. Merriam chuckled. "What else did you think I wanted?"

Milo forced a laugh. "I was joking. See you in the morning."

He disconnected the call and scratched his head. Now where was he going to find old books and DVDs?

THIRTY-TWO

LYRA WAS IN GOOD SPIRITS WHEN THEY GOT back into the car. She had her subject for her film project now, and with Father Henry's help getting the parents of the first graders to sign permission slips, she could start filming as early as next week or the week after, assuming she finished the script in time and met the first deadline.

"Did you see how happy those children were?" she asked Sam.

"I saw how happy Father Henry was when you handed him that check. I thought he was going to do a backflip in that dress he was wearing."

She laughed. "It's called a cassock." The thought of the priest doing gymnastics made her laugh again.

"I also saw how much fun you were having with those children. What were they doing?"

"Playing a game they had made up, and I *was* having fun."

"When do you have to have this film project done?"

"I reread the rules to be certain," she said. "My script must be postmarked no later than the fifth. That's a Friday. If it makes the top five, then I'll be notified, and I have another week to send the film."

Sam got on the entrance ramp to the highway. "How long do you have to wait to find out if you're in the top five?"

"Up to six weeks. So I have to have a film ready."

"At least this time you won't have to breathe toxic fumes."

"True, and I'll have more fun with this one, too. I'm surprised Mahler gave me this opportunity. I'm hardly one of his favorite students."

A few miles later, she asked, "Did anyone drive by the house last night?"

"No."

"Were you watching?"

A quick smile, then, "Yes."

"Why do you think they didn't come back?" She said it as though a dinner guest had rudely not shown up.

"Maybe there was too much traffic coming and going at the house," he said. He reached over and patted her hand. "Don't worry. They aren't going to disappear. They'll be back."

"That isn't comforting news." She crossed one leg over the other, and Sam automatically looked and appreciated how long they were. He remembered how they'd felt around him when he was inside her . . . He cleared his throat. How often did psychiatrists say a man thought about sex? Every ten seconds? Twelve? Since he'd met Lyra, it was simply all the time.

"Let's concentrate on what we know," he said. "We know there have been at least four different men trying to kill you. Two are in jail without bail, and then there are the two who broke into your apartment. They also could be the two who drove by Gigi's house. Mind you, that's just a guess."

"I hope it's true. Otherwise, I would have six men trying to kill me." She looked up with a weak smile. "You don't suppose someone's out recruiting killers just for me, do you?"

He laughed as he switched lanes. "No, I don't think so."

Her expression turned somber again. "What did I ever do to any of them?"

"I'm sure it isn't personal. We know the two in jail work for Michael Flynn.

"He's an Irish immigrant, and he's been head of an organized crime family in L.A. for a long time. They're into money laundering, prostitution, graft, but no drug trafficking, as far as we know. Up until now, he's been able to lawyer his way out of any charges leveled against him. Detective O'Malley told me Flynn is willingly going down to the station for questioning."

"I want to be there when they talk to him. Is that possible?"

"I don't see why not. You can watch and listen through the glass, but you can't say anything to him or let him see you."

"So shooting him would be out of the question."

"That's my job, sweetheart."

"Do you think he'll tell us anything?"

"No."

"Then why bother?"

"Because Detective O'Malley wants to give Flynn some information. See what he does with it. We know who most of his business associates are, so maybe he'll give us some leads." Sam got on the phone and made arrangements for them to be there for Flynn's interview.

When he finished his call, Lyra switched topics. "Why can't I go back to my apartment? With a bodyguard at my side—"

"No."

She prodded. "Why?"

"I want to sleep through the night without getting blown up. There are other tenants to consider as well. It's better if no one knows where we're staying."

He had a valid point. She didn't want anyone to get hurt. "Okay," she said.

"Do you need something from your apartment?"

"No. I packed clean clothes from my closet at Gigi's house."

"So we don't need to go back to campus?"

"Not today, but . . ." She knew he wasn't going to like what came next. "I have to switch out the memory card at the park."

"Hell, no," he said. "We're not going back there."

"Sam . . ."

"I know you're curious, and you want to find out who's planting flowers—"

"It's more than curiosity," she argued. "I might

want to do something with it in the future. A short film maybe. Just let me shoot another week."

"No."

"All I'm asking for is a week, and then I'll dismantle and be done."

"No," he repeated, his voice firmer.

"What if I bought new camera equipment and replaced what I have at the park? I could get something with more memory and a longer battery life. It could record for a couple of weeks and I wouldn't have to go back and forth so often."

"Why didn't you get that in the first place so you wouldn't have to climb around in that garbage?"

"I wanted to use my camera. It takes such clear pictures. But I'm willing to change if you'll just let me go to the park a couple of times."

"I'll think about it."

Frustrated, she shifted in her seat. "Sam, I'm afraid I'm going to have to pull rank on you. A bodyguard's job is to protect. He doesn't set the schedule. I'm going to that park with or without you."

He didn't laugh at her, but she could see amusement on his face as he kept his eyes on the road. "Ah, that's sweet."

"What is?" she asked suspiciously.

"You, thinking you can pull rank."

Okay, she had been bluffing, but did he have to get such a kick out of it? Lyra stared out the window at the landscape while she made a mental list of what she could be doing to help the investigation. As they arrived in L.A., her thoughts kept returning to the yard sale. She firmly believed whoever was trying to kill her was somehow connected to that yard sale. The man the shooters worked for, this Flynn, must think she had something that belonged to him. When she mentioned that to Sam for a second time, he shook his head.

"There was nothing in those boxes that would warrant this, remember?"

"But maybe they think there was."

Sam leaned his elbow on the armrest between them. She took his hand and traced the scars on his arm. "Did you get these when you went through the window to help Alec?"

"No, those are rugby scars."

She thought he was making that up until he held up his other arm. "I got *these* scars when I went through the window."

"This arm is much worse," she said, touching his right arm. "You don't play rugby anymore, do you?"

"Yeah, I do. It's a great way to let off steam."

"You're too . . . calm, too relaxed to play such a rough game. Rugby players are aggressive. They're . . ." She stopped before she offended him.

"They're what?" he pressed as he pulled into the police station parking lot.

"Brutal," she said. "On the field," she qualified.

He laughed. "Yeah, I guess you're right."

Sam parked the car and walked close to her until they were inside.

"O'Malley's upstairs," a policeman who recognized Sam called out.

The second floor of the police station was wide open with desks in three rows. Detectives sat at computers. Some were taking statements from people who sat in front of them, and others were dealing with suspects handcuffed to their chairs. Two unsavory men sat against the wall with their hands cuffed behind their backs. They were conversing in a language Lyra didn't recognize.

"Get those two in an interrogation room," a detective shouted to no one in particular. "The Russian interpreter is on his way."

Sam listened to the two men snickering and mocking the detective. Then one of them said something that made him smile. When Lyra slowed down to look around the large room, Sam took her hand and pulled her along. Detective O'Malley was in a glass office at the end. Spotting them, he hurried out. After asking Lyra how she was holding up, he turned to Sam. "Flynn should be here in about fifteen minutes. You're early."

"Good. Lyra can look at the footage from the campus security cameras."

"No problem. I'll pull it up."

O'Malley went to his computer and brought the security video onto the screen. The parking lot came into view. It showed routine movement of people and cars, nothing unusual. O'Malley pointed to the upper-right-hand corner and said, "There he is."

Lyra leaned close. The picture wasn't clear, but she could make out a dark figure circling their car. His head was covered by the hood on his raincoat. He dropped down beside the car for a couple of seconds and then stood up and strolled away.

O'Malley reversed the video to the spot where

the man had disappeared and said, "Here's where he's planting the bomb."

Lyra shook her head. "I can't see his face. I don't know who he is."

A policeman stuck his head in the door. "Flynn's on his way up."

O'Malley shut down the computer and led the way through the office.

When they walked by the detective who had called for the interpreter, Sam paused to read the name on the desk and said, "Detective Muren, those men you want to interrogate aren't speaking Russian."

Muren didn't bother looking up. "I've got it covered. Thanks."

Sam had a bit more vital information the detective should hear, but he didn't tell him. He knew Muren would be coming around in a little while.

While O'Malley entered the interrogation room, Lyra followed Sam into the observation room and stood in front of the window. They watched two men enter. The taller man handed his card to O'Malley and introduced himself as Mr. Flynn's attorney. He sat next to his client.

Michael Flynn was a strange-looking man. He had more hair sprouting out of his ears than on his head. Lyra didn't know why she had assumed Flynn was an old man, but he looked to be in his fifties.

"Lyra, have you ever seen him before?" Sam asked.

She shook her head. "Absolutely not. Trust me, I'd remember."

The gigantic ring on his pinky finger drew her

attention to his manicured nails, and his suit appeared to be Italian, probably hand-tailored. He could be the poster boy for "Crime Pays," she thought.

"He's Irish," she commented.

"Yes."

There was a tap on the door, and the detective who had given Sam the brush-off entered the room. "Sir, do you have a minute?"

Sam turned to him. "Yes?"

"I'd like to apologize for being rude." He put his hand out to shake Sam's and introduced himself. "Detective Muren. Bill Muren. I know who you are. Three guys out there told me already. They also called me a . . ." He stopped when he realized Lyra was listening.

Sam shook his hand but didn't say anything more.

"It's been a bad day," Muren said. "Those two creeps have given me a run for my money. If they're not speaking Russian, then what are they speaking?"

"Czech," he said.

"It sounded Russian. Could someone who knows Russian interpret?"

"Not necessarily. There are similarities in the two, but they're different languages."

"You wouldn't happen to speak Czech, would you?"

"Yes."

"My day just might be getting better. What do you do for the FBI?"

"I'm a language specialist."

Muren started laughing. "This is now a good day."

"I'll make it even better. They know you have a key, but they don't think you'll figure out what it unlocks."

"Did they say—"

"Pier twenty-three, locker seven. You might want to lead with that."

Muren rubbed his hands together. "You're right. Since I met you, this day just keeps getting better and better." He opened the door and said, "When you're finished here, do you think you could help me out with the interrogation?"

Sam nodded.

"Take as long as you need. They can wait."

Nothing was happening with Flynn. No matter what the question, he consulted with his attorney before answering. Then he danced around the question and never really answered.

"If the detectives asked him if he likes the weather, I bet he'd talk to his attorney first," Lyra said.

O'Malley had been civil and restrained up to now. He put two photos on the table in front of Flynn. "These men work for you, don't they?"

"No, they don't."

"Have you ever seen either one of them before?"

"Not that I can recall."

"Those are the men who shot at us, aren't they?" Lyra asked Sam.

"Yes."

Ten minutes of evasions were enough for Lyra.

She was about to suggest that Sam go help Detective Muren when the conversation in the interrogation room suddenly got interesting.

O'Malley was no longer polite; he had become hostile and antagonistic. He informed Flynn that he would probably need him to come in three or four times a week because he could never quite remember all the questions he wanted to ask. He told Flynn that he should be prepared to spend a lot of time at the station. O'Malley thought it would only take a month or two.

Flynn didn't consult his attorney this time. The smirk gone, he started yelling at O'Malley, calling him a disgrace to the Irish community and threatening to sue him for harassment. Flynn's attorney put a hand on his arm, but Flynn flicked it off.

"Do you know a woman named Lyra Prescott?" O'Malley asked, undaunted.

Flynn's eyes narrowed ever so slightly, but Sam saw it and so did O'Malley. "So you know who she is?"

"I've never heard of her."

"Your two goons," he said, tapping the photos, "tried to kill her the other day. Tried to kill the FBI agent who was with her, too. That's gonna get them a lot of years."

The attorney stood. "We're done here."

"I'm going to connect you to those men, and when I do you're going down with them," O'Malley warned.

Flynn shoved the attorney to get him moving. "Michael, let's leave."

"See you boys tomorrow and probably the day after. I'll let you know. Keep your schedule open."

"I'm filing suit . . ."

"Go ahead," O'Malley said.

Once Flynn and his attorney were gone, O'Malley opened the observation room door.

Smiling, he said, "Did you see that look on Flynn's face when I mentioned Lyra's name?"

"Why are you happy about that, Detective?" she asked.

"We think Flynn's doing a payback or a favor for someone else. We can't connect him directly to you any other way. From everything we've learned, you've had no interaction with any of Flynn's crew."

"A favor?"

"That's what we're hoping. If we can put enough pressure on him, he might get fed up. It looks like he's got several men working on this. Two are in jail and at least a couple more are still out there. That's a lot of payroll and not very cost effective for him, I'd say."

"You think he'll just quit?"

"No, we're hoping he'll now go have a chat with whoever wanted his help."

THIRTY-THREE

LYRA WAS HAPPY TO BE BACK AT THE DUPLEX. For a hideout, it was quite comfortable; everything was brand new, and she hadn't stubbed her toe once because, unlike her apartment, it was spacious. After her shower, she dressed in a silky gown and robe and went downstairs to the dining room table to work on her script. Now that she knew exactly what she wanted to do, the ideas came freely. According to the rules, the film couldn't be more than ten minutes long, which didn't sound like much, but to a budding film-maker, it could just as well have been ten hours. Every second had to count.

She closed down her computer at eleven. Sam was in the kitchen, having just come in from the backyard.

"What were you doing out there?" she asked.

"Just checking."

"Checking what?"

"The yard," he said. He raised his eyebrows at her outfit. "I like that on you, but . . ."

"But what?"

"I like it off you better."

"I'm going to bed." She turned and slowly saun-
tered toward the stairs. Glancing seductively over
her shoulder she said, "Are you coming?"

Sam made sure all the doors were locked before
heading upstairs. He took a quick shower, wrapped
in a towel, and knocked on Lyra's door.

"Who is it?"

He opened the door and walked in. Lyra was lying on her side, propped up on her elbow with her
head in her hand. She didn't say another word.
She simply lifted the sheet. Her robe and gown
were already off. When he pulled her to him, he
sighed with pleasure.

Lyra wanted to be the aggressor. She pushed him
onto his back and straddled his hips. Her eyes
locked with his while her hand slowly moved down
his body.

"Had any fantasies lately?" she asked, her voice
a sultry whisper. Her fingers circled his navel. "I
have," she said. "Do you want me to show you?"

He swallowed hard. She took that as a yes and
began to kiss every inch of him. As her tongue
playfully titillated, her fingertips drove him out of
his mind, her touch arousing him to an ecstasy he
had never before experienced. When they both
found release, she collapsed on top of him. She fell
asleep as he stroked her hair and tried to calm his
heartbeat.

Sam was shaken. Lyra was so loving and giving.
She wasn't shy with him. Beth had been a loving

wife, but she had never initiated sex. He hadn't experienced anything like this with her. The two women were so different.

He knew that Lyra would not have made love with such passion if she didn't care for him. Perhaps she was falling in love with him. And what did he have to offer her? Lyra deserved to have someone who would share his life with her, and he had vowed he would never marry again. He still felt the pain of losing Beth. If anything happened to Lyra, he couldn't bear it.

But how could he leave her?

He fell asleep without an answer.

THE FOLLOWING MORNING, Lyra went right to work on her script, and Sam spent time on the phone and computer. He was frustrated with the investigation and was pacing while he thought about all the possibilities. O'Malley was monitoring Flynn's conversations and was hoping the Irishman would be angry enough to make a few calls that would shed some light on why Lyra had been targeted.

Lyra closed her laptop and stretched. She was stiff all over. "It feels like months since I worked out. No one knows where we are. Do you think we could go for a run?"

A run sounded good to him. "It's hot out, but I'm up for it if you are."

He usually ran five miles every morning during the week and ten on Saturdays and Sundays. Lyra, on the other hand, was usually happy with three, but she was determined not to slow him down, so she ran alongside him matching his stride. By the time they returned to the duplex, she was soaked with sweat and gasping for air.

"Are you okay?" he asked when he saw her red face. He lifted his shirt and wiped the sweat from his brow.

"I'm fine," she said breathlessly. "It's sizzling out there."

Her wet clothes clung to her body. He gave her the once-over. "You sizzle. Let's get you upstairs and cool you off." He took her hand and led her toward the steps.

He ran a cool shower and then stripped out of his clothes before undressing her. Together they let the spray of the water take the heat away.

Later, as Lyra was standing at the sink slicing an apple, she said, "Do you have plans for this afternoon, Sam?"

He came up behind her and kissed her neck. "You're my plan." He reached over her shoulder, took one of the slices, and popped it into his mouth.

"Would you mind if we went out? I want to buy the new camera and some extra equipment. The camera can take pictures for up to a month, but I'll keep it there for only a couple of weeks."

"As long as you promise not to go back before then, and when you do, you go with your body-guard."

Go with your bodyguard. The phrasing was a subtle reminder he would soon be leaving. "I promise," she said.

Since they were going to be walking in trash,

Lyra ran up to change from shorts to jeans. She put on her flip-flops, grabbed a fresh pair of socks, and went to the garage to get her boots.

They didn't take long at the camera shop. Lyra knew the exact model she wanted and had called ahead to make sure they had it in stock. She purchased two extra battery packs and was back in the car before Sam could point out the time or tell her to hurry. With the help of the camera store owner's instructions and the manual, Lyra got the camera ready while Sam drove to Paraiso Park. All she had to do once there was remove the old camera, set the new one in place, and flip a switch.

"One, two, three, easy as can be." Gigi used to say that to her whenever Lyra complained of homework.

"What did you say?" Sam asked.

"Nothing important. Do you have only one gun?"

He didn't answer. Instead, he told her he had finally scheduled his lecture to the cadets.

"In L.A. or San Diego?"

"L.A. first, then I'll drive to San Diego early the next morning, give the lecture, and be on a plane back to D.C. that night."

Lyra felt as though an elephant had just landed on her chest. Fortunately, she had been looking away from him when he dropped the news, and was able to recover before she turned to look at him.

"Am I getting a new bodyguard?"

"Yes."

"When?"

"I'm not sure. I'm thinking tomorrow morning."

"Okay."

If he said, "If you're ever in D.C.," she knew she'd start crying. When he left, it had to be completely over. She couldn't handle seeing him every now and then, or eventually running into him with another woman. Lyra wasn't angry with him. He hadn't forced her to fall in love with him, and he would never have touched her if she hadn't allowed it.

She'd get over him. Absolutely. She would pour herself into her work, and eventually she would forget all about him.

Like that would happen.

She felt a burst of anger. No one to blame but herself, she decided. She would not make him feel guilty, but by God, she wouldn't say good-bye to him either. That was asking too much.

THIRTY-FOUR

MILO HAD A PROBLEM. WHERE WAS HE GOING to find a bunch of old smelly books? Old DVDs and CDs weren't a problem. He had shoplifted enough of those from various stores over the years, and he could toss those in a box. But old books?

Then it hit him. The library. He could grab all the books he needed, pack them in grocery sacks, and outrun the librarians to his car.

Milo hadn't been inside a library since he was eight years old, so he didn't know about all the changes. He was unaware that there were detectors that would set off an alarm if even one book was taken out without being stamped, but he found out about them when he passed through the metal bars and a loud pulsating beep brought people running.

He also vastly underestimated librarians. They weren't at all like the ones in old movies on television. No, these women didn't wear their hair in buns or walk around in ugly, black, tie shoes with thick soles. The two women he encountered were kind of hot, and if he hadn't been trying to get away from them with two grocery bags loaded with books, he might have tried to ask one or both of them out.

Man, those women loved their books, and there was no way in hell they were gonna let one get out without a fight. Fearing that they would beat the crap out of him when they caught him, he ran down one aisle after another, A to D, E to G. They were closing in on him in the self-help aisle when he had to slow down to catch his breath. Panting, he finally dropped the sacks and sprinted for the door, high-jumping the metal bars to get out before more alarms could go off.

Now what? Fortunately, it didn't take long for Milo to come up with another brilliant idea. He would buy new books and throw them around the house until they looked old and worthless. He knew there was a big bookstore across the street from the mall, so he drove there and asked the clerk behind the information desk if he had any new books that looked old.

The young man said "Excuse me?" three times before he understood. Then he said, "No." He did, however, turn out to be helpful. He took Milo to an area he called the classics, and some of them had real dark covers, like the ones Lyra had taken from the yard sale. The clerk brought him a cart and told him he'd be happy to help him find titles.

"No, I just need old-looking books," Milo said as he began pulling books off the shelves.

The clerk left him alone, and Milo cruised

through the stacks tossing in anything that had a dark cover or an embossed print. He had learned his lesson from the library and knew he couldn't steal these books because the store had the same kind of shoplifting detector panels just inside the front doors. What's the world coming to, he thought, when books had to be protected from thieves?

He filled two boxes, and when he paid cash at checkout, he mentioned to the clerk that he needed more old books. She gave him two extra empty boxes from the back and suggested he try Mary Ann's New and Used Book Store on Nall and 89th. Since Milo had never bought books before, this was all news to him. He wished the clerk had said something about the cheaper used books before he'd paid so much money.

Mary Ann's had just what he wanted. Once again, he didn't bother to read any titles. All he was interested in were the old covers. He dropped his books on the counter and tapped his foot impatiently waiting for his purchases to be rung up. The nerdy clerk in his rimless glasses and long unkempt hair took his sweet time and delighted in reading each title as he scanned it.

"Let's see, what do we have here?" He turned the book over to find the bar code and read, *The Basics of Toilet Training*. He swiped the decoder gun over it. "Check." He reached for the next. "*Lady Chatterley's Lover*. Check." He picked up another. "*The Trials of Menopause*. Check." He looked quizzically at Milo. "Eclectic choices. Are these for you?"

Milo didn't like the nerd's haughty attitude. "I like a lot of different stuff," he huffed defensively. "Just hurry up."

Milo left the store with two full bags and transferred them to the extra boxes in his car. When he shut the trunk, he was all set to impress the boss. Recovering the *missing* books and CDs would remind him that he could always count on Milo. He could just imagine the praise his boss would heap on him and wished he could call Mr. Merriam right then and there to tell him he was on his way, but phone calls to the boss's office or personal cell phone were strictly forbidden. Milo would have to wait for his adulation.

MR. MERRIAM WANTED TO see the park that Milo had told him about. It sounded like the ideal place to bury a few incriminating articles. Like a safe.

Keeping the safe in his office was borrowing trouble. He kept it hidden, but he worried that one day a cop would come in with a warrant and find it. He needed to get rid of it as soon as possible, and the more he worried about it, the more nervous he became. He sent Charlie and Stack out to buy a tarp, a couple of boxes of Clorox Wipes, and rubber gloves.

"Make sure you get three pairs of leather gloves, too."

When they returned to the office, Charlie put the tarp on the floor while Stack locked the door. It took the strength of all three men to move the safe to the middle of the tarp, and then Charlie and Stack put on the rubber gloves and started wiping it down.

Charlie backed his van to the service door, and they changed into their black leather gloves to carry the safe downstairs. Grunting like hogs, they lifted it into the van.

Paraiso Park was a dream come true for Mr. Merriam. He was so happy about it, the smell didn't bother him at all.

"Drive around to the back side of that hill in case someone comes in behind us to dump. It looks like there's more garbage here in front. Guess people don't want to take the time to drive around." A few minutes later, he said. "Will you look at that. A bunch of flowers found a way to grow in this cesspool. Go ahead and park. We'll dump the safe behind that heap on the other side of the flowers."

When they got out of the van, they looked all around while they put on their leather gloves.

"Now remember," Mr. Merriam said, "try not to let your clothes rub against the safe and leave fibers on it. I don't want anything to lead back to us."

They shuffled like old men as they carried the safe across the little garden, trampling the flowers as they went. They reached a tall pile of trash with a torn and stained mattress lying on top.

"Okay, drop it here, but watch your feet."

After getting the safe to the ground, they pulled the mattress over it.

Mr. Merriam strutted back to the van peeling off his gloves. He looked up at the blue sky and let the sun's rays wash over his face as he smiled with relief. Glancing back, he made sure the safe wasn't visible amid all the other junk surrounding it. No one would ever know it was there.

Better yet, no one could connect it to him.

THIRTY-FIVE

SAM AND LYRA WERE ON THEIR WAY TO THE park when Lyra got a call from her apartment manager. He had some bad news to report.

"Someone vandalized your car," he began. "Broke every window in your SUV, even the back one. Glass everywhere," he added. "I think whoever did it used a hammer. Dented your doors, too."

After thanking him for the call, Lyra dropped the phone in her lap. "We have to turn around."

Sam noticed her frown. "What's wrong?"

After she explained what the call was about, she said, "I guess I'll need a tow service."

"You'll need to file a police report, and you should get photos for your insurance company. O'Malley will want to take a look at it first, though. We've got to let him know."

Depressed, Lyra rode to her apartment in silence. When they reached the parking lot, Sam parked a good distance away from her SUV and told her to wait in the car.

Tears of anger flooded her eyes when she saw her shattered SUV. She was seething. "I'm getting real impatient with these creeps."

Lyra nervously tapped her feet on the floor as she watched Sam walk around the car and bend down to look underneath. What if he touched it and, boom, the car exploded? He'd be blown to bits.

She jumped out of the car. "Sam, let the bomb squad do that."

"Get back in the car, Lyra."

"Damn it," she muttered. "If you get blown up, I'm going to be seriously mad."

Sam finished examining the exterior, careful not to touch it and smear any fingerprints. He carefully reached inside the driver's window and pulled on the handle to open the door. Brushing aside the broken glass, he leaned in. He found a pair of sunglasses in a pink case under the driver's seat and a CD wedged between the seat and the armrest. Under the passenger's seat was a DVD, and in the back cargo area he pulled out a thin book of poetry. He carried the loot to Lyra.

"Oh, there are my sunglasses. I've been looking for those. What's this?" She looked at the book first and then at the DVD and CD. Finally recognizing them, she said, "These are from the yard sale. Everything in my car went flying when I swerved on the freeway, and these must have landed under the seat. I missed them when I boxed everything up for the ranch." She looked at the CD and didn't recognize the singer's name. Holding up the DVD, she said, "*The African Queen.* I've never seen it, and I love Humphrey Bogart. Want to watch a movie tonight?"

"Sounds good," he said. "I guess these vandals weren't the creeps after your yard sale finds. Do you have your car keys? We'll drop them with the apartment manager for the tow service."

After making the necessary calls, they were finally ready to drive to the park. Unfortunately, it was rush hour, and rush hour in Los Angeles was like running with the bulls. If you didn't keep up, you got crushed. The speed limit on the 405 was 65 miles per hour, but most drivers thought that was just a suggestion. The bumper huggers and the lane changers usually made Lyra so tense, her hands were welded to the steering wheel by the time she pulled off the freeway. Sam didn't seem bothered by the traffic. Now that she thought about it, he was rarely bothered by anything. She envisioned him knocking people down on the rugby field. The image was such a contradiction, it made her smile.

Lyra exchanged the camera equipment at the park while Sam stood watch, his hand resting on his gun the entire time. No one came or went while they were there. In fact, there was an almost eerie silence as the wind blew through the trash, picking up papers and tossing them from one heap to another. Once they were away from the park, Sam relaxed.

They arrived back at the duplex around seven with two pizzas from one of Lyra's favorite pizza shops. It was a buy-one-get-one-free night and each came with a large bottle of Diet Coke. They had enough food to feed an army. Lyra put the boxes on the kitchen table, thought about making salads, and changed her mind.

"Would you like to watch a film while we eat?"

"Sure."

They moved the food to the coffee table in the living room. Sam leaned back on the sofa ready for her to put the DVD of *The African Queen* in the player, but instead, she sat down next to him with her laptop and inserted the latest memory card.

"I have thousands of pictures," she explained, "but what's great is that I can zip through them until I see a car or a person. Then I slow it down. I've had two memory cards without a single person in any frame. Do you mind if I take a look before we watch the movie?"

"No, go ahead." He put his arm on the back of the sofa and waited.

Lyra tilted the screen back so both of them could see, inserted the memory card, and sped through the slide show of pictures. When she saw a van, she quickly paused it, then backed up to watch the sequence of photos again.

"Do you suppose that's someone coming to tend the garden?" he asked.

"I'll bet you that van is loaded with junk they want to get rid of," she said. "We'll know in a few seconds."

She reached for two slices of pizza and handed one to him. They both propped their feet on the coffee table and leaned back on the sofa, their shoulders touching. She felt comfortable with him, and sitting close like this seemed so right, as though they were a couple who had been together for years settling in for the evening.

So that she wouldn't forget this was temporary, Lyra had to ruin the moment.

"Are you leaving tomorrow morning?"

"Yes," he said. "I talked to Alec, and he has another bodyguard to replace me. He'll be here early."

Deep calming breath, she told herself. "Okay."

She started the pictures again. The shots showed three men coming out of the van. They put on gloves, which made sense considering where they were. One of them wore a suit and topcoat, which seemed out of place considering the eighty-degree temperature. In a couple of photos, the men seemed to be looking around with anxious expressions on their faces.

"They sure look nervous," Lyra commented. "Maybe they're going to change their minds."

Then the safe came out. The three men looked strained as they carried it away from the van. When the shots of them shuffling across the garden and trampling the flowers came on the screen, Lyra sat up. "They couldn't bother to walk around the flowers?" she said indignantly.

"They're illegally dumping," Sam reminded her. "They don't care about flowers."

He had a point, but she was still angry. "I hope they get caught."

They watched the men leave the safe under an old mattress. In the next picture, they were heading back in the direction of the van, and the man in the topcoat had stopped and looked upward. The camera got a straight shot of his face. The photos that followed showed them getting into the van and the van pulling away.

"Back up," Sam said. "I want to see the license plate number."

Lyra reversed the photos, cheered by the thought that they might get arrested.

Sam grabbed a pen and wrote the number on one of the pizza boxes. "Mind if I make a copy of your card? I'd like to email some of these pictures."

"Not at all."

After Lyra and he finished watching the rest of the slide show, he took the memory card to copy onto his laptop. She inserted another card and viewed the entire thing, but there wasn't anything interesting there. She couldn't understand why the person tending the little garden hadn't come back. Where was he or she?

She filed the memory cards in her metal box, and while Sam worked on his computer, she worked on her script. She liked what she had so far. She added a sentence to the narration she would use at the beginning and completed a list of the segments she wanted to shoot, hoping she could get enough footage of the children to fit into her plan. When she looked at the clock, she was shocked. She'd been sitting there for two and a half hours. Sam was still at the table, focused on his computer screen. She didn't want to bother him, so she put her laptop in her backpack and set it in the corner. The case with *The African Queen* DVD still lay on top of the television waiting to be played, but it was late, and she knew there was no way she could stay awake through a movie now. So, without a word of farewell, she quietly went upstairs. After washing her face and brushing her teeth, she put on a robe and walked into the bedroom. She had determined she wouldn't have sex with Sam again, but she left the door open. Perhaps it was a subconscious hope.

She fell into bed exhausted. The worry and tension from all the craziness surrounding her was slowly chipping away at her nerves and making her jittery. She had more than enough angst in her life right now. She didn't need her feelings for Sam to add to it. Getting involved with him had been a mistake. Her only consolation was that he would be gone tomorrow.

Her cell phone, charging on the table next to her, vibrated, signaling a text. Thinking it might be Sidney, she picked it up. There were two texts: one from her mother and one from her father. Her mother was letting her know that she and Lyra's father had decided to sell Gigi's house in San Diego. They planned to have an appraisal made the following weekend. The next text from her father confirmed what her mother had told her. He offered more. They expected to get close to eight hundred thousand dollars and would put it in their account for safekeeping. Gigi would either live at the ranch or come and live with them in La Jolla. Lyra's parents must have gotten a new lawyer, and they were making another play for Gigi's money and property.

Lyra sent a four word text back: *Gigi doesn't own it.*

Yawning, she rolled onto her stomach. She fell asleep wondering how those people were going to take the news. She hoped badly.

THIRTY-SIX

Lyra was sound asleep when Sam got into bed with her. She must have felt his nearness because she scooted up against him. He kissed her shoulder, put his arm around her waist, and went to sleep.

He heard a knock on the door at six a.m. He picked up his jeans and stumbled into them as he grabbed his gun. Quietly shutting her door, he went downstairs.

The new bodyguard was holding up identification. Sam opened the door, took one look, and muttered, "Oh, hell no."

Alec had sent Mr. Chippendale. How could a stripper protect Lyra from a bullet? Gyrate around her? The man was dressed in a button-down shirt and pressed navy slacks, but he looked as though he belonged on a stage surrounded by screaming women thrusting dollar bills at his underwear. Bet there's Velcro holding those pants on, Sam thought. He couldn't care less what the bodyguard's credentials were or how much experience he'd had in the security business. Lyra didn't need some muscle-bound pretty boy hovering around her. No, this one had to go, too.

Sam was nice to the guy and told him he'd make sure he was paid for his time, but he turned him around and suggested he go back to the dance floor.

After closing the door, Sam went into the kitchen, gulped down his orange juice, and went back upstairs to undress and get into bed. He fell asleep almost instantly.

Lyra woke up at eight. She opened one eye and looked at the clock inches from her face. Rolling over, she opened both eyes and saw Sam. Not again! How much torment could one person take? Twice now she'd prepared herself for him to leave, and twice he didn't. She thought about poking him to find out what had happened, but he was naked, and so was she . . . and she knew how that would end. Instead, she put her robe on and went downstairs. She decided she would wait until he came down—fully clothed, she hoped—before she returned to her room to dress.

Two bowls of cereal later, Lyra was back on the sofa with her laptop. She reread what she'd written last night and no longer thought it was brilliant. She tried a couple of other versions and finally was satisfied. She'd probably hate it in the afternoon, but for now it worked.

Sam came into the living room as she was typing. He was prepared to tell her that the new bodyguard didn't work out and that he was determined to make certain that she would be safe when he left her—all of which was true—but Lyra didn't ask why he was still there. She just smiled at him and went back to what she was doing.

"Lyra, do you want to go for a run before it gets too hot?" he asked.

"I ate two bowls of cereal."

"How long ago?" he asked, walking toward her.

She looked at the clock on the computer screen. "A little over an hour."

"Then let's go."

Lyra decided a run might get rid of some of the tension she was feeling. She hurried upstairs, put on shorts and a tank top, zipped her cell phone into a back pocket, and tied her running shoes.

Sam was waiting at the door. He watched her pull her hair back into a ponytail. Was there anything wrong with her? Perfect body, perfect smile, perfect . . . everything.

Lyra needed to run, to wear herself out so she would be too tired to worry about anything. It worked for a while. By the end of her three and a half miles, her mind was clearer. When she got into the shower, the water relaxed the rest of her. She stepped out of it energized.

She looked across the hall and saw Sam sitting on the bed, still sweaty from his run. She closed her bedroom door and hurriedly dressed. When she heard his shower running, she raced downstairs. As ridiculous as it was to admit, Lyra was hiding from him. She was determined to keep her distance.

Her cell phone rang. It was Detective O'Malley. "Where's Agent Kincaid?" he asked after the preliminary how-are-you's were finished. "I tried to call him, but it went to his voice mail."

"He's coming down the stairs now," she told him. "Sam, Detective O'Malley's on the phone."

He took the phone and dropped down on the sofa next to her. After a minute of listening, Sam said, "Hey, you know I'd like to help, but I gave you a list to check out, and so far I haven't heard a word—"

"Look," O'Malley said on the other end of the line, "I've been swamped. You've got the entire FBI you could ask."

Sam wasn't quite so nice when he responded. "I'll tell you what. Why don't I get some agents in there to take over the case? I'll call them right now."

"Sam , it's not your jurisdiction," O'Malley argued.

"Now it is." Cursing, he ended the call and put Lyra's phone on the coffee table.

Lyra was stunned by the anger she'd heard in his voice. "Tell me what happened."

"I'm tired of waiting. They're dragging their feet on this."

She touched his hand. "Didn't you notice how crowded the station was? This is L.A. The police are underpaid and overworked. They have other investigations, and maybe I'm not a priority because I already have an FBI agent protecting me."

"Screw it," he snapped. "There was a bomb under the car. That alone makes it a priority. I'm getting a couple of agents in there to get copies of their reports. I'm not waiting any longer."

"You're frustrated because you're not actively investigating. You're babysitting me."

He didn't respond to her statement of fact.

"What list were you talking about?" she asked.

"I gave O'Malley some names I wanted checked out."

"And he didn't?"

"Right."

"Why wouldn't you ask your associates?"

"I did last night. Agent Trapp's on it."

She sat up. "Then why are you all over O'Malley?"

"He didn't do what he said he'd do."

"Who did you send the pictures to last night?"

"Trapp," he answered.

"What about O'Malley?"

"No."

Lyra was right; he was frustrated. She calmed him down and he didn't even realize it. He watched her for a while as she sat engrossed in the research on her children's film. Every now and then she would smile. He mentioned it to her.

"I had no idea how much I would enjoy this," she said. "Even if my script doesn't make it into the top five, I kind of think I'd like to do more of this sort of work."

"Maybe a career is born."

AGENT TRAPP CALLED SAM that afternoon. "You gave us an early Christmas present, Kincaid."

"How's that?"

"We looked at the pictures you sent us, and then

went out to that park and hauled that safe in. You wouldn't know about the case, local, happened over a year ago. An office was robbed, and the owner went out the window. Only thing of importance that was taken was his safe. The same safe we picked up today, thanks to your pictures. Owner's name was engraved on it, too deep to file off. We ran the license plate of the van. It's registered to a Charles Brody."

"Did you get the other two?"

"Yes. All we had to do was follow good ol' Charlie. He led us to Frank Merriam. He's the one in the suit. Lou Stack's the other one."

"Merriam," Sam said. "I know that name. He's connected with a guy named Rooney."

"That's right. A murder/suicide. Rooney worked with Merriam. They each had their own company, but they did a lot of bad deals together. We never had enough to put 'em away."

"When are you picking them up?"

"Waiting on a warrant now. They say a picture is worth a thousand words? Those pictures of the three of them being so careful not to touch the safe, and after they drop it, Merriam looks up at the camera." Trapp sounded giddy. "Priceless," he crooned. "We're finally getting Merriam with a picture."

"This isn't locking together the way it should," Sam cautioned.

"What do you mean?"

"How did Merriam know about Paraiso Park? All of these pieces should fit together. Merriam knows Rooney. Rooney's wife has a yard sale. Lyra takes some books, DVDs, and a few CDs. And what about Flynn? How is he involved?"

"They've looked through every book, watched every movie, and listened to every CD."

Not all of them, Sam realized. "Let me call you back."

Sam looked around the room. "Lyra, where is that DVD and the CD I found in your car?"

She could hear the urgency in his tone. "On top of the television." She closed her laptop and got up. "Do you want to watch it now or after dinner?"

Sam found them. He opened the CD, saw the label, then opened the DVD case. No label. *Bingo*.

"We're going to watch it now."

"Okay," she agreed. "Do you want some popcorn or a drink?"

"If I'm right, this isn't *The African Queen*."

She folded her arms and stood in front of the television while Sam inserted the disk. He pulled her back to the sofa and sat down next to her.

The camera was focused on a heavyset man. He had a glass of whiskey in his hand. The back of a man's head was visible in the corner and he was talking.

"That's the man at the park yesterday," Lyra said in amazement.

"His name's Frank Merriam. He's the one Bill Rooney worked with."

"But how . . ." she began, confused.

"Just listen," Sam told her as he propped his elbows on his knees and leaned forward.

"How did you ever manage to push him out of the window?" the man asked Merriam.

Merriam chuckled. "You should've been there, Rooney. He never saw it coming. I'm only sorry I couldn't get more out of him." He took a sip of his whiskey and reached in his breast pocket for a cigar. "He opened the safe for me. After I took everything out, I decided it was a nice safe." He shrugged. "I should have looked closer. Anyway, Charlie and Stack got a dolly from the basement and rolled it out to my car. The thing was so heavy, I thought it was going to pop my tires."

"What did you do about—" Rooney started to ask.

"Bernie? Oh, that was easy. I went back up to the twentieth floor, opened the window, and tossed him out. He was just coming to as I shoved him over the sill."

"What about Tunney?" Rooney continued.

Lyra was mesmerized. Rooney brought up three different "accidents" to Merriam as he poured glass after glass of whiskey.

"He has absolutely no guilt," she said.

"It's a business to him," Sam replied.

Merriam talked about shaking down men and women who had borrowed money from him at an exorbitant rate.

When the screen went black, Sam ejected the disk and said, "I want to get this to Trapp."

"You should make a copy in case something happens to this one."

"They'll do it down at the field office," he assured her.

"So that's what all of this has been about. The disk is what they were looking for. I told you it had something to do with that yard sale."

"Rooney must have taped it as blackmail. Merriam had to be desperate. He knew he'd go away for life if this DVD ever got out."

Lyra looked up at Sam with tremendous relief. "I can't believe this. It's finally over."

THIRTY-SEVEN

WAKING UP WITHOUT HIM BESIDE HER FELT strange. Lyra looked in the other bedroom just to be certain he was gone, and there wasn't even a hint that he had been there.

It was better this way, she thought. Watching him leave would have been too stressful.

Vick, the new bodyguard, was in his late forties. He was stocky and had a thick mustache. He was polite but didn't engage in conversation, and he was very serious about his job. Lyra knew he would do his best to keep her safe, and she appreciated that he left her alone to work.

Detective O'Malley called her in the afternoon. "Watch the evening news. The three men in the pictures you took are in custody. The man in the suit was Frank Merriam. The two guys who worked for him are already talking, trying to make a deal."

"What about Michael Flynn?" she asked. "Has he been arrested?"

"Not yet, but soon," he promised. "Merriam won't talk until he gets a deal."

"Will he get it?"

"Oh, yes. If he can hand over Flynn . . . that would be a real coup. Merriam might hold out awhile, but the D.A. will sit down with him and his attorney real soon."

They talked for a few minutes, then O'Malley said, "Kincaid was right to get angry. He gave me that list of names and I didn't look into all of them. Might have caught Merriam sooner if I had."

"He's locked up now," she said.

"You can breathe easy, Lyra. Just let us wrap up a few things on our end, and you should be able to get back to your routine in no time at all."

That evening, all the local news channels reported the arrest of Merriam and his two accomplices for the alleged murder of Bernie Jaworski. The police weren't releasing any of the details of the case, but they stated that they planned to expand their investigation to include Merriam's possible involvement in other criminal activity. Lyra switched back and forth among the various channels to see if one offered more detail than the other, but they all said and showed the same thing: Merriam in handcuffs being led into the police station. His head was down and he said nothing as reporters pointed their microphones at him and pressed for a comment.

Agent Trapp stepped in front of the microphones to represent the FBI. He talked about the collaborative effort of the FBI and the L.A. Police Department in bringing Merriam to justice. He singled out the work of Detective O'Malley and promised that they would continue to work together until everyone involved was arrested.

Lyra watched the reports and listened carefully to the interviews, but she was just as intent on scanning the faces of the people in the background. Was Sam there? She didn't see him, but she wondered if he was involved with the case. Or had he moved on? Maybe he had delivered the disk to Agent Trapp and resumed his regular duties, which meant that, after he presented his last two lectures in California, he would be returning to D.C. Lyra switched off the TV and reached for her laptop. She needed to keep busy so that any thoughts of Sam would stay out of her head. Nothing good would come from wondering about him.

LYRA WASN'T ALLOWED TO go home for two more days. She assumed the detectives and Agent Trapp were wrapping up the case and wanted her out of the way. She had spent as much time as she could on her project, researching children's psychology, reading articles about play and the development of the imagination, and she was anxious to begin filming. Once she'd finished all of her research and had outlined the specifics of her project, she gathered her work, printed it out, and got it in the mail before the deadline.

Vick drove her back to her apartment and then left for another job. Without a car, she felt trapped. She called the service department at the dealership to find out when her car would be ready and got more bad news. The manager gave her a rough estimate which was outrageous, so Lyra called her friend Lucy and asked her to drive her over to the SUV dealership. She paid for the repairs that had already been made, then drove to the BMW dealership, traded in her clunker, and purchased a brand-new car.

The first night back in her apartment, she was all alone. Sidney had gone back east to stay with her family for a few days and wouldn't be coming home until tomorrow. Lyra unpacked her things and went to the kitchen to find something for dinner. The refrigerator was bare, except for a carton of milk, a block of cheese, and two bottles of beer. The expiration date on the milk had come and gone days ago, so she poured it into the sink and tossed the carton in the trash. She grabbed the cheese and a bottle of beer, found a box of saltines in the cabinet, and took them into the living room. Sitting cross-legged on the floor with her back against the sofa, she ate her meager meal.

The quiet made her uncomfortable. She had been alone in her apartment hundreds of times, but she'd never felt this emptiness before. She was used to having a guard. Maybe that's why she was feeling lonely now. She had grown accustomed to having someone around. No, not someone, she finally admitted to herself . . . Sam.

The tears came in torrents. She cried about Sam and how foolish she had been to fall in love with him. She cried about her dysfunctional family, and she even cried about less important things, like not having the faintest idea where she was going to get a job after she finished school, which would be soon. When all those tears were shed, she heaved a sigh, feeling completely spent. She wiped her eyes with her fingers, and tried to think of something pleasant. The image of Sam getting Gigi to drop her feud with Mrs. Castman popped into her head, and she smiled. She knew Gigi had grown fond of him and would miss him. Lyra would miss him, too. And that thought brought a new round of tears.

THE FOLLOWING EVENING Father Henry called to tell her he had secured the permission slips from the parents of the first graders.

"I'll see you in a couple of days then, Father," she said. "Thank you."

Sidney arrived home an hour later. She looked exhausted, but she was happy because she was able to announce that all of her projects were handed in on time. The two friends talked for hours.

Sidney noticed that Lyra brought Sam's name into the conversation as often as possible, and it didn't take long for her to see that her friend was miserable. "You need to keep busy," she said. "It's the only way you'll get through this."

Lyra knew she was right, so she packed a small bag, gathered up her camera equipment, got into her new BMW, and drove to Gigi's house in San Diego. Even though she thought of it as her grand-mother's home, the house actually belonged to Lyra. She had purchased it for Gigi when she de-cided to move to California, and if Lyra stayed in the area after finishing school, it would be her home as well.

The day was sunny, and it was a nice drive to San Diego. She parked in the garage, walked around to the front of the house, and only then saw the For

Sale sign. A real estate broker was coming out the front door with a couple.

Lyra saw stars. She marched up the porch steps and asked the broker what she thought she was doing.

The well-dressed woman looked uneasily at the couple she was with before turning back to Lyra. Flashing a toothy smile, she said, "I have an agreement with the owners, Mr. and Mrs. Prescott, to sell the house."

"They don't own this house."

"They believe they do," she said belligerently.

"No, I'm the owner, and I have papers to prove it. You need to get off my property or I'm calling the police. And take that sign with you."

"Listen here, young lady," she snapped, "I've got three couples fighting over this property, and I'm . . ."

Lyra pulled out her cell phone and announced that she was calling the police chief. "Hi, Paul. I'm fine, thanks. There's a Realtor at my house. She trespassed and is trying to sell my home." She listened for a minute, then said, "Thanks." She turned to the woman. "He's on his way."

Ms. Realtor wasn't willing to lose such a high commission. She clung to the hope that Lyra was bluffing . . . until the police car pulled up in front of them. "You called the police," the woman said incredulously.

"Yes, I did."

"You actually own this house?"

"That's right."

The couple who had toured the house looked crestfallen.

"If you ever want to sell . . ." The broker took a card from the side pocket of her briefcase and handed it to Lyra.

As she and her clients were walking to the street, the policeman called out to Lyra from his squad car, "Do you want to press charges?"

"No," Lyra answered. "She's leaving."

The Realtor was appreciative and turned around. "Mr. Prescott changed all the locks. Would you like this key to get in?"

"No, thank you. I'll have them changed again," Lyra assured her.

Lyra called the locksmith, and an hour later she sat on the porch swing while the locks were being replaced. Not even the ocean breeze or the sunny afternoon could diminish her anger, however. Once inside, she dropped her bags in her bedroom and left again to run a few errands. The mundane activity should have calmed her, but she was still seething when she returned home. She was putting her groceries away when her temper exploded. Not even chocolate could stop it.

"They tried to sell my house!" she shouted. No one was there to hear her, and yelling didn't help. She was still fuming and had to tell someone. She reached for her phone and called her brothers.

Owen answered. "Hi, kid. What do you want?"

Owen was the oldest of the three and couldn't seem to grasp the fact that his little sister was no longer a child. Of course, whining to him about their parents' latest escapade probably reinforced that notion, but at the moment, she didn't care. Her voice shook as she told him what had happened. Owen wasn't very sympathetic. He laughed.

"Stop that," she ordered. "People were going through my house with a real estate broker."

"I know, I heard you, but Lyra, our parents can't sell what they don't own."

"They must know that, so tell me, why are they doing this?"

He sighed. "They think they can pressure Gigi and end up with control of her money. I'll bet they've already got another attorney working on it."

"They want all of it."

"Yes, they do." He said, "Hold on," and yelled, "Hey, Coop, the parents are trying to sell Lyra's house."

Lyra heard Cooper's laughter. "It's not funny," she said.

"Yeah, it kinda is."

"Do you know how much money those people have gone through? They've spent all of their inheritance, and the monthly amount they get from the other trust is generous."

"Not to them," he said.

"What am I going to do?"

"Nothing," he answered. "Coop and I have your back. And Lyra," he added, "when you need us to gang up on them, we will."

"May I talk to Gigi?" she asked.

"She's out with her *girlfriends*. Honest, Lyra, that's what they call each other."

"How is she?"

"Happy. She's happy to be home. She's said so a dozen times. I think she moved to San Diego so you wouldn't be lonely."

"She has lots of friends here."

"But this is her home."

"I know. Tell her I'll call her tomorrow. And Owen . . ."

"Yes?"

"I love you."

"Oh, God . . ."

She was laughing when she hung up.

In a much better mood after talking to her brother, Lyra finished straightening the kitchen. She suddenly remembered the panic room and wondered if Harlan had finished building it. She walked back to Gigi's bedroom to see. Not only was the work finished, but finding a way to open it was almost impossible. The wall looked perfectly smooth. In the corner maybe? She tried pushing and pulling every piece of molding or hardware she could find, even looking at the floor for some kind of button or board to push.

Finally, she called Harlan. Since he was on his way for ice cream with his girls, he stopped by and showed her the exact place to push in the middle of the wall. He applied pressure with the palm of his hand, and the hidden door sprang open. Harlan reached inside and switched on an overhead light. The little room was perfect. Bottled water sat on the floor next to a small daybed, and the only other item in the space was a cell phone plugged into a charger.

"She had the room built for you, you know," Harlan said. "Gigi worries about you staying here alone."

Lyra saw the irony. All this time she'd worried about Gigi being alone when, in fact, Gigi had been worrying about Lyra.

"I've got a good family," she said, thinking of Owen, Cooper, and Gigi. "I'm very fortunate." She was calm again. Lots of children, she supposed, had parents who didn't want to grow up.

Later that night, as Lyra was drifting off to sleep, the funniest thought came into her head. She didn't crave chocolate anymore. Unfortunately, she couldn't say the same about Sam.

THIRTY-EIGHT

MILO WAS BEGINNING TO THINK MR. MERRIAM was a real jerk. He had a trunk full of books and DVDs to give him, and his boss hadn't bothered to call him to let him know he could bring them in. He still remembered how excited Mr. Merriam had been when he told him he'd found everything the girl had taken. Of course, it was a lie, but Mr. Merriam would never know that.

Now the boss was being just plain rude. Why didn't he call? Milo bet Charlie and Stack had something to do with it. They were trying to squeeze him out.

Two entire days and nights went by without a word. Milo had half a mind to throw the boxes in the Dumpster, but he talked himself out of it. The boss was depending on him.

He made sure he took his disposable cell phone with him when he went out to get a triple cheeseburger with chili fries. He didn't like eating in restaurants by himself, so he stopped for carry-out. When he got home, he tore the grease-stained sack open on his ottoman, and spread his food out.

Picking up the oozing cheeseburger with one hand, he reached for the TV remote with the other and turned on the television. Usually, he watched cable channels, but there weren't any good movies on, so he tried the network channels.

If he hadn't paused in his channel surfing to dip a fry in the chili, he wouldn't have heard Mr. Merriam's name.

On the screen was the prosecutor, standing in front of a dozen microphones held by zealous reporters.

"Frank Merriam, Charles Brody, and Lou Stack are now in custody. The three men were arrested in connection with the murder of Bernie Jaworski."

One reporter shouted, "We understand they were caught on tape destroying evidence at Paraiso Park. Is that true?"

Uh-oh, Milo thought.

"I'm afraid I can't comment on that just yet," he answered.

"What about a tape with Merriam confessing to other crimes?" another asked. "Is it true that he's been implicated in other murders?"

The prosecutor remained calm and restrained. "I can't answer that either."

"What about bail?"

"We will be asking the judge to deny bail. We consider Mr. Merriam and his associates to be flight risks and also to be highly dangerous. All I can say is that the evidence we've collected thus far is compelling, and we feel confident we will have a conviction."

"Wow," Milo whispered. "No bail."

The picture turned to Merriam's office where policemen were carting off boxes marked "Evidence."

"No bail?" Milo repeated. It suddenly hit him. He didn't have a job any longer.

What was he going to do with all those books?

THIRTY-NINE

Sam couldn't stop thinking about Lyra. God knows, he tried. Right in the middle of the lecture he was giving to the cadets in Los Angeles, she popped into his mind, and he lost his train of thought. The same thing happened in San Diego.

He thought a lot about the investigation, too. Agent Trapp was keeping him informed. He told Sam that neither the FBI nor the L.A.P.D. had been able to link Flynn to Merriam or Rooney.

"Go back to D.C. I'll call whenever we have anything new. Don't worry about Lyra. We're not letting Flynn anywhere near her."

Sam couldn't do it. He couldn't leave. He called and canceled his reservation, and drove back to L.A.

The case wasn't tied up to his satisfaction. Something wasn't right. Merriam hadn't been given an offer he liked yet, so he'd clammed up, but his two accomplices, Charlie Brody and Lou Stack, were making deals right and left. They agreed to hand over information that would seal Merriam's conviction on a dozen counts if, in return, they got light sentences. Seemed like a fair trade to the police, so they conceded. When it came to Flynn and his men, however, Brody and Stack revealed nothing. In fact, they said they not only didn't know Flynn, they'd never heard of him, and nothing could get them to change their story.

There was a good chance that Merriam and his men feared the Flynn gang more than they did a prison sentence, but Sam wouldn't rest easy. Everyone assumed that Merriam had hired Flynn's men to go after Lyra, and now with Merriam behind bars, that the threat was over. If Sam had to get Flynn alone in a room to make the connection, by God, he'd do it, even if it meant losing his job. Better the badge than Lyra. The thought of anything happening to her made him crazy.

He never should have left her. He knew he could come up with at least ten reasons—or excuses—for leaving, but none of them held up under scrutiny. The truth was, Lyra scared him. Sam had left because he didn't want to love her, and how stupid was that? He'd been an idiot and a coward. And, damn, he did love her.

He called her apartment and her cell phone to tell her he was coming, but no one answered. He decided to check in with Detective O'Malley.

"Anything new on the two guys you picked up?" he asked.

"No," O'Malley answered. "Trapp probably told you we haven't been able to connect them to Merriam yet. Johnson and Foley, the two who shot at you in the park, won't give us anything. As much as we'd like to prove Merriam hired them, we don't have the evidence. Same with the car bomb. We can't connect that to Merriam either. We'll keep trying."

"Good," Sam said. "We can't let go of this until you do."

PER THE D.A.'S INSTRUCTIONS, O'Malley arranged to have Johnson and Foley brought to the interrogation room. They had been sitting in their cells long enough to get worried, and it was a last attempt by the D.A.'s office to make a deal with whoever talked first. O'Malley didn't think there was a chance in hell that either one of them would rat out Flynn. He could be more terrifying than any prison.

Sam was a few miles from Lyra's apartment when the detective called him and asked if he would like to observe. Sam immediately turned around and drove to the station. He had no intention of simply observing. He had questions of his own.

O'Malley spotted him coming up the stairs. Sam was wearing a comfortable pair of jeans and a white shirt. O'Malley, in the same old rumpled blue suit he wore three out of five days, envied him.

"Nice dress code you feds have."

"I'm not at work," Sam informed him.

As they walked down the hall, O'Malley said, "Look, I slacked off on that list you gave me, and I'm sorry about that. I also want you to know I appreciate getting the recognition as head of the joint operation."

"Trapp did that."

"Yeah, but you told him to. Anyway, thanks."

"Are they here yet?"

"Just arrived. We've got Johnson in one room and Foley in the other. We're waiting on the D.A.'s assistant."

"Let's go."

"You're not going to wait for the D.A.?"

"No."

Sam went into the observation room and looked through the window at Johnson, who was nervously biting off a fingernail and spitting it on the floor. He was young, barely out of his teens. Sam watched him for a minute, then crossed the hall to look at Foley. The middle-aged man leaned back in his chair and looked bored as he tapped his fingers on the table.

"I'll start with Johnson."

O'Malley followed Sam into the room where Johnson waited. The young man smirked when O'Malley introduced the agent.

Sam couldn't see Johnson's hands under the table. "Is he shackled?" he asked O'Malley.

"You afraid of me?" Johnson snickered, but Sam ignored him.

"Why does it matter?" O'Malley asked Sam.

"I can't throw him into the wall if he's shackled."

The way he stared at Johnson when he made the threat was so intimidating, O'Malley thought he might really do it.

Johnson wasn't convinced. "You can't do that. You're an FBI agent."

"Not today," he said. "I'm on vacation." He

turned to O'Malley. "You want to take my gun and wait outside a few minutes?"

"You can't touch me," Johnson snarled. "I know my rights. It's illegal."

Sam took a step toward the table, and Johnson recoiled.

"I'm not just any agent," Sam said. "I'm the agent you tried to kill in Paraiso Park, and *that's* illegal. I can do pretty much anything I want to you."

The assistant D.A. was watching from the other side of the glass when Johnson shouted he wanted his lawyer present. "Great," he said. "Agent Kincaid has him so scared, he won't say another word."

Detective Muren stood beside him. "Hold on just a minute. Let's see what Kincaid does."

Sam smiled at Johnson then said to O'Malley, "Get him his lawyer, but make it quick. As soon as they move him out of here, he's a dead man." After dropping the news, Sam stood as if to leave.

Johnson shouted to him, "Wait! What do you mean 'I'm a dead man'?"

"You didn't hear?" Sam asked. Turning to O'Malley, "You didn't tell him?"

The detective played along. "I didn't want to scare him."

Sam shook his head. "You're leaving that to Flynn, huh?" He once again started to leave.

"What have you heard?" Johnson blurted.

Sam turned, leaned against the wall, and folded his arms across his chest. "Flynn thinks you talked. He's got people out there just waiting for the chance to take you out. That's the word, anyway."

"But I didn't talk. Why would Flynn think I did?"

Sam smiled. "I told him you did. Say your prayers, Johnson."

For a third time, he turned to leave. He got as far as the hall when Johnson screamed, "I want to make a deal. I'll talk but I want witness protection and . . ."

When Sam returned to the interrogation room, he was followed by the assistant D.A. Johnson knew who he was because he'd been questioned by him twice before.

"I'll take over from here," he told Sam. "I'll let you know—"

"I'm staying," Sam said.

"This is a—"

Sam cut him off. "He shot at a federal agent. I could take total control of this case with one phone call."

"I don't want to argue with you. If you want to stay, fine. Just don't interfere."

O'Malley decided to stay, too. Like Sam, he leaned against the wall and listened as Johnson talked.

Johnson directed his statements to Sam. "I didn't shoot at you. I drove the car, that's all. Foley was the shooter. He'd been told to kill the girl."

"Who told him?" the assistant D.A. asked.

"Flynn."

"Did he say why?"

"No, but Foley and I figured it out. It was payback for an old friend. I heard him tell Foley that, several years ago, the friend had some very incriminating evidence on Flynn. The guy could have put this out to the world and ruined Flynn, but he didn't do it, and he didn't try to blackmail him. This friend told him, like in *The Godfather,* if he needed a favor someday, maybe Flynn could help him out."

"And now that favor was to get rid of Lyra Prescott?"

"Yes."

"Who's the friend who wanted this done?"

"I don't know. Flynn never mentioned his name to Foley or me. Now can I have my deal?"

"He didn't tell you *anything* about the friend?" Sam demanded.

"Just that he met him a long time ago, and the friend didn't rat on him."

"What did this have to do with Merriam?" the assistant D.A. asked.

Johnson laughed. "You guys have that all wrong. Flynn never would have done anything for Merriam. He had some dealings with Merriam a couple of years ago, and the jackass tried to swindle a couple hundred grand out of him. No way would Flynn do him a favor."

"So why was Lyra Prescott the target?"

"Flynn said something about the girl messing things up for his friend and him. They couldn't keep dumping things they didn't want found."

Sam felt an urgency to find Lyra. There were unanswered questions racing through his mind, but he was clear on one thing: the man who wanted to hurt her was still out there.

O'Malley followed him as he hurried out of the station. "What are you thinking, Sam?"

"Lyra caught something else with her camera. I need to look through all her film again."

He hurriedly drove to Lyra's apartment. Sidney answered the door, immediately sensing something was wrong.

"What's happened?"

"Is Lyra here?"

"No. Sam, what's wrong?"

"I need to make sure she's all right. I need to see her."

"She came back from San Diego with a lot of footage of some kids, and she's still working on her project after class. She told me she had a full day ahead of her. She has to meet Professor Mahler and give him all her research materials and her memory cards. Then she has to show him she's finished the children's film. She's not getting home until really late."

"Thanks, Sidney."

Sidney stopped him as he was leaving. "Lyra's safe, isn't she? On campus she—"

"I'll find her and stay with her. Don't worry."

Sam was putting it all together, but he needed to be sure. The campus was almost empty. Classes had ended for the day, and the streetlights were just coming on. He was racing across the quad when he saw two young men approaching. He recognized them as two of Lyra's friends, Carl and Eli.

"Hi, Sam," Carl shouted and jogged over to him.

"Have you seen Lyra?" Sam asked.

"She was just in Mahler's class with us."

"Brutal, as usual," Carl muttered. "Just a couple more classes with that creep, and I'll never have to hear about tentacles again."

Sam frowned. "What are you talking about?"

"Tentacle of Greed," Eli said. "That's the name of the documentary Mahler made. It's his only claim to fame. He won a little nothing award, but he never stops talking about it. No wonder his wife left him."

Carl added, "It's about a couple of small mob families out here, and— Hey, where are you going?"

Like one of Lyra's slide shows, the pictures flashed across Sam's mind. The poster of Paraiso Park in Mahler's office, Lyra sitting in Mahler's office while one of Flynn's men was planting a bomb under the car, Mahler telling her to concentrate on a children's film instead of going back to the park. Last was the image of Lyra's metal box with all the memory cards. Mahler wanted them because he thought there was something there that would damn him.

Running, Sam pulled out his phone and punched a number. When O'Malley answered on the other end, he shouted, "It's Mahler."

FORTY

LYRA WAITED AS THE LAST STUDENT FILED OUT of the classroom. This was the last class of the evening, and people were usually eager to clear out. There was little time left in the day, and Lyra was anxious to get to the lab to continue editing her film, but Professor Mahler wanted to see her in his office first. He had called her apartment late the night before and told her he'd been trying to reach her for a few days. He had noticed she'd missed a couple of his classes. With all the turmoil surrounding her on campus—namely the bomb—he'd hoped she was safe, but he stressed that she still would need to make up for the classes she'd missed. He was also concerned that she wasn't devoting enough time to the children's film. When she explained that she'd been out of town filming first graders and was now beginning the editing process, she expected him to berate her for leaving town when the filming could have been done right here in Los Angeles. Mahler could always find something to say to keep his students in their

places. He liked to make them feel small and insecure. She thought he did it to make himself more
important.

Over the phone he cleared his throat, and she'd
known a lecture was coming. "You need to take
your studies more seriously or you'll never make
it in media, especially the film industry."

"Yes, Professor," she dutifully replied.

"There are eager young people out there dying
for the opportunity to attend my classes."

"Yes, I know."

"Good. Now Lyra, I want to offer you praise."

She nearly dropped her phone. Praise from
Mahler? Unheard of.

"Your documentary on the park was quite good,"
he told her. Coming from Mahler, this was effusive
applause.

"Thank you, Dr. Mahler," she said. "It wasn't
what I had set out to do, but I think it makes a
statement about—"

"Yes, yes," Mahler interrupted. "The reason I'm
calling is that I think I might be able to present
your documentary at a symposium in New York
next week. If it gets the sort of recognition I think
it will, you'll have the opportunity to show it in
screenings around the country."

"That would be wonderful." Lyra grew excited.
If more people saw her film, it might actually do
some good. Maybe Paraiso Park would be cleaned
up, and some of the vandals and garbage dumpers
would be brought to justice, or at least stopped.

"In order to make my presentation of your film,"
Mahler went on, "I'll need to see all of your re-

search, and I'll need to know what your process was, what equipment you used, and all the images you collected."

"My pictures are stored on my memory cards," she explained. "I transferred the ones I selected for the documentary to a computer file, but there are thousands more still on the cards."

"Bring everything in," he said. "Even the pictures of the charming garden you told me about. I'll give them back to you later so you can consolidate them onto a disk if you want."

"Okay," she agreed. "I have my evening class with you tomorrow. I'll bring everything with me then."

Mahler hung up without saying good-bye.

Sitting in the classroom now, Lyra impatiently looked at the clock over the door to the professor's office. She hoped the meeting with him didn't take long. She wanted to spend the few remaining hours of her day working on the children's film. Carl and Eli had stopped to ask the professor a couple of questions, and he was ushering them to the door with curt, one-syllable answers.

Once he closed the classroom door, Mahler turned back to Lyra.

"Come into my office," he said, pointing the way.

Lyra picked up her backpack and the file folder with all of her printed research and followed him. Closing the door, Mahler gestured to a chair and then took his seat behind the desk. Lyra noticed that the poster of Paraiso Park was gone. A faint outline remained in the spot where it had hung.

She thought it was a little sad that the professor removed the one picture in his office that was the least bit uplifting, but then Mahler was not the cheerful sort.

"Do you have all of your materials with you?" he asked.

A student knocked on the window in his office door.

"Now what?" he muttered. He rushed to open the door and said, "Can't you see I'm with a student now?"

"I'm sorry, Professor, I was just wondering—"

"Make an appointment with my assistant."

"I was just going to ask—"

Mahler shut the door in her face, locked it so there would be no more intrusions, and pulled the shade down.

He sat heavily in his chair. "Where were we? The materials," he said, nodding. "Do you have them with you?"

"Yes," she answered. "I have printed copies of all the articles and records I found." She laid the folder on his desk and reached for her backpack. "I've also got the tapes of the interviews I did. I've thought about transcribing them, but I haven't had time to do that yet." She opened the flap to her backpack and brought out a couple of small metal boxes. "And here are the memory cards with all the pictures from the park."

He tapped the box. "And the garden? Are they in there?"

"Yes."

Mahler picked up the file and the tapes and put

them in a briefcase. He opened a drawer and pulled out a canvas tote and placed the two boxes of cards in it.

"You're sure that's absolutely everything?" he asked.

"Yes," she said.

"Good, I think the people at the symposium will be impressed." He leaned back in his chair. "I wish you could come with me, but I'm afraid the event is for professionals like myself. As a student, you'd be out of place."

While Lyra would have liked to present her own work, the thought of a long trip with Professor Mahler made her cringe.

"There's just one other thing I'm going to need before I can exhibit your documentary," he said.

"What is that?" Lyra asked, thinking she had given him every possible piece of material she'd collected.

"I'm going to need to see Paraiso Park, and unfortunately, this is the only free time I'll have before leaving for New York. My car is just outside. I'll drive." He stood as though the matter was settled.

Lyra was surprised. "But, Professor, it will be dark by the time we get there. Besides, I have lab time scheduled, and—"

"That will have to wait," he said impatiently. "We won't stay at the park long. We'll use my headlights to see."

"Couldn't you go there on your own? You said you lived near the park at one time, so you know the area well."

"I know how to get there, yes," he admitted, "but I'll need you with me to explain how you chose your camera angles, how you set up your shots, what environmental factors you considered in your photographs."

She didn't want to go anywhere with him. Her instincts were telling her to get out of his office. Something was wrong. Mahler had become so emphatic.

"I'm sorry. I'm going to have to decline."

"You would pass up the opportunity to have your documentary shown? You cannot be serious."

"Of course I want it shown. I'm simply declining to go with you to Paraiso Park."

"I'm going to have to insist. I'm afraid not only your documentary but your entire evaluation in my class could depend on this." He opened the side drawer on his desk. When he looked up at her, his face was red and his jaw was clenched.

Lyra didn't refuse again. He was acting so strangely, she was becoming alarmed.

"All right," she relented. "I'll meet you there." She pulled her cell phone from her pocket and said, "I'll call Sidney, my roommate, and ask her to ride with me. She's been wanting to see the park, and I—"

"Hand me the phone."

She looked up. Mahler held a gun pointed at her.

Lyra was so shocked, she stammered, "Professor . . . what are you doing?"

"I said, give me that phone." His anger was so

fierce that she could see the pulsing veins in his forehead.

ONLY THE LENGTH OF a desk separated Lyra from a bullet, but instead of being frightened, she became furious. Her hand holding the phone dropped to her lap. She pushed 911 and muted the call.

Mahler could barely contain his rage. "Of all the parks in this city, you had to choose Paraiso Park! If I had known before you started taking your ridiculous pictures, I could have gotten you onto another project."

"I chose that park because of the poster in your office."

"You're saying this is *my* fault?"

Lyra didn't know how to respond. "Please put the gun down and explain to me what has you so upset."

"Upset? I'm enraged," he growled.

"But why?" she asked again.

"You pointed the damn camera at that garden. If it got a picture of my car or me, I'll be screwed. I can't chance that."

She took a deep breath. "Is that *your* garden? Did you bury something that—"

"No," he said. "Not there. Not there. But if your camera got the garden, it got what was on the other side." He wore a sick smile.

"What?" she asked.

"Not what, who," he corrected. "Yip, yip, yip. That's all she did. Constantly picking at me. I couldn't stand it one more second." Almost as an afterthought, he said, "And I needed the money."

"Your wife?" Lyra asked incredulously.

"I couldn't divorce her," he said. "She was the one with the money."

Lyra's heart sank to her stomach. She and everyone else in her film class had thought that Mrs. Mahler had left him. He was so mean and bad-tempered, it was easy to believe.

"Money? How can you get money if her body isn't found? It could take years before the insurance is paid."

"Think you've got it all figured out? You don't. You're all wrong. I don't want her body found. As long as everyone believes she's left me, I can continue to dip into her accounts. I can't touch her money if she's dead. She saw to that, all right." He shook his head. "That park could have been ignored for years. If they start digging around now . . ."

He suddenly realized she hadn't given him the phone. "Give me your phone."

She held it up, and he slapped it onto the floor. Blessedly, it was still in one piece. Lyra prayed that her 911 call had gone through.

He kept the gun on her as he paced a couple of steps back and forth, thinking. His anger was turning into panic.

"If you'd just gone to the park quietly . . . Now I have to figure out how to do this. It was all going to be so easy. Your two friends are waiting about a mile from here. All I had to do was hand you over. They'd do the rest."

Lyra was trembling and desperately trying to stay calm. Her mind raced from one crazy idea to another to get that gun away from him. And still live to tell about it. She could see the turmoil inside him. His scheme hadn't gone as planned, and now he had to scramble for a new one. All she could think to do was to keep him talking.

"What friends?"

"The men Flynn sent to your apartment. You pepper-sprayed one of them, and he can't wait to see you again."

Lyra was confused. "You sent Flynn's men after me? What does this have to do with Frank Merriam?" None of this was making sense.

"Who the hell is Frank Merriam? All I know is that if Flynn's thugs could have found those pictures in your apartment, this would be over. When the pictures weren't there, I couldn't take a chance you or anyone else could see them. I had to let Flynn call the shots after that. He's not going to help me out again." He looked at her resentfully. "I wasted my favor on a damned student."

He picked up his cell phone and pushed some numbers while keeping an eye on her. Lyra thought if he would just stretch his arm out a little more, she could knock the gun out of his hand.

The phone was up to his ear. "She's not cooperating. You'll have to come and get her. Campus should be cleared out by now. Come in the back door on the lower level."

Lyra couldn't just sit there and wait to get dragged outside. If she didn't do something soon, it would be three armed men against her.

*   *   *

THERE WERE TWO ENTRANCES into Mahler's office. The door facing the hall, which the students were encouraged to use, and the private entrance through the classroom.

Sam tore into the building and ran up two flights of steps. The building was empty and when he came to the hallway to Mahler's office, he slowed down. He moved quietly past the first door, then another and another until he reached Mahler's door. His name, like all the professors' names, was etched on the glass. The window shade was pulled down. Sam knew before he tried the door that it was locked.

He could hear Mahler talking. His voice was loud and angry. But there was more to it, a hysterical pitch. Mahler was breaking down, which meant the least little thing could set him off. Sam was certain Lyra was inside, but he needed to hear her voice so that he would know she was all right. It made him crazy to consider any other possibility.

He flipped his gun safety off as he ducked down to get to the classroom door. It was closed, so he quietly turned the knob and slowly pushed it open a couple of inches. Mahler stood in profile, but Sam saw the gun. He knew Lyra must be on the other side of the desk. Since Mahler kept his gun on her, she was alive and conscious.

Mahler was agitated and moving back and forth. Sam couldn't get a clear shot. Any thought of getting the angle he needed without being seen was futile.

He heard heavy footsteps. They sounded as

though they were coming from the stairwell. Two men were arguing. Their voices were becoming more distinct as they climbed the stairs, but they were speaking in such hushed tones, he could only catch a few words. He heard one of them complaining about having to dig up something and move it so it wouldn't be found. The other agreed it was a lousy job.

Their voices became clearer as they got closer. "We're grave diggers is what we are. And now we've got to dig two new graves if we're going to dig up the wife's body and move it," one whispered.

"I brought some pepper spray just for her. Let the bitch know what it feels like."

Sam couldn't wait any longer. He went back to Mahler's office door and knocked.

Mahler didn't answer at first, and then cautiously said, "Who is it?"

Sam didn't answer.

"Lyra, go open the door, and don't try anything or you'll be getting a bullet in your back," Mahler ordered.

"No."

"Get up and open the door," he demanded.

Sam kept his eye on the door to the stairwell. The two men should be stepping out any second.

Lyra screamed back. "No, I'm not getting up."

"Bitch," Mahler muttered. He kept his eyes on her as he edged around her chair and backed toward the door, his left hand reaching for the lock.

Sam used all his might and kicked in the door, sending Mahler flying. He landed on the floor beside his desk. Lyra leapt up and ran to get Mahler's gun, but he scrambled forward and got there first. When Mahler rolled on his back and aimed the barrel at Sam, Lyra sprang at him. Mahler swung the gun toward her, and a shot rang out. The bullet from Sam's gun struck Mahler in his throat, severing his carotid artery. He fell to the floor with blood pooling around him.

Lyra shook uncontrollably. "Sam." She called his name, but her voice was so faint he couldn't hear.

He wasn't looking at her. He lifted the door and propped it in the opening. Then he grabbed a chair and pushed it against the propped door to hold it. The glass was cracked but still intact. Sam pulled the torn shade down as the footsteps pounded in the hallway. The men outside had heard the shot and were running toward Mahler's office. Two large file cabinets stood against the wall next to the door. Sam grabbed Lyra and pushed her into the corner, hidden by the cabinets. He stood in front of her, pushing her back even farther.

Just as Sam hoped, the men kicked down the door and started shooting even before they rushed in. They aimed at the desk in front of them, riddling it with bullets. "You check, make sure you got her."

"Oh, I got her," the other boasted.

"I'm still squirting pepper spray in her eyes."

"Drop the guns!" Sam ordered from behind.

The vengeful thug whirled around, and Sam

shot the gun from his hand. His friend ducked down behind the desk, but his arm came around the side to shoot wildly. Sam shot him in the shoulder, forcing him to drop the gun.

After Sam kicked the guns away from the injured men, Lyra collected them and put them on the desk. She added Mahler's gun to the collection.

One of their attackers was now screaming that he would never use his hand again.

"Your shooting hand?" Sam asked casually. "That'd be a real shame."

Lyra was watching the other man. He had a bullet in his shoulder, but he remained stone-faced. Of the two, she thought he was the more dangerous. She heard footsteps pounding toward them and turned around. Sam had stepped into the hallway and was holding his badge up for the three approaching policemen to see.

Within minutes they were surrounded by police officers and paramedics. Lyra stood in the corner of the tiny office so they could get past her. Her racing heart had finally slowed, and her hands were no longer shaking. She noticed her phone on the floor and remembered her 911 call. She picked it up and held it to her ear. "Is anyone there?"

"Yes, ma'am, we're here."

"Did you record all that? Did you get every word Mahler said?"

"Yes, ma'am, we sure did." Lyra could hear a smile in her voice.

Detective O'Malley arrived on the scene, and Sam was filling him in on the details. She waited for Sam to say something to her, but he was preoccupied, acting as though he didn't even see her. The door was blocked by people, so she went through the classroom and into the hall. She wondered why Sam had kept her in the office instead of running in this direction. She looked down the hallway and had her answer. If they had turned one way, they would have met a dead end. If they had turned the other, they would have run past the office, and the gunmen would have had an easy shot at them. She and Sam would never have made it to the exit. He had made a good call, she thought. By pushing her into that corner and then placing himself in front of her, Sam had kept her alive.

Lyra thought she would have to give her account of what had happened at least two or three times, but only one policeman had any questions. He explained that the 911 operator had heard and recorded every word, so they knew exactly what had taken place. She was free to go home.

Sam was still talking to O'Malley, and she felt foolish waiting around. He had obviously put the pieces of the puzzle together and realized that Mahler was behind the horrible things that had been happening. If she stood there waiting for him, and he didn't say anything more than, "Nice to see you again," then what?

She wasn't waiting. She didn't even try to get her memory cards or her backpack. They were now part of the investigation. She tucked her phone in her pocket, turned around, and walked away.

She didn't get far. She had just turned the corner in the hallway when she felt strong hands on her shoulders.

FORTY-ONE

SAM DIDN'T GIVE HER A CHANCE TO THANK HIM for saving her life.

"You scared the hell out of me, lass." His voice shook with emotion, and his grip on her shoulders tightened. His brogue was so thick, he sounded as though he'd never left Scotland. Did he just call her "lass"?

Before she could say a word, he jerked her into his arms and hugged her fiercely. "Don't you ever do that to me again." She could barely understand a word he said. He *was* speaking English, wasn't he?

The side of her face was pressed against his chest, and she heard his heart pounding. Lyra was still shaken from the ordeal she'd gone through, but in Sam's strong arms, she was comforted.

"Promise me," he demanded.

"Yes, whatever it is, I promise."

He tilted her chin up and kissed her almost savagely. His tongue swept inside, and there was such passion in his kiss, such desperation.

Lyra didn't resist. She wrapped her arms around

his neck, and her fingers spread through his hair as she kissed him with equal fervor.

When he finally released her from his arms, he took her hand and began walking. "Let's get out of here." Calmer now, his brogue wasn't as thick.

Outside, a crowd had gathered. Spotting the TV news vans parked across the quad, Sam muttered an expletive.

O'Malley rushed up behind them and said, "You need an escort out of here?"

"No," Sam answered. "But you deal with them." He motioned to the cameramen.

"Yeah, sure," O'Malley said, and headed to intercept the reporters.

They had almost crossed the quad without being mobbed, but Carl spotted them and shouted Lyra's name. Everyone who heard him ran toward Lyra and Sam.

"Is it true? Is Mahler dead?" Carl asked.

Lyra nodded, and Carl turned to Sam. "I know Mahler was a jerk, but we only had two more classes with him. Now what happens? You don't think we'll have to retake the entire class, do you?"

Before Lyra could answer, Eli said, "You couldn't have waited until—" The look Sam shot him stopped him cold, and he hurried to get out of the way.

Sam didn't say another word to Lyra until they reached her apartment.

"Pack something, and let's get out of here."

"No."

"No?"

Sidney opened the door, shouted, "Oh my God,"

and hugged Lyra. "You're okay? Oh my God," she repeated, but this time she threw herself into Sam's arms. "I heard there was a shooting," she said as she backed into the tiny living room so they could come inside. "I've gotten at least twenty texts, and I prayed it was you doing the shooting, Sam."

"Lyra," Sam said, "why don't you pack a bag while I tell Sidney what happened."

"No," Lyra said again.

Sidney looked from one to the other, then scooped up her purse and keys. "I've got to run an errand. See you later." And she was gone.

"Look what you've done," Lyra said accusingly. "You made her leave her own home."

Sam turned her toward him. "What's the matter with you?"

"I'm not going anywhere with you, and let you leave me again. I won't do it."

"But I'm not leaving you. Not ever."

The tenderness in his eyes made her believe him. Almost.

"Until when? Sam, I know you can't let yourself be hurt again, and I understand. You loved your wife and you lost her. I wouldn't want to go through that again either, but I—"

His kiss stopped her. He held her tighter still as he whispered in her ear. "I never want to be scared like I was today. I knew you were with Mahler, and I swear my heart stopped beating. Damn it, Lyra, I don't want to live without you." His hands cupped the sides of her face. "I love you, lass."

The brogue was back full force. His voice was low, but she got the gist of what he was telling her.

"I can't move in with you, Sam. Gigi would—"

"I guess I'll have to marry you," he said offhandedly.

"What?"

"You heard me."

She pushed his hands away. *"Have to marry me?"*

He grabbed her before she could walk away. "When I have the ring, I'll drop on one knee and propose officially, but know this, love: you are going to marry me."

"My family . . . I won't put that burden on you. I have responsibilities. . . ."

"I know . . . to protect Gigi from her son. I can help with that."

"And my parents . . . they're always going to cause trouble. I can't change them. I used to think I could, but—"

"Your brothers and I will help you with them."

"Oh, God, my brothers. You won't be good enough for me. That's what they'll say."

"I'm *not* good enough for you, love, but I'm still marrying you."

"Your parents are diplomats. Mine are con artists."

Sam was slowly unbuttoning her blouse. She was nibbling on her lower lip while she was thinking about the differences between their families.

"I have money," she said, a point in her favor.

Sam lifted her into his arms and carried her into the bedroom. He lowered her to her feet and slowly undressed her, pausing only long enough to shed his own clothes.

Lyra was breathless when she said, "If I have to, I'll use all my money to fight those people. Honestly, my parents keep finding new lawyers. . . ." Sam was kissing her neck.

He loved the way she smelled, the way she felt, everything about her.

"Lawyers are expensive. . . ." she continued

"I know. I'm a lawyer," he said as his kisses moved down her breasts.

Sam was driving her to distraction, and she couldn't remember what she was trying to tell him.

They fell into bed and made love. Sam tried to take his time, but she became so demanding, he couldn't hold back. When they had both climaxed and were content, she told him that she loved him, too.

Later, after they were dressed, Sam told her to expect to be hounded by reporters.

"Mahler's class would have been my only one tomorrow. Since I won't have that, I think I'd like to go home."

"To San Diego?"

"Yes. Do you think the police need me to stay here?"

"No, I'll talk to O'Malley."

After writing a note for Sidney and packing a little bag, they were on their way. No traffic to speak of, and only after they had passed the exit that would have taken them to Paraiso Park did Lyra remember the camera that was still taking pictures.

"O'Malley will have a crew out there digging for Mahler's wife's body. I'm sure they'll have to dig up that little garden, too."

"My camera—"

"I told him where it was. He'll get it for you." He reached across the console and took hold of her hand. "I imagine Flynn's been picked up for a nice long conversation," he said.

"Will I get those yard sale books back?"

"Eventually. What are you going to do with them?"

"I think I'll have them auctioned for Father Henry's church. They're desperate for money. Bingo doesn't pay the bills."

He smiled. "You've got a good heart, Lyra Prescott."

A few minutes passed in comfortable silence, and then she said, "I can't believe it wasn't the yard sale that started this. I was so sure people were trying to kill me because I'd taken something. I never would have suspected Mahler."

"Look at it this way, if Merriam had known for sure you had the DVD, I'm sure he would have tried to kill you."

"Is that supposed to make me feel better?" She laughed.

"I should have homed in on Mahler sooner. I almost lost you, and I—"

"You got there in time," she reminded him.

They talked about Mahler and his attempts to manipulate her away from photographing the park by steering her toward the children's film competition.

"I guess I don't have to rush to do the film now," she said.

"Why not?"

"You shoot your professor, and it pretty much dooms your chances of his endorsing your film."

"I'm sure as hell not sorry I shot him."

"I'm not sorry either. You had no choice."

When they were pulling into the garage at Gigi's house, Lyra said, "Wait until you see the panic room."

"It's a real panic room?"

"One wall has metal reinforcement, so a bullet couldn't get through, but only one wall. No reason to do any other. It works."

Sam was impressed with the construction when he saw it. "You ever want to hide from relatives, this is the place."

"I love this house. It's comfortable."

"We can keep it," he promised her. "I might be able to transfer out here for a little while."

"Then what?"

"We'll get everything tied up, and then we'll go home."

Lyra liked the idea of keeping Gigi's house. Her brothers would have a place to get away, and Gigi might want to come back for a vacation away from the Texas heat.

Gigi would be happy about the marriage. She had immediately taken to Sam, and she wouldn't have to worry about her granddaughter any longer.

"I'm exhausted," Sam said, breaking into her thoughts. And with that, he picked her up and carried her to bed. They slept with their legs entwined.

The next afternoon, O'Malley called. Sam was on the phone for a long time, and when he hung up, he grinned at Lyra and said, "Cat."

"Excuse me?"

"They found the bones of a cat in the garden. Apparently all those pretty flowers were part of a memorial for someone's dead kitty."

Lyra had been certain the story behind the garden was something more romantic. She took a bottle of water from the refrigerator and went out to the porch swing. Sam followed her.

"A cat, huh?" Lyra shook her head.

"Well, there was a woman's body buried nearby, too—apparently the late Mrs. Mahler."

"D.C. isn't anything like this, is it? Living there will take some getting used to for me."

"We won't be living in D.C.," he told her.

She sat up to face him. "But you said—"

"I said we're going home." He smiled as he put his arm around her and pulled her close. "You'll love the Highlands."

FORTY-TWO

MILO SAT AT THE BAR SIPPING A COLD BEER while he stared intently at the television. The eleven o'clock news was on, and he was watching Lyra Prescott being led out of a building by a man the reporter identified as an FBI agent.

"See that beautiful woman on the television?" he asked the man sitting next to him. When the man didn't respond, Milo nudged him and said, "I had to break up with her. It was the only way to keep her safe."

The stranger, bleary-eyed and drunk, patted Milo's shoulder. "You did the right thing, buddy," he slurred.

"I don't watch the news regularly," he told his new friend, "but I'm sure glad I watched tonight. You know, I gave up everything for her. I don't regret it because, like you said, I had to do the right thing. Now I'm out of a job. I'm thinking about getting into another line of business, something less stressful."

He couldn't believe Merrian was in jail, and Charlie and Stack, too. All this time he had thought they were behind the break-in and the shooting. Oh well, can't be right about everything.

"In other news," the newscaster continued as Milo ordered his second beer, "Councilman Bill Jackson has resigned effective immediately so that he can mount a defense against the charges pending. The councilman was indicted on . . ."

Milo stopped listening. "There's going to be a job opening if that councilman resigned." He scratched his jaw. "That's what I can do. Politics. I'll go into politics."

His friend patted him again. "You're a natural, buddy. A natural."

EPILOGUE

SAM AND LYRA WERE MARRIED AT ST. AGNES'S Church. Father Henry happily officiated.

Lyra had thought it would be a small affair, but by the time the guest list was complete, the San Diego church was packed with family, friends, and, according to Sidney, a veritable who's who of the political and diplomatic arena, including ambassadors and other dignitaries.

Both the ceremony and the reception at the Coronado Hotel went off perfectly. Lyra thought it was probably because her mother and father had declined to attend. When Lyra told her mother that Sam had asked her to marry him and that she had accepted, her mother's reaction wasn't surprising.

"Oh, Lyra, what are you thinking? With your looks, you could do so much better than an FBI agent. If he's after your money . . ."

Her father's reaction wasn't much better. "I'm sure he loves you, but just to make certain he isn't after your money, I think you should consider transferring your trust to me. You'll want to assure that the assets stay in the Prescott family, of course, so if you'll . . ."

When Lyra refused, an argument ensued. It ended with her parents threatening to boycott the wedding, but despite their coercive tactics, she held her ground and did not give in.

She pretended she didn't care, but the reality was that she was embarrassed that her father wouldn't walk his own daughter down the aisle unless paid to do so. Owen and Cooper were enraged by their parents' conduct, but neither was surprised, either.

Owen stepped in for their father. Sidney was Lyra's maid of honor and walked down the aisle with Cooper. A cousin and two friends from Texas served as bridesmaids. Sam's best man was his cousin Tristan, and Jack and Alec were groomsmen. In addition to the wedding photographer, there were photographers from newspapers and magazines outside the church covering the elegant event.

Lyra loved Sam's parents, who were the complete opposite of her own. They were kind and generous, and welcomed her into their family with open arms. They offered to host a reception for Sam and her in the Highlands so that their Scottish friends and family could also welcome her. Gigi promised to attend.

Sam and Lyra spent their honeymoon at the house in San Diego. They had only three days before Lyra had to return to Los Angeles for the awards ceremony. Her entry into the competition for the Dalton Award had been disqualified last semester because, after Mahler's death, she no longer had a sponsor. Nevertheless, she continued to work on her children's film, and with another professor's blessing resubmitted it the following semester. She won first place. She received multiple offers from production companies in Los Angeles and New York, but she declined them all. Lyra didn't want to work for anyone. She loved the freedom of writing and directing her own work, and had come up with an idea for a children's series she wanted to pursue. She could work from anywhere, which was fortunate, because three months later Sam took her to their home in the Highlands.

Her husband was full of surprises. The first surprise was that their home was a castle. It had been built centuries ago and was magnificent, but cold and formal. Fortunately, their small apartment on the second level was cozy and charming. The estate, or holding as Sam called it, was the most beautiful place she'd ever seen.

The second surprise was that Sam would inherit a couple of titles. As a landowner, he would become Laird Kincaid, but he was also in line to become Earl of Cairnmar.

The third surprise was the most astonishing to Lyra. Her sweet, loving husband turned into a brutal warrior on the rugby field.

Sitting beside Sam's parents on a hill, Lyra watched with great trepidation a match between Sam's team and the one from the next town over. At one point in the game, when she saw Sam emerge from a pile of huge, muscular men, she grabbed her father-in-law's arm. "Did he just break . . . ? Did his elbow . . . ?"

Sam's father, seeing the horrified look in her eyes, sympathetically patted her knee. "Do you know what's been said about rugby? It's a hooligan's game played by gentlemen. Don't worry, he's fine, my dear."

Nodding, she turned back to stare at her husband. He was covered in mud, and his uniform was spotted with blood, which she didn't think belonged to him. His teammates were just as beaten up. What she found most amazing, however, was that once the game was over, both teams laughed and carried on as they dragged one another off the field.

Sam saw her in the crowd and made his way over to her. He had a cut over his eyebrow, and he was muddy from head to toe. Oblivious to the fact that she was wearing a white blouse, she threw her arms around his neck and hugged him. That wasn't good enough for Sam. He kissed her passionately, ignoring his cheering teammates.

When he finally came up for air, he said, "Now that's the way a husband should greet his wife when he returns home."

Blushing because of their audience, she said, "You were thirty feet away from me."

"Exactly," he replied, and kissed her again.

She leaned into his side. "I'm relieved you're still intact."

"It's a sport, sweetheart."

A sport? They actually called the mayhem she'd

just witnessed a sport? "Does it have to be so rough? I don't want you to get hurt."

He laughed. "A few minor cuts and bruises won't kill me."

He picked up his duffel bag, put his arm around her shoulders, and began walking toward their car. "I got a call from the FBI this morning. They want me to fly to D.C. tomorrow to consult on a case. I'll be leaving before dawn. Want to come with me?"

"I can't," she answered. "I'm visiting the Cairnmar school tomorrow to film for my new series."

"Then I guess we'll have to say our good-byes tonight." He lustfully inspected every inch of her body and then said, "In fact, if you're up to it, I'll say good-bye all night long."

As Lyra waited by the car for Sam to drop his rugby gear in the trunk, she looked all around her. She was in a field bordered on one side by a lane of quaint stone cottages and on the other by a pasture with sheep peacefully grazing. In the distance were the magnificent Highland mountains. How different this all was from where she had been less than a year ago. Because of Sam, everything was new and exciting and wonderful.

He turned and smiled at her, and her heart swelled with love.

Life with Sam was going to be full of surprises.